Luck of the Draw

Luck of the Draw

Anthony J. Cardieri

MINOTAUR BOOKS

A THOMAS DUNNE BOOK

NEW YORK

A THOMAS DUNNE BOOK FOR MINOTAUR BOOKS.
An imprint of St. Martin's Publishing Group.

LUCK OF THE DRAW. Copyright © 2009 by Anthony J. Cardieri. All rights reserved. Printed in the United States of America.
For information, address St. Martin's Press, 175 Fifth Avenue, New York, N.Y. 10010.

www.thomasdunnebooks.com
www.minotaurbooks.com

Library of Congress Cataloging-in-Publication Data

Cardieri, Anthony J.
    Luck of the draw / Anthony J. Cardieri.—1st ed.
        p. cm.
    ISBN 978-0-312-56502-2
    1. Police—New York (State)—New York—Fiction.
    2. Serial murder investigation—Fiction.   3. Serial
    murderers—Fiction.   4. Manhattan (New York, N.Y.)—
    Fiction.   I. Title.
    PS3603.A7347L83 2009
    813'.6—dc22

                                                    2009012744

First Edition: December 2009

10 9 8 7 6 5 4 3 2 1

This book is dedicated to my father, retired New York City Police Detective Vincent J. Cardieri. Without his tireless support, on all levels, the writing of this book would not have been possible.

Luck of the Draw

Chapter One

Friday, December 22, was shaping up to be a great day. The storm system that had just dumped six inches of heavy snow on the New York City area was finally beginning to pull out, leaving a biting cold in its wake. All the romantics hoping for a white Christmas would be satisfied with the fluffy powder that settled on their windowsills, and all the travel-conscious could be thankful that it came early enough to have the streets cleared in time for them to get to where they were going.

Mike Nevalo was one of the few people who fell into both groups. The cold weather and snow were a staple of his youth while growing up in northern Minnesota. Back then, a white Christmas was more the rule than the exception. In New York, however, it was surprisingly rare.

He was awakened by the sounds of his children running up and down the hallway, laughing and playing. He rolled over in bed and opened his eye a crack, trying to focus on the clock. As it came into view, he quickly tossed aside the blankets and sat up, wondering why his daily alarm hadn't done its job.

His alarm was busy today doing many other things, and it had completely slipped her mind. Normally, she's in at seven ten

1

on the nose getting him up for work, but today she was busy planning for their weekend getaway, a getaway that was a long time coming, a Christmas weekend in Florida. She took care of the hotel reservations months ago, planned the daily itinerary weeks ago, and now all that remained was the packing of the small odds and ends that would be needed. Nothing would be forgotten, for Victoria Nevalo was all over this one. She scurried about the place stuffing things into the carry-on suitcase like a pack rat in a junkyard. There was a little voice in her head that kept nudging her, though, trying to tell her that she might have indeed missed something. That little voice didn't talk long, as the one thing evading her consciousness at the moment had just come stumbling from the bedroom looking for a cup of coffee.

"Anything slip your mind, Vick?" Mike said as he passed her in the hallway.

"Oh my God, I'm sorry. What time is it?" she yelled.

"About a quarter after. Don't worry. I was only over a few minutes. No big deal. It actually was kinda nice. We should do this every Friday."

"You shouldn't scare me like that. I'm doing a million things here. Coffee's on in the kitchen if you want some."

"Thank goodness for self-timing coffeemakers," Mike mumbled softly.

"What was that?" his wife asked demandingly.

"Huh? Nothing. I didn't say anything," came the reply with a smile that Victoria could not see.

Mike stopped by the living room to say good morning to his little noisemakers. There were two of them, Tommy, who was nine, and little Ginny, only four. Tommy's existence was planned from day one. Ginny was a complete surprise, and a very happy one at that. They were the typical brother-sister duo, agreeing on certain things, disagreeing on most. Tommy could deal with sitting and

2

watching the cartoons she liked, but he absolutely drew the line when it came to playing with her dolls. Some things were just too sacred.

"G'morning, guys," Mike boomed as he entered the room. "What's doin'?"

"Hi, Dad," Tommy said matter-of-factly.

Ginny was way more exuberant. "Daddy!" she screamed as she came running toward him. Mike picked her up from the floor and lifted her almost to the ceiling.

"Hey, baby. How is my little girl today?"

"Tommy won't play Barbies with me."

"That's right," Tommy answered, never taking his eyes from the TV. "Tell her to leave me alone with that, Dad."

"He's mean," said Ginny, leveling her green eyes so they stared directly into dad's blue. Her little hands held Dad's face tight for effect. Mike smiled and quick-kissed her on the nose before she could pull away and then lowered her gently to the floor.

"Who's ready for tonight?" he asked excitedly.

"Me!" Ginny answered, jumping up and down, blond hair bouncing off her shoulders.

Tommy played it cool. "I am," he said passively, with a fast wave of the hand.

"I think Ginny may be right about you," Mike said as he tickled Tommy's belly, causing him to convulse with laughter. "You always have to be Mr. Nothing Impresses Me." He looked at the cable-box clock. "All right, I need to start getting ready for work. You guys behave."

As he neared the kitchen, he turned around to take a glance at his children. Ginny was his big love, his heart. She was thirty-six inches of sweetness, always ready with the hugs and kisses. Her blond hair was crazy-curly, but her face, with those light green eyes, was the oasis in Dad's desert. Tommy was the brain in the family.

He had effortlessly navigated grades one through three and was cruising through number four. He'd said his first word at six months old and hadn't shut his mouth since. He was Dad's pride, the one who would outaccomplish all the others—on both sides of the family. He even had Dad's eye color, though the blue was much deeper. He would be a tall one, too, but probably wouldn't reach the six foot four his dad enjoyed. He was a lanky kid, and Mike hoped he could someday avoid the paunch around the middle he himself was stuck with. There was plenty of time for both of the kids, and Mike hoped they would grow up nice and slowly.

He took his coffee black, hastily pouring it into a cup and heading for the bathroom. He perched the cup on top of the shower door frame and drank it while bathing. When the shower was done, so was the coffee. As he lathered his face for a shave, he hollered for Victoria to bring him a refill.

"Wouldn't it be easier to just set the pot up in here?" she asked facetiously.

He answered her in the same way. "Well, it's not like you're doing anything anyway."

A love tap on the back of the head was his reward for the snide comment as Victoria went back to her gathering. "Feed yourself," she shouted, heading toward the bedrooms. Mike stuck his head into the hallway and marveled at Victoria as she walked away. In his eyes, she was more sexy at that moment than she was on the day he met her. The few pounds she'd gained since then only added to her beauty. He always told her she was too thin, that he could see her bones, but those words only came when he could actually take his eyes away from hers for a moment. He had a thing for green-eyed women, and Victoria's were emerald. He had found himself lost in those perfectly shaped eyes many times over the years and was extremely pleased to find that they were carried on through Ginny. Eyes like that shouldn't be a rarity.

Mike made himself the only breakfast he was qualified to cook. When the hot pastries popped up from the toaster, he grabbed them and headed for the door. "I'm late. I'll see you guys tonight."

"Bye," everyone yelled in unison.

Victoria actually stopped to look at the clock. Tommy had to get ready for school, and she knew that if she didn't push him, he'd lie there all day watching cartoons. *If only he were as ambitious as he was smart*, she thought. She took out his clothes and laid them on the bed. His sneakers were right there at the foot. She went into the living room, grabbed the remote, and put an end to the cartoons. She pointed one finger at Tommy and another in the direction of his bedroom. They stared at each other for a few seconds before Tommy reluctantly got up off the couch and trudged toward his clothing. As he dressed, Victoria brought Ginny into the kitchen and sat her at the table. She poured some cereal and milk as a quick breakfast for each child. A cup of orange juice and a chewable vitamin completed the meal.

She sat with them as they ate, making sure there was no dilly-dallying. "Sorry about the cereal, guys, but I am too busy to cook right now, what with trying to get ready for tomorrow and all. There's a lot of things we need for the weekend."

"Why can't we go now?" Tommy sighed. "I want to go on the rides."

"Me, too," Ginny added.

"No, you silly gooses. Dad's gotta work. Tomorrow will be here fast enough. You'll be on those rides before you know it. Besides, you have the plane ride tonight."

"Whoopee," said Tommy in his typical fashion.

Victoria smiled at him. "I should have sent you to work with your father," she said jokingly.

On the other side of town, Mike Nevalo arrived at work a

few minutes later than normal, which made no difference since it still put him there twenty minutes early. He walked in with a couple dozen doughnuts, one of those coffee boxes that hold ten cups or so, and a bag that contained the creamers, sugars, and stirrers. This sight was not lost on one single co-worker. His boss was the first to speak up.

"Hey, Mike, what's the story? You get an inheritance or something?"

"Why's that, Mr. Johnson? Can't a guy do something nice for his office?"

"Sure," Johnson answered skeptically. "I think I may need to go and check the books again. I smell embezzlement here."

The rest of the office erupted in mild laughter as the boxes were opened and the doughnuts scavenged. Mike stood by patiently as he waited for his turn with the coffee box. He watched, amused, as each person filled his cup just a bit higher than normal, in an effort to polish off the coffee box before he could get to it. With great success, the last drop was poured by the person with the last coffee cup before his. Mike watched as the box was shaken and then tapped on the bottom to ensure emptiness.

"All yours, Mike." Shelly grinned as she handed over the box. "Enjoy."

Mike smiled defiantly. "Thanks, Shelly, but you keep that," he said. "I'll drink this here." He reached into a white paper bag and pulled out a cup of coffee and a blueberry muffin. He then spoke up to the room. "In case some of you may have forgotten, I invented the 'kill the box before the buyer gets some' method. I'm always one step ahead of you guys. Remember that."

Mike gingerly and victoriously made his way over to his desk. His closest friend in the office, Ted, another accounts manager, met him there. Mike had broken Ted into the numbers job almost a decade earlier. Ted stood in front of him with the morning newspaper held straight out with both hands.

"Unbelievable, eh, Mike?" he said, holding the paper steady so the headline could be read. "This is out of control now."

"Again?" shouted Mike as he scanned the front page. "What the hell is going on here?"

"I don't know, but this thing is way, way out of hand."

"Big-time!" he agreed. "Looks like I'll be getting out of New York at a good time. Those sandy, sunny beaches are calling to me. Wait, shh, shh," he said as he put his cupped hand to his ear, "you hear 'em? They're saying, 'Mike, come sit on us. Mike, come run your toes through us.'" His smile could've been stolen straight from the Cheshire cat. It was huge and absolutely said it all. He glanced at his watch. "Twelve hours from now, honey, I will be in paradise!"

Ted glanced out the window at the white frozen powder that was everywhere; the icy misery that he would be trudging through while Mike was busy sunning. "Yeah, well, ya know what?" he began. "You still have twelve hours—and I am gonna do my best to make them as miserable as I possibly can. Maybe I can get you to jump out the window so I can take your place on the plane tonight."

"You are a sick man," laughed Mike, "but you don't have much of a chance. I am in way too good a mood. Besides, you're still on Vicky's hit list from the last time you were at my house. That girl's gonna knock your lights out."

Ted tipped his head and gave a half hearted salute. "Always nice to be loved." The boss's glare caught his eye. "Hey, Johnson's looking over here. I think maybe we should get to work now."

Mike turned his head, grinned, and waved. "He's probably looking for another doughnut. All right, I guess we might as well do something. My Lotto numbers didn't come through again last night, so I think I'll need to stay in the workforce a bit longer."

"You still playing those numbers, dopey? It's a waste of money. When are you gonna learn that your numbers will never hit in a million years?"

"Maybe not, but like they say, buddy, you never know. All it takes is just one lucky night. One hit and I'm set for life. I am the ultimate dreamer."

"OK, you dream on, champ. I'm going to knock off some of these accounts before Johnson comes in here and busts us. You might want to get your head out of the clouds and do the same."

"Yeah, why not. I do have a lot of loose ends on accounts I want to rectify before I leave. Unless, of course, you'd like to do them for me while I'm gone."

"Boy, you weren't lying, were you! You really *are* the ultimate dreamer. Let me see if I got this straight. You'll be sunning on a sandy beach in Florida, and I'll be up here, freezing, doing your work?" Ted waved good-bye. "Happy rectifying."

Mike yelled to him as he walked away. "There goes your souvenir T-shirt!"

The rest of the day moved by fairly quickly for Mike as he dotted all his i's and crossed all the t's. At home, Victoria had every base covered. All of the suitcases were dragged to the front door and stacked up, one on top of the other. The kids were taken to and picked up from school. Afternoon snacks were doled out to the troops, and dinner was waiting in the oven for Mike's return home. He came through the front door right on time and with an ear-to-ear smile. "I'm home!" he yelled to no one in particular, eliciting the same blasé response he got every night.

"Hi, Dad," Tommy said, still being Mr. Cool. "What time are we leaving?"

"Right after dinner. Where's Mom?"

"I think she's changing Ginny's clothes."

Mike sank down into his brown leather couch and waited for the dinner bell to be rung. He grabbed the remote control and bounced from station to station looking for something that he and Tommy could agree on. Mike wanted the financial report, and Tommy was hoping for more in the way of cartoons. The regular news channels were all bypassed quickly, as Mike didn't want Tommy being frightened by the crisis that was currently engulfing the city. They settled on a minor league baseball game that, ultimately, they never even watched. Instead, Mike muted the TV and got down to basics with Tommy concerning his "rules of transit" for the trip. There would be no fighting with Ginny in the car on the way to the airport. There would be no scaring her on the plane by telling her she would fall out the window. He was ordered to leave her dolls alone and not pull their heads off and use them as soccer balls.

Tommy had a look on his face as if Dad had told him he couldn't go on any rides in Florida. "Aw, come on, Dad! That's really gonna make the flight seem longer now!"

Mike was about to make it even longer. "You're gonna sit right between me and Mommy on that plane. I don't want them landing in Georgia and kicking us off because you had Ginny screaming the whole flight."

"Come on!" Tommy yelled, hands in the air. "That's not fair!"

"Sorry."

"How about this, then," Tommy said. "You said we have four seats next to each other, right?"

"Correct."

"OK, you could put me by the window, then comes you, then Mommy, and then Ginny. Me and her will be far away from each other."

"She and I," Mike corrected him.

"Whatever!" Tommy responded anxiously.

"All right, but promise me that you'll look out the window the whole way and not bother Ginny once."

"Yeah . . . OK," Tommy conceded.

Mike smiled and unmuted the TV, knowing that he had just pulled a fast one on Tommy. The seating arrangements Tommy came up with were the way it was going to be from the get-go, but now Mike had a pretty big bargaining chip in his pocket. Tommy was willing to do anything to stay out of that seat right between Mom and Dad.

Victoria came into the room and saw Mike sitting in his chair. "Heyyy," she said joyfully. She carried Ginny on her hip. "I didn't hear you come in."

"Sure you didn't," he answered, smiling. "You never do for some reason."

"Did Tommy get the riot act read to him yet?"

"All done. We've struck an agreement."

"Really? I guess we'll see with that. OK, who's hungry?"

At the dinner table Tommy said the prayers of thanks and Mom did the serving. The conversation centered on Disney World and what they were going to do on their minivacation. Everyone had a different wish. Dad wanted a round of solo golf, Mom wanted a day at the spa. Tommy wanted to be allowed to bug Ginny and then go on every ride there was, and Ginny wanted a picture with every character from the movies. They talked and planned it out so that everyone's wish would come true. Before they knew it, the plates were all empty and dinner was done. Mike and Ginny cleared the table and put the plates and utensils into the dishwasher. Tommy stuck close to Victoria to help with anything she needed. Everyone was pitching in to get to the airport on time.

When Mike was finished with the kitchen work, he slipped

off to the bedroom to change from his work suit into some casual clothing. Victoria already had an outfit laid out for him on the bed, all neat and pressed. He sat down and started unbuttoning his shirt, marveling at the luck that had brought him into such a perfect family situation. Things, he hoped, would only get better from here.

In the living room, Ginny and Tommy sat on the couch while Mom got everyone's coats out of the closet and placed them with the luggage. She found Tommy's sneakers and tossed them to him for self-installation while Ginny's were put on her feet and tied. As Mom double-knotted the laces, there was a knock on the front door. "Car service is here," she hollered.

"Tell him to wait," Mike answered from the bedroom.

Victoria opened the front door and was greeted with a beautiful bouquet of fresh-cut flowers and a shivering delivery-man. "Flowers?" she said, astonished, and then smiled know-ingly in the direction of the bedroom. "He can be so thoughtful sometimes," she said to the delivery guy. "Come on in a second. Let me give you something. Tommy, honey, go get my pocketbook, please." She turned from the front door and went to pull a vase from her display shelf. She ripped the paper covering the flowers and took a peek inside. "Oh, how beautiful they are."

When Tommy came back with the pocketbook, he stopped dead in his tracks. His eyes were open wide as saucers, and his breathing came to a stop. Gone was the smile from his face. His teeth were clenched so hard that Victoria could hear them grind-ing on each other. Puzzled, she spun quickly to get a glimpse of what was going on behind her. She found herself staring down the barrel of a high-caliber pistol—thick, black, and heavy. Her face then became the mirror of her son's. Before she could utter a word, a large muzzle blast blew a bullet straight through her brain. It entered at the bridge of her nose and exited a little above the base of her skull. She fell to the floor like a wet towel, and the blood that was once contained within her body now flowed freely onto the beautiful white carpeting she was so proud of. The fresh-cut flowers she had happily received were crushed beneath her.

Tommy dropped the pocketbook and tried to comprehend the scene his eyes were showing him. His heart was pounding, and his breathing went rapid as he tried to muster enough energy to scream for his dad. He noticed the gunman's attention shift from the person on the floor to the one that had just dropped the pocketbook. Something in his brain finally clicked and told him to run. In the blink of an eye, he bolted for his bedroom and what he hoped was a safe hiding place. Ginny, on the other hand, saw Mommy on the floor and ran straight to her. As she knelt over Mom and began calling and shaking her, trying wake her up, the barrel of the gun was trained on the back of her little blond head. The trigger slowly started pulling back as Mike came tearing down the hallway and into the living room. He didn't even have the chance to utter a word before the gun was quickly repositioned on him and a bullet tore into his chest. He fell to his knees and caught a glimpse of Victoria as she bled to death. Another bullet to the stomach caused him to fall forward onto the floor, and a burning pain began to sear through every crevice of his body. As his vision began to cloud up, he could see Ginny still trying to wake up her mommy. Her little hands were pulling on the reddening, saturated hair as she yelled into a much bloodied ear. Mike began pulling himself toward the gunman with every ounce of strength he could muster as it became clear that the gunman was once again focusing on Ginny.

"Leave her alone!" He tried to yell but could not get the words past the blood in his mouth and an excruciating lack of air in his lungs. As he neared the gunman's feet, Mike could hear Ginny talking to Mommy. He had never heard her voice this way before. It was muffled and distorted, sounding almost cartoonish. Mike knew he was slipping away fast. Any move made to save Ginny had to be done right now—but the strength just wasn't there. He could hardly drag himself along. He was completely overcome with unbearable pain, and also with a feeling he had never known before—insurmountable fear. Not for himself, though. He knew he was done. It was for his beautiful little baby, who was being targeted for death, right there in front of him. Life pictures passed before his eyes, Ginny's life, from birth right up until this moment. She counted on him for everything. He was her hero, her protector. She was Daddy's little girl. He couldn't just let this piece of crap blow her away on a whim. His already increased heart rate surged, pumping more and more blood out of his body. His adrenaline was so high he could taste the bitterness in his mouth. With every remaining amount of strength he had, Mike inched himself closer to the gunman until he was within reach.

This effort was not lost on the killer. He crouched down and grabbed a fistful of Mike's hair and yanked his head up so he could see little Ginny more easily. "Here, let me help you out," he said callously. Her beautiful pink travel dress that Victoria had put on her earlier was now completely stained with rich, organic color.

The killer then implanted some parting words into Mike's ear. "Not today, my friend," he said in a cold, gravelly voice. "There's no room in my world for heroes."

Mike's head was held in perfect position as he watched the barrel of the gun take direct aim on the back of Ginny's head. His mind then screamed the words his mouth could not speak as his life oozed out of him with each pint of blood that was lost.

Ginny kept calling for Mommy, never even realizing that Daddy was behind her. Her obliviousness probably made for a more merciful end. She never knew what hit her. The bullet that ended her tiny life burst through her brain like a baseball bat versus a melon. It destroyed everything from back to front and exploded her entire face, leaving one eye dangling from the socket and the other lying loosely on the floor. Her small body had come to rest on top of Victoria's, her diminutive hand still holding tightly to Mommy's hair, both of their bodies twitching in a morbid dance of death.

The gunman, more agitated now, ripped Mike's head in the direction of his feet. "Look at this!" he said angrily. "She went and got her brains all over my new shoes!" He looked into Mike's lifeless eyes and shook his head violently in an effort to revive some consciousness. It was useless. Mike's spirit had slipped from his body at almost the same moment Ginny's spirit was ripped from hers. The gunman released his head, and it smacked against the carpeted floor. The blood that flowed from his mouth and chest now pooled together with Victoria's and Ginny's, helping to join them in death just as their love had joined them in life.

Little Tommy was now the last Nevalo still breathing, albeit heavily. Gone was Mr. Cool and in was Mr. Panic. When the killing started, Tommy took off for his room and hid under the bed. The monsters that he always feared were under there now paled in comparison to the one lurking in the living room. Jumping out the window or grabbing a phone and calling 911 never even occurred to him. Finding safety in what he hoped was a good hiding spot was the only instinctive move he could make. In his mind, Dad was going to win out there, and it would only be a matter of time before he was out of danger. He heard the popping of the gunfire only a second or two after blowing by Dad as they passed each other in the hallway. Once he got under the bed, all he could make out was the faint murmur of voices. Then one more pop hit his ears, and then nothing but silence. He tried his best to keep his sniffling and crying to a minimum so there would be nothing to attract the bad man to his room in case Dad fell short out there.

The bad man, unfortunately, had a memory, and it was one that told him exactly how many people he started with, how many were now dead, and what he was left with. He briefly stepped into the kitchen and lifted the wall phone from its handset. The dial tone in his ear assured him that the police were not on the way; such a call would have taken a greater length of time than he had used to wipe out three-quarters of the Nevalo family. He rested the phone on top of the kitchen table and walked away, comforted in the fact that no calls could now be made. He worked his way back into the living room and stood at the edge of the hallway leading to the bedrooms. The drone in his head kept buzzing and buzzing, ensuring that there would be absolutely no compliance between his mind and sanity. His wits, left just outside the front door, would not be with him again until this mission was accomplished. There was one more battlefield to fight on. One more toy soldier to defeat. He tucked the gun in his belt and began a slow, methodical walk down the hallway in search of the final victim.

Tommy could hear the squeaking of the wooden, parquet floorboards underneath the hallway carpeting. He knew someone was coming his way. From his vantage point under the bed, he had a good view of the lower half of his doorway and anything that passed it. He covered his mouth tightly with his hands and tried not to breathe. Into his sight line came a pair of bloodied shoes as they made their way past his door. Tommy accidentally let out a little shriek as he immediately realized the shoes weren't Dad's. The squeaking of the hallway floor stopped, and the bloodied shoes backtracked their way into Tommy's room. His breathing grew extremely fast and shallow as the shoes closed the gap between life and death. He started whispering for his mommy as a large, gloved hand reached under the bed and grabbed hold of the wooden side rail. Effortlessly, the bed was lifted up, exposing Tommy to the eyes of the last person he would ever see. He shivered in fear as the gun was pulled into sight and brought down toward his head.

"Mommy!" he cried loudly. "Mommy!"

The gunman pulled the hammer back slowly. "Mommy's sleeping, kid."

The gun fired, and another body lay flat against the soft carpeting, more blood and brain scattered all about. The bed was then carefully lowered to let it come to rest exactly on the indents it had originally left in the carpeting. The killer then walked back into the living room, pulled a handwritten note from his pocket, and placed it carefully on Mike's body. He walked to the front door and shut off the outside light. He peered out into the darkness for a couple of seconds to check for a quick escape. He then shook the cobwebs out of his head, blew a kiss to the Nevalo family, and slipped out the front door into the cold winter night.

He walked briskly down the street, his hands tucked deep into his pockets. His right hand gripped the gun tightly, and his finger was at the ready on the trigger, just in case. As he passed a house on his right side, a house adorned by many beautiful Christmas lights and decorations, he heard the faint singing of children playing inside.

"Ring around the rosie, a pocketful of posies, ashes, ashes, we all fall down."

The killer grinned an evil grin. "Yeah, you all fall down," he snickered. "Dead!"

He stopped walking when he got to a desolate stretch of street where no one could, or would, see him. He scraped his shoes along the curb, getting as much of Ginny's brains off as he could.

"Little bitch," he muttered to himself, looking angrily back in the direction of the Nevalo household. "Fucking ruined these on me."

A dog barking in the distance brought the killer's attention back to the situation at hand. He ducked behind a tree as the headlights of an approaching car caught his eye. He waited there until it passed, its driver on his way to wherever, oblivious to the carnage that had taken place not far from his vehicle. When the car was out of sight, the killer quickly scanned the area for any changes that might have taken place. Once appeased, he resumed his pace down the sidewalk, hands back in the pockets, finger on the emergency button. He continued on, unnoticed and undeterred, as he cruised into his most coveted destination—the background of society.

Chapter Two

Deke Durgess had just entered his fifth consecutive hour of broken, agitated sleep. He tossed, he turned, he punched and fluffed his pillow numerous times. He rolled all over his king-sized bed in hopes of finding just the right spot where comfort would meet with haggardness. It was useless. Every time he drifted off, his mind would jump in and reflect on the previous day's tumultuous events. His brain was racing through a million things, different scenarios and possibilities, but no outcomes.

Once again, he had begun to drift off. Once again, he was pulled back as the telephone ripped him into consciousness. As it rang, he just lay there and watched it, almost expecting to see his wife's hand reach over and pick it up. There was no hand, however, and no wife either. She'd been gone for months after it became painfully clear, once again, that *the job* came before her and anything else in Deke's life. She gathered all of his possessions and threw them out onto the front porch one Sunday morning when he should have been home with her but instead was out somewhere tracking down the bad guys. Her absence only made his large bed seem that much bigger, that much lonelier, and way tougher to sleep in on nights like this.

This ringing of the telephone was exactly the reason she was no longer next to him. It never stopped. It came in the middle of the night, it came at kids' birthday parties, it came in the middle of anniversary dinners and holidays. It even came when he was on vacation. Any time that phone rang for Deke, he was up and out and on his way to whatever situation beckoned him.

That part of his persona had changed very little since his days growing up in Bensonhurst, Brooklyn. He was always the guy his friends turned to in a pinch, seeking his help whether he was eating a family dinner or fast asleep in bed. Once they called him, up and out he went. He was considered a tough guy because he had a mouth that roared, one that talked a big game but rarely had to back it up. The mouth was the one thing he never quite left behind. While he wasn't the same street tough he was back yonder, he still had that Brooklyn way of talking, bunching two or three words together to form one new one or leaving letters completely out of some words. It made him appear to lack intelligence, something he loved because it only enhanced his ability to sneak up on and catch the bad guys.

The phone continued ringing, and Deke just lay there listening to it, knowing instinctively what it meant. Phones that ring at five o'clock in the morning rarely bring good news. His stomach twinged as he made his way over to the phone and picked it up.

"Durgess," he said.

"Deke, it's Captain Murray. Get in here, we got another one."

"Jesus Christ! Where?"

"Out on Staten Island. A whole family." Frustration resounded in the captain's voice. "This is out of control. We're pulling everybody in. Move your ass!" The phone was hung up.

Deke flopped back on the bed and looked up at the ceiling. Numbness washed over his entire body at the thought of investigating yet another murder scene, seeing more blood and bodies, and knowing how it would all add up to another night's useless attempt at sleep. It wasn't that he was unaccustomed to seeing bodies. In his line of work he'd seen quite a few, almost becoming indifferent to it. It was the frequency with which they were turning up that was getting to him. His normal caseload was maybe a new murder every week or two. Now they were coming in by the day, three and four bodies at a time, all at the same scene. It was almost overwhelming, but this was what he had signed on for. This was why he lost his marriage. This was why he and his two kids were no longer under the same roof. Such is the life of a homicide detective. Always on call and always called. It had been this way for all twelve years he'd been in homicide. At first, if it wasn't his home phone ringing, it would be a beeper. When they moved into the age of cell phones, well, it only became that much easier to get him.

He was good, real good, at what he did. All the truly tough cases came his way because he was so thorough and determined in his investigations and had an uncanny ability to play a hunch that usually produced a successful result. Detective work was in his blood, tracing all the way back to childhood. He had a knack for reading people—eyes, body language, the little quiver in one's voice when telling a lie. He also possessed a mind like a steel trap when it came to details. When he played the game Clue with his friends, he didn't even need the notepad to keep track of all the clues. He followed along closely and always knew where, what, and who were in the little yellow envelope way before anyone else even had an idea. Whenever he played Electronic Detective, the computer was eliminated before it could gather its own clues. He had just the right makeup for figuring things out, plus a brain that could stay level when things got totally out of whack.

Before he'd even gotten into the Homicide Unit he was considered to be one of the top minds in the detective ranks. When he first made detective and was assigned to a small-crime task force, he went out and bought himself a police scanner so he could listen in on the more prestigious homicide calls during his days off. Homicide was always where he wanted to be. When a call came in, he would go to the scene, wherever it was in the city, and try to help solve the case. Some of the established veterans of homicide would get pissed off when Deke would show up. Many times it was easier for them to rule a death a suicide, especially in the case of a prostitute or druggie. Nobody ever missed people like that, and often it was much simpler just to write the case off as them killing themselves and closing the paperwork right there.

It wasn't the easy way out all the time, though. Sometimes the detectives were careless, lackadaisical, or just plain blind and missed things that caused them to file a homicide as a suicide. On some of those occasions Deke would swoop in with his little police scanner and ask if he could have a look around and learn from the big boys. Then he would pull the rug right out from under their feet and solve the case with a clue that no one else even sniffed. This didn't bring him favor with the homicide detectives that were relatively new to the unit or the ones that were looking for the easy ride. Guys didn't like to be shown up by a hotshot upstart who wasn't even a part of their ranks, and they often complained to their commanding officer, asking him to keep Deke out of crime scenes during his off time.

On the other hand, there were a few grizzled veterans who actually liked it when Deke's car rolled up. Behind closed doors, they would champion his case to the commander in an effort to continue his access to the murder scenes. They had an appreciation for a kid with a keen nose for clues that even they could miss. Plus, Deke never looked for any of the credit on a case. He merely pointed out things to the other detectives and let them tell him if he was barking up the right tree or not. Most of the time he was right on target, and before long a couple of the elite detectives took him under their wing and really showed him the ropes of homicide. When it came time for their retirement, they put in a strong recommendation for Deke to be brought into the unit. The higher-ups making those decisions knew of Deke's determination and passion for solving cases and how he would never give up on a case even if everyone else had. On the day he was finally transferred in, he was one of the few detectives to be rewarded with an assignment into homicide without a major bust under his belt. Well, at least none that he was credited for.

In the twelve years since, he had become widely known as the detective with the most homicide convictions in the history of the department. Some were easy, open-and-shut cases. Others were more difficult. None had ever weighed on his mind the way his current case did. On this one, his shields were holding but definitely weakening.

He sat up on his bed, grabbed the phone, and dialed back into the precinct, asking for Captain Murray. The call was transferred and picked up harshly.

"Murray," the captain growled.

"Yo, Cap, it's Deke."

"Are you still there? I thought I told you to move your ass!"

"Listen, I'm goin' directly to the scene. I gotta get there before CSU screws it up."

There was a second or two of silence. "OK, Deke, go ahead. I'll clear it with Central. It's in Great Kills, Staten Island, 9773 Armstrong Avenue."

"Great Kills? Sounds about right," Deke said, making a mental note to himself to check on the neighborhood names where the other murders took place, just in case this guy was playing word games. "You got everyone else comin' in, too?"

"Yeah."

"OK, good. Do me a favor, Cap. Get Ronnie, Jimmy, and Larry workin' on trackin' down all the local workers. Tell 'em to get names of meter readers, mailmen, garbagemen, and anyone else in the area. I don't care if it's the paperboy. I want a name and a way I can talk to 'em. Have 'em find UPS and the phone company guy, too. Have 'em start matchin' names up to the lists from the other scenes, and let's see if anybody pops up more than once."

"Done. Now shake your ass!" The phone was abruptly hung up again.

Deke staggered to the bathroom and threw water on his face. He placed both hands on the sink and took a close look at himself in the mirror. He looked like he felt—crappy. His graying hair was pointing in fourteen different directions. His normally oval-shaped brown eyes were all bloodshot and half closed. The face was as stubbly and abrasive as high-grit sandpaper. Gone was the olive skin color, replaced with a paleness one can only get from a week's worth of sleeplessness. He gave the appearance more of a drunken hobo than of an elite detective. Showering and shaving were considered luxuries right now, not necessities. Those two events would have to wait until imperativeness gave way to convenience. Getting to the crime scene while it was still intact was paramount at the moment. No thoughts were given to the stringent NYPD policy on uniform requirements that demanded a clean-shaven face. What were they going to do, send the lead detective on the highest-priority case the city had ever seen home because he had two days' worth of beard on him? He wet his fingers and ran them through his ragged hair and quickly brushed his teeth. He grabbed his keys, badge, and gun off a table by the front door, and out he went.

The drive to Staten Island from Brooklyn took half the time it normally did. Traveling at five thirty in the morning sure did cut down on traffic. As he zipped over the Verrazano-Narrows

Bridge, Deke programmed the address into his global positioning system. It flawlessly led him directly to the murder scene. The entire street was cordoned off, and police cars and lights were everywhere. News cameras, news vans, and news reporters were all over the place. The reporters tried to talk to anyone and anything that moved. This was the sixth day in a row of the killing spree, and the police, Deke included, were completely baffled. So far there was nothing that tied the killings together, except for a cold-hearted note left on one of the bodies at each crime scene. That might change once ballistics finished matching slugs from the bodies to calibers and guns. At the moment, though, the notes were by far the most important clue they had, giving every assurance that it was the same lunatic pulling the trigger each time.

Deke was well aware of this. He was the lead detective at the very first killing, in Manhattan, as it happened to occur in his precinct. As the killer branched out to the other boroughs, the police commissioner instructed the detective squad to keep Deke as lead detective over the case as long as it went on. His reputation earned him that right.

Blocked by the blue police barricades that had closed off the street and not willing to get out and move them, Deke parked the car at the end of the block and walked his way in, badge hanging around his neck for identification. The badge and his stature as one of the elite were not recognized by the just-out-of-the-academy rookie officers placed at the front entrance, instructed to let only the Crime Scene Unit into the scene.

"Sorry, Detective, those are the orders we got. Only CSU inside."

"Listen, Officer"—he squinted at the officer's nameplate—"Jenkins, I'm runnin' this case. Get out of my way so I can do my job."

"Sorry, Detective, no can do."

"No can do, eh? Well, how 'bout this, then. Go in there and get me the lead crime scene guy and bring him out. Do it now before you get yourself in even more trouble."

The officer nervously stepped inside while the other kept vigil over the entrance. Within a minute or so, he came back out, followed by the top CSU guy.

"Deke, what the hell are you doing out here?"

"Yo, Bobby," Deke said, surprised, "you're runnin' the scene out here?"

"Yeah, this thing is front-page news all over the country. All our top guys are on the case now. Come on inside. You didn't eat yet, did you?"

"No, I've done this enough times."

"Good, 'cause it ain't pretty in there—blood everywhere, two kids down. This bastard totally ruined the little girl. We have a picture of what she looked like on the wall inside, and it's not her anymore. Friggin' shame."

"How old you figure on the girl?" Deke asked.

"Hard to tell from what's left of her, but judging from the size of the body, I'd say anywhere between three and six."

"Shit," Deke said, "I got a little girl just turned five."

"My daughter's ten. There's a boy in there about that old. You better catch this guy before I do, because I swear to God I'll waste him—and I'll do it slow and with as much pain as I can."

"Believe me, Bobby, he won't be any safer with me. Let's get in there."

As they entered the house, the first thing to hit Deke was the smell. Bodies immediately begin to decompose upon death, but it usually takes a few hours to stink up the place. Deke looked around at the room size and the location of the bodies. "Sometime around seven or eight last night, right?"

"Yeah, that's what the medical examiner said after judging the temperature of the bodies. Good guess there."

"Wasn't a guess. I can smell it," Deke answered as he ran his fingers along the doorjamb and keyhole for any sign of forced entry.

"A real nose for news, eh, Deke?"

"Who found 'em?"

"Car service guy. Came to pick them up for the airport around 10:00 P.M."

Deke crouched down over the bodies and had a good look. The crumpled shell of the little girl had fallen on top of what appeared to be her mother. Dad was just to their left, facedown, hand reached out toward them. Deke leaned over toward the father and had a look at the note that was left on his body. "Anyone touch this, move it at all?"

"No, that's right where we found it. Don't move it, though. We still haven't finished photographing the scene. When we're done flashing, you can go through whatever you want, and then we'll bag everything."

Deke looked back at the note and shook his head. "Same wordin' as all the others. It's like a friggin' calling card."

"Yeah, and still no real leads. We have a huge problem here with this guy."

"OK, we gotta start movin'. He's probably already plannin' tonight's murder. You said we had four bodies here. I see Mom, Dad, and baby. Where's the boy?"

"In the back bedroom, under the bed. He did his best to hide. Bastard couldn't just let him go. He had to go back there and finish him."

"Kid must've seen him. Couldn't leave a witness that could identify him."

"Still, put yourself in the kid's shoes. Imagine how scared he must've been."

"Yeah, I know." Deke stood up. "This son of a bitch got no conscience. He obviously don't give a crap about no one standin' in front of him. Totally heartless." He noticed the pictures on the wall and walked over to one. "This is the little girl, huh?"

"Yup."

Deke's stomach tightened up a notch. "There's no need for this . . . friggin' psycho. Let's get him off the street. What did you guys find out so far? How'd he get in? You check all the other doors and windows?"

"Sure did. Doorjambs, locks, keyholes, all fine. All the windows are sealed tight and locked from inside. Whoever did this walked right in."

"Hadda be someone they trusted, then, or maybe had no reason to fear." He looked around. "I doubt it's a neighbor or an acquaintance. The killer's gotta know that's the first place we'd look. No, our boy's got a different angle."

"I agree. We already started compiling a list of all the working people with access to this area. Could be a meter reader or something."

"I'm already on that, but I'm not so sure. The more I think about it, the less likely it seems. Meter readers don't usually come by at night."

"Maybe he was here in the daytime, liked what he saw, and came back."

"Could be, but why would they let him in twice in one day? I think that would raise a red flag for me."

A small protrusion from under the mother caught Deke's eye, its dark green color standing out grossly against the bloodied carpet. "Who gave her the flowers?"

"I would assume the husband. When she fell, she must've been holding a bouquet or something."

Deke looked at the woman and then at the door. "What if

the husband didn't give 'em to her? What if they were delivered? That'd be a pretty easy way to get in here. Look around, find me a card, wrappin' from the florist, anything that could identify where these flowers came from. Let's start hittin' all the shops around here and see what we come up with."

"Already done. We rolled the woman back a little so we could clip a piece of the paper from under her. Was hard trying to find a piece without blood on it. I have two guys out there now checking out all the local florists."

"Good, good. Very good."

"Hey, you taught me well when I was in homicide, buddy. Some things stick."

"Maybe not everything. Have you looked for the shoes yet?"

"What shoes? The father's?"

"The shooter's. Look at this space here on the carpet near the mother and daughter. It's a reverse footprint. Instead of somethin' being transferred from the bottom of the shoe to the carpet, it actually prevented some of the blood spatter from stainin' the carpet. Look how clean it is here." Deke put his foot into the void. "Fits very well. Somewhere out there there's a shoe that fits this spot perfectly that has blood and junk all over it. Get someone in here to take measurements on this. The shoe size'll give us a rough estimate of how tall this guy is."

"You got it, Deke. When my guys are done with the florists, I'll get them started checking out all the shoe stores in the area and see how many shoes have been sold recently that fit the size on the carpet."

"No, don't use the florist guys; they'll be busy enough. Find two other guys for the shoe detail. Listen, there's no budget on this one. You need to authorize overtime for any of this, do it. You need extra men, get them. Anyone says anything to you, drop my name. If they still give you a problem, send 'em to me."

"OK, no prob. Sounds good. When I hear something back from the florist detectives, I'll find you."

"All right, but listen, don't let 'em just stop at checkin' the delivery guys. I want copies of every receipt, every address, every surveillance tape taken of every customer that passed through every one of those florists covering the last twenty-four hours. When that's done, let 'em check out every person on that list and find out if they can be placed near any of the other murders."

"Understood, Deke. That's gonna take some time, though, and if there's no budget on this, how 'bout letting me get my crime scene guys back and giving this to some of your guys?"

"Yeah, you're right, lack of sleep's getting to me. When you hear from them, call my squad and give 'em what you got. We'll take it from there."

"You got it, Deke."

The vibrator on Deke's cell phone started buzzing away in his pocket. He pulled it out, looked at the caller ID, and flipped it open. "Durgess, go, Cap."

"Deke, I need you back here. Right away."

"Are you kiddin' me! I got a crime scene here."

"No shit. You think I'm in a goddam closet here?"

"Well, then, leave me be. I barely started processin' the place. I'm not even out of the first room yet."

"Forget the crime scene. Let CSU process it. The mayor just held a press conference. I need you here now."

Deke looked at his watch. "It's 6:30 A.M.! What the hell's he on the air this early for?"

"He's calling for assistance from the FBI. They'll be here within the hour with an entire forensics team and a profiler. I want you in here to help brief these guys on what we have so far."

"I'm bein' taken off the case?" he asked, not sure if he felt angry or relieved.

"No, they're here to help you. This is your case all the way, but I need you within the hour."

"Yeah, yeah, yeah." The phone was smacked shut and shoved back into his pocket. Deke said a few words to the CSU guys, gave them his card that had both his home and cell phone numbers on it, and headed for the front door. An icy blast of winter air greeted him, and he was thankful for it. Even cold, blustery air was preferable to the stench of mutilated, decaying bodies. As he walked down the front pathway and headed toward his car, he could clearly see a huge gaggle of reporters begin to mass just on the other side of the blue police barriers, right in line with him. Once he was within ten feet of them, the questions and the camera flashes began.

"Detective, is that the work of the Daily Killer in there?"

His stride was never broken. "No comment."

The reporters and their questions followed. "Does this have any connection to the fact that the mayor has asked the FBI for help in the murders?"

"No comment."

"Detective, a preliminary search on this house says it's owned by a man named Mike Nevalo, his wife, and two children."

Deke's head whipped around as the question continued.

"Are those the victims that were found in the house?"

Deke was livid and yelled an answer this time. "Hey, haven't you ever heard of next of kin! Dammit! Don't be putting names out there without first getting confirmation." The the flashes from the strobes intensified, and the cameras zoomed in on his angry face. The next words out of his mouth were spat over the entire group, like a blanket covering them all. "That question was off the record, people. Do not be using those names unless you get a briefing from us. Give us time to confirm identities and notify next of kin before you go throwing names over the air." He reached

31

for and ripped open his car door. "What happened in that house is still bein' investigated, and we will update you as information becomes available. At the present time, I am not prepared to say that this situation is in any way connected to any other case. Am I clear on that?"

"Can you tell us how many victims are in the house, Detective?"

Deke jumped into the car and closed the door without answering another question. He knew it was useless trying to reason with these people. He peered through his windshield at the crowd of overzealous, heartless newshounds. Nothing pissed him off more than people who did their jobs at the expense of others. Reporters were the worst of that lot for him. In his eyes, there was more to life than just bylines, deadlines, and headlines. There was a family in that house back there. It was a living, thriving, cohesive unit flourishing and basking in what each person had to offer. There were happy pictures all over the walls of wonderful memories that they shared. Those people had done nothing wrong to deserve a fate like this. To Deke, these murders, and all others, were a complete and utter travesty.

To the reporters, however, they were little more than words on a page, possibly a bigger paycheck, a way to put some higher-quality food on the table. There was absolutely no connection drawn between what they were writing about and what Deke was seeing. It was a pretty simple equation. Reporters report, that's all they do, and the one who does it first and gets the story in ahead of the others will probably get the lion's share of attention. It's as easy as that. Reporters don't have time to feel. If they stay too long on a story because they are emotionally involved, they might miss the next one. It's all about beating the other guy to the front page. Deke understood this. It didn't mean he had to like it. Or even respect it, for that matter.

In one aspect, though, he wasn't much different from them. He was racing to a deadline also. Only his deadline truly was a matter of life and death. His deadline, and some other unsuspecting family's, was probably just hours away. This lunatic was wiping out people by the day. The murder scenes were coming too fast, and the clues were noticeably nonexistent. For Deke, that meant he'd always be two steps behind. Somehow, some way he had to find the card with the ice cream float on it, or at least a double red. He needed to close the gap on the guy. Better yet, if only he could figure a way to jump ahead. Deke knew he had to come up with something. Right now, it was real hard following along behind the killer. He absolutely needed that connection from one murder to another to catch up.

Unfortunately, the murderer either thought of this or was just plain lucky. The only consistency from one scene to another was a callous calling card, a note that was always written the same, word for word, and dropped on the body of one of his victims. BETTER LUCK NEXT TIME, it would say. Was it a clue or just a cruel joke to piss off the cops? Was it a message to the victims or to the cops trying to catch him? The answer was somewhere in the killer's warped mind. Deke wasn't the least bit interested in that answer, though. As far as he was concerned, the only thing he wanted in the killer's mind was a slug from his old-fashioned .38 Special.

He drove his car down the street away from the murder scene, noticing the camera lights and police lights glistening smartly off his rearview mirror. The thought hit him that he was driving that car from one part of hell directly to another. There were now six murder scenes in six days, fifteen dead bodies in all. New York City had once again become the focal point of the world, as it had five years earlier when time seemed to stand still as two of earth's proudest symbols came crashing down. That situation was mass murder, though, and it was carried out by fundamentalist extremists. This time it was, more than likely, one individual terrorizing the city. Deke was now riding in the front car on this roller coaster of death, the lead investigator on the highest-profile murder case of the century.

When he was first assigned the case, he only had to deal with one murder scene and just two bodies. There wasn't even a hint of a clue that this would turn into a daily event. On the surface it appeared to be just another murder case involving drugs, money, or infidelity. Those were the usual motives, and each case always came with its own usual-suspects list. There was the jealous husband, the jilted boyfriend, the crack addict looking for a fix. Insurance policies were also a good place to start. They usually get bumped up right before a victim gets bumped off. Point was, the victims more often than not had some connection to the killer. Seemingly not so in this case. This guy appeared to be picking victims right out of thin air, on some psychotic whim, and he was good at it, very well prepared. How he managed to do it on a daily basis and continually get away undetected was almost a clue in itself.

Deke understood that the killer *had* to know beforehand who, where, and when he was going to strike. It had to be. The key to the whole thing was in his process of selecting the victims— although he certainly made it appear that there was no selection process. The victims he chose came from all walks of life. They were men, women, and children. They were black, white, and everything in between. They were old, young, married, and divorced. One victim was even transgender. There was no merit given to financial status either. Wealthy or poor, both were deemed insignificant. Basically, it made no difference whatsoever who you were. If you came up on his list of things to do today, tomorrow was no longer in your future.

What stood out above all else was the frequency with which the murders occurred. Most serial killers pick and choose their spots over days, weeks, months, sometimes even years. They seem to take a little break after a killing before moving on to the next poor soul in their sights. They plot their course of attack, so to speak, and usually an escape plan. Mostly there is some type of method to their madness. Not here, though. This case had fast become its own precedent. If not for that sloppily hand-scribed note, there would be no evidence connecting any of the murders. There would be six different investigations going on to catch six different killers.

This guy didn't want the police wasting their time on that. Whatever his agenda was, he had no fear of being tracked down for his dastardly deeds. He almost encouraged it with his notes. This "better luck next time" nonsense was a real kick in the crotch for Deke because it meant that there would be a next time. Sometime in the next twenty-four hours he would be getting a call informing him of yet another bloody scene to investigate, unless he could solve this thing before another unfortunate family met their demise. He knew there was no way that was going to happen unless the killer decided to walk into a precinct and give himself up—and the chances of that happening were slimmer than none. Hopefully, somewhere this guy would slip up and give Deke the break in the case he needed. For now, though, with six separate murder scenes on six different days yielding no clues to the identity of the killer or his selection process, many more innocent people out there were in harm's way. Nothing could be done to save them.

Deke arrived at detective squad headquarters and was pissed to find that a four-door black sedan with government plates now filled his regular illegal parking spot up on the sidewalk in front of the place. The rest of the block was filled bumper to bumper with cars identical to the one occupying his spot. He double-parked his car and grabbed some papers from the backseat.

A soft knock on the driver's window grabbed his attention. He pushed a button on the door console and lowered the window. "Who are you?"

"Good morning, Detective. Agent Williams," the man said while flashing a small black wallet containing a badge and ID card. "You can leave your car here with the engine running. I'll look after it while you're in there."

Deke scanned the badge with his eyes and committed the information on it to memory. He exited the vehicle and lumbered his way up the front steps, nodding his reply to each of the FBI guys that wished him good morning. Any one of them could plainly see that it was anything but a good morning for Deke. He was exhausted, and his walk surely showed it. The mind was still crisp but beginning to get a bit overloaded. He did smile at the identical black suits the FBI guys wore. He'd always heard about it but thought it wasn't anything more than a joke.

He swung the door open into Captain Murray's office and was greeted by another sea of black. FBI guys were all over the place, sitting, standing, leaning against walls.

"What was it, a buy one, get a hundred free sale at the clothin' store, guys?" Deke asked cynically.

"Deke, get over here," Captain Murray ordered. "This is Assistant Director Miller of the FBI's Serial Murder Profiling Squad," he said, motioning to Miller with his hand.

"Serial Murder Profiling Squad?" Deke remarked. "Ain't heard that one yet. I guess it's pretty freakin' convenient, though," he continued sarcastically.

"I'd say it's more lucky," the captain replied. "Assistant Director Miller, this is Detective Harlon Durgess, our lead investigator on the case."

Durgess put his hand out first. "I prefer Deke," he said, grabbing Miller's hand firmly. "Good to meet you, Director."

Miller quickly replied, "Listen, there's no need for titles between us. We're on the same team now. Just call me Dom."

"Will do. I appreciate that."

"OK, talk to me. What have you got so far on this guy?"

Deke looked around. "Can we clear the room? I don't like playin' to a crowd. Besides, my voice is tired. I'll brief you, and then you can brief your men."

"Not a problem." With a wave of the director's hand, the sea of black funneled itself into a stream of black headed out of Captain Murray's office. The last suit out grabbed the knob and quietly pulled the door closed. "OK, I'm listening."

"Well, what we're dealin' with here is either a criminal genius or a lucky-ass amateur."

"We get that feeling in almost every one of these cases. Eventually, it becomes clear. What gives you the feeling?"

Deke chuckled. "Almost everything."

There was no laughter from the Fed. "Explain."

Deke cleared his throat. "All righty, then." He took a seat and pulled his notebook from his inner jacket pocket. He flipped though the pages as he spoke. "So far we got six murder scenes, fifteen bodies, very few clues, and hardly any forensic evidence left behind. Not once has there been a witness, or at least anyone who admits to seein' anything."

Miller pursed his lips. "Ballistics?"

"We're still waitin' on that. Maybe you guys can speed things up a bit there."

"Done. What else?"

"Personal stuff. It seems this guy's a real wiseass; likes leavin' notes on the victim's bodies to piss us off." He looked at Miller with a direct stare. "So far, it's workin' on me pretty good."

Miller sat up in his chair. "Where are these notes? What do they say?"

"Same thing every time." Deke glanced quickly at the notes in his hand. "They say, 'better luck next time.'"

"Is it the same wording, written six different times? Or is it a photocopy of the same note six times?"

"No, it looks like he wrote each one individually."

"All right! We may have something here. Where are they now?"

"They were taken down to the evidence hall by whatever CSU team was doing that particular murder scene at the time."

"OK, let's get them here. I have handwriting specialists with me that can study this guy's writing and develop a profile on him on that alone."

Deke was a bit skeptical and feeling a little infringed upon. "How accurate is that? I don't wanna be chasin' wild gooses here."

"It's fairly accurate in about sixty percent of the cases we do involving handwriting."

Captain Murray jumped in before Deke could shoot it down. "Sounds like a starting point to me," he said as he picked up the phone and began making the necessary calls to get the notes over to his office. "What else you got for the man, Deke?"

"You know what?" Miller said as he took a small tape recorder out and set it on the desk. "Let's do this case by case."

Deke whistled softly as he scrolled backward through his notebook. "OK, murder scene one. December Seventeenth, Upper West Side, Manhattan, West Seventy-second Street. Two victims. Male white, thirty-six years old, shot in the head at about five feet, body found in the living room by the couch. Second victim, female white, thirty-four years old, also shot in the head at close range, body found just outside the kitchen near the living room. She must've heard the commotion going on and walked right into it. Time of death somewhere between 7:00 P.M. and midnight. Both victims were fairly affluent, held high-profile jobs, and had no criminal record. Nothin' of note stolen from the home, no ransackin' whatsoever, no sign of forced entry." He took a breath. "Couple was married, no children, no family livin' in New York area. All bills paid up to date, no outstandin' gamblin' debts, no drug addictions of any kind. They just seemed to be a typical hardworkin' couple doin' the right thing." Deke took a peek at Miller to see if he had any questions or comments on the first set of facts. A stoic face was his answer, and Deke continued.

"Murder scene two. December eighteenth, Maspeth, Queens, Fifty-eighth Avenue. Three victims. Male Hispanic, sixty-nine years old, shot in head point-blank, body found just inside front door. Second victim, female Hispanic, sixty-five years old, shot in upper back, apparently as she tried to flee the attack, and then once again in the neck at close range. Victim three, male Hispanic, two years old, shot in head as he slept in portable playpen in rear bedroom. Kid was the grandson of victims one and two and was dropped there by his mother on her way to work. Time of death roughly around two in the afternoon. The mother discovered the bodies when she came to pick the kid back up after work." Deke paused a second and shook his head. "Imagine that poor woman comin' to get her baby and seein' that." He shook his head again. "I had to interview her that day. I saw the bodies, and there was nothin' left of that kid. That one right there made this personal for me."

Miller interrupted. "Why were you at this scene? You knew there was a connection that quick?"

"The note. As soon as CSU saw it, they called me. We put out a memo to all the CSU units after the first murder to find out if any had come across any notes in previous crime scenes, or just in case any came up in future scenes."

"Yeah, that's what I figured. I was hoping there might've been something else there also. OK, please go on."

"All right, let's see." Deke scanned the notes. "Mother found the bodies . . . oh yeah, here we go. Victims one and two were retired, rent-stabilized apartment, livin' comfortably on Social Security and small pension. No debts, no enemies. Other neighbors in buildin' said they were very quiet yet helpful. There was no sign of forced entry and no prints or forensic evidence left behind. No one in buildin' saw nothin' comin' or goin' and didn't hear nothin' neither."

"How many shots were fired at scene two?"

"Four," Deke responded. "One in the old man, two in the woman, and one in the kid."

Miller sat up straight, then leaned forward, put his elbows on his knees, and clasped his hands. He looked at Deke with squinty eyes. "Four shots and no one heard anything?"

"Apparently not."

"No shell casings found at any of the scenes?"

"Not one."

"Maybe he uses a revolver and a silencer, then."

"Or he could just be a neat freak with an automatic and a pillow that likes to clean up after himself. He could be pickin' up the shell casings for all we know. I have no idea right now. What I can tell from the damage done to the victims is that he's usin' nothin' smaller than a .38 or 9 mil."

Miller shot his hand up. "Hold on a sec." He took a small walkie-talkie from his shirt pocket, pushed two or three numbers, and clicked the button.

A deep voice quickly came back to him. "Go, boss."

"Listen, contact the New York office and get one of our ballistics teams over to the NYPD ballistics lab and speed this process along. I want to know what caliber and gun was used for each killing by the end of the day."

The answer was short and sweet. "On it."

The talkie was put away. "I know you said your ballistics team was slow. I've seen some take as many as ten days to come back with a result."

Deke smiled and nodded. "Yeah, probably here."

Miller motioned to Deke's notebook with his head. "All right, what else?"

"OK, nothin' missin' from the apartment, nothin' out of place, at least accordin' to the daughter. No criminal history on the parents' or daughter's part, but the daughter's ex-boyfriend did do a stint in Rikers for armed robbery."

"You check him out?"

"Not personally because murder scene three rolled in, but a couple of my guys looked him over real good. His alibi's tight. He was actually up in Ossining with his parole officer. We looked into his past. No one out there lookin' to get him or get even with him. He was a dead end."

"Is that all you got on two?"

"Pretty much," he answered, peeking at the notes. "The rest is just filler."

"Let's hear three, then."

"Murder scene three. December nineteenth, down in the Village, on East Sixth Street. Two victims. Time of death was about 7:30 to 10:30 P.M. First victim, male black, fifty-six years old, shot twice in the face, body found in bedroom on the floor. Second victim, male—or female dependin' on which way you look at it—Chinese descent, approximately twenty-five to thirty years old, shot three times in back of head, body found next to victim one." Deke noticed the odd way Miller was looking at him.

"What do you mean, male or female?"

"Victim two was transgender, although we got no positive ID on him . . . or her."

"I see. Go on."

"More than likely this person was an illegal with no documentation. What exactly their relationship was we don't know, but victim one's family stated that he was involved with someone they didn't approve of. We checked out the whole family to find out how much they didn't like this person and turned up nothin'. They're mostly churchgoin' people that didn't like his lifestyle, so they disowned him. Anyhow, there was absolutely no connection between them and any of the previous murder victims."

"Nothing stolen?"

"Nothin'. Killer seems to come in, do his business, drop his note, and leave. There's no screwin' around. Like in the other two, there was no forced entry and nothin' left behind in the way of evidence."

Miller leaned back in his chair and stretched his legs. He laid his head back and looked up at the ceiling. The perfectly pressed black wool suit he'd walked in with was now unbuttoned and hanging open. The vest, while still buttoned, was being pushed to its earthly limits by a potbelly jammed full of an early breakfast of bacon, eggs, and toast. "I see what you mean with this guy," he said as he pulled himself back into a straight-up position. "Let me hear the rest."

"I hope you got enough room on that tape there," said Deke, alluding to the recorder on the desk.

"It's voice activated. More gigs of space than I can count. We're good."

"Cool. OK, let's go, then. Murder scene four. December twentieth, Gravesend, Brooklyn, little nothin' street called Applegate Court, two victims, time of death roughly eight o'clock at night. First victim was a male white, forty-six years old, shot once, dead between the eyes, body found at the foot of the basement stairs below the side-door entrance. Victim two was female white, seventy-eight, shot once in the head, once in the left ankle. He probably caught her as she tried to run up the stairs to the second floor. Body was found three steps from the top. Victim one was the son of victim two, divorced six years, college-age kids. Poor guy was put through the wringer by his ex-wife, lost pretty much everything in the settlement and had to move back home with Mom and Dad. Bodies were discovered by woman's husband, age eighty, who then took a heart attack and is now in ICU at Coney Island Hospital. As usual, nothin' missin' from home, no forced entry, and no evidence left behind. Interviewed all the neighbors and came up empty. Small street, tight houses, you'd think someone would have heard somethin'."

"If I recall, the first three killings were all over the news at that point. News media had it put together that these were serial?"

"Not at that point, but they were gettin' there. We didn't release nothin' about the note   still haven't. They ain't stupid, though. Different murders with similar circumstances always get connected somehow by the media."

"So the public wasn't really clued in yet. That might explain the lack of witnesses. People weren't keeping their eye out."

"They're keepin' their eye out now, and we still ain't got no witnesses."

Miller did his best to hold back on the snide comments. The way Deke spoke, he found it hard to believe he was the lead detective on the case. He sounded more like he should be flipping burgers somewhere, or better yet scrubbing toilets. Like Deke, though, Miller had learned long ago not to judge a book by its cover, or in this case its wording. "Someone has to know something," he said. "It'll just be a matter of time, you'll see. We're up to number five now?"

"Yup, murder scene five. December twenty-first, Brooklyn again, Marine Park, Brown Street. Two victims. Time of death between 4:00 and 8:00 P.M."

Miller broke in. "Almost every one of these was late afternoon to early evening. Looks like your guy is a working stiff, can't get off during working hours to do his dirty work."

"Yeah, we thought of that, too. We're checkin' the meter readers, mailmen, delivery guys, pretty much anyone with access to these areas durin' work hours. We're hopin' for someone's name to pop up more than once."

"That's where he's going to be, just watch."

"Well, we're on it. Hopefully it'll pan out." Deke flipped the page in his notebook and continued. "Two victims at this scene. First was a male black, twenty-four years old, shot once in the chest and once in the neck. Victim two was also a male black, age twenty-three, shot once in the head and once in the chest. Now, here's where it gets really interestin'. Both victims were found on the livin' room couch with about an eight ball of coke on the table in front of them. We found scales and small distribution bags on the table also."

"Small-time drug dealers, huh?"

"No doubt. We also found two fully loaded semiautomatics, more than five thousand in cash, and a delivery of L&B on a chair."

"What's L&B?"

"Oh yeah, sorry. I guess you gotta come from Brooklyn to know. L&B is Spumoni Gardens. It's a local pizza place."

"I see. So, any way this could be just a drug deal gone bad? Maybe it's just a couple of guys from the 'hood taking revenge. Might not be your guy." His hand quickly went up as a thought blew into his head. "Check that . . . the note."

"Yup, dropped right on top of the twenty-four-year-old."

"No forced entry? No kicked-in door?"

"No, and you'd think there would be, right? Two guys, coke all over the place—and two guns ready to go."

"Well, what's your theory?"

"I think he came in with the pizza. L&B says they didn't take no orders goin' to that address. We showed 'em pictures of the victims, and no one remembers either of 'em comin' in for a pie. The guy probably showed up with the pizza and, in the confusion of whether it was ordered or not, either pushed his way in or threatened 'em with the gun to make 'em let him in, and that was that."

"Nothing like the element of surprise. Really evens up the sides. No witnesses here either?"

Deke shook his head.

"How can that be?"

"These guys were blarin' rap music at the time of the killin'. Any sound was drowned out. Didn't make a difference, though. All the neighbors we interviewed were happy to be rid of these mopes. They wouldn't say nothin' even if they did see somethin'. Guys were thugs in the buildin'."

Deke's cell phone began buzzing wildly in his pocket. He pulled it out, saw the caller ID, and immediately answered. "Durgess . . . Yeah, go ahead . . . OK, OK . . . Yup . . . OK, do me a favor, fax me a copy of that report to Captain Murray's office. Yeah, I'm there now. Very good . . . Hurry up." He slipped the phone back in his pocket and looked at Miller. "I guess we didn't need your guys after all. Ballistics just came in on the first three murder scenes."

"What's it look like?" asked Captain Murray.

"Slugs are all the same, .38 calibers, all fired from the same gun. The report's on its way."

"Dammit," Captain Murray said, "thirty-eight is a very common bullet. It's not going to be easy tracking the gun it came from."

The fax machine started ringing and beeping, and before long it was spitting out a piece of paper full of black and white. Deke ripped it from the machine and took it to the copy machine. He then handed one copy to his captain and one to Miller so they could view it simultaneously and all move at the same pace.

"I can tell you right now," Deke began as he scanned the pictures that had come with the report, "by the grooves on the slugs it looks like a snub-nose or somethin' pretty close to it. They ain't too deep or defined."

"I agree," Miller responded. "The slugs are fairly intact, too, so he's not using hollow-points. They're distorted but not fragmented."

"I wish these pics were color," Murray chimed in. "I can't tell if they're straight lead or copper jacketed."

"No, those ain't cop killers," Deke said. "They look like straight lead. There'd be some kinda shine to 'em if they were cop killers."

Murray lifted his gaze from the paper. "Copper jackets would make it easier to track if that's the kind of ammunition he's buying. At least we can trace them back somewhere."

Miller pulled his talkie again and pressed some buttons. "Pick up," he ordered.

"G'head, boss" came back.

"When you get to ballistics, I want a complete report of the type of bullet used and its composition. Get me some color pictures and scan or fax them over to me immediately."

"I'm about ten minutes out, boss. You'll have it in fifteen."

"All right. Shake it."

Deke and Captain Murray were still bouncing ideas off of

each other when Miller returned to the conversation. "You'll have color pictures of the bullets inside of twenty minutes."

"OK, good," Deke answered and then turned to Captain Murray. "Ya know, this guy's pretty friggin' economical with his firepower. He don't waste no bullets. Every one he fires hits its target. We ain't come across a stray shot yet."

"Your point?"

"It's gonna be next to impossible trackin' down where these bullets came from. Think about it. Whaddaya get in a box, twenty-five? Fifty? He's only averagin' about four per scene. He coulda got a box a year ago and waited till now to do his thing."

"Deke, it's all we got right now."

"I know. Fuck!" he yelled. "These bullets are gonna take a lot of legwork."

"That's OK. Relax. We have a lot of legs on this one."

"Deke," Miller said, "while we're waiting on my guys here, why don't you give me the rest on these murders. Are we done with the fifth one yet?"

"Yeah, pretty much." Deke took a deep breath and slowly let it seep out. He moved back around the desk within voice range of the recorder. "You ready?"

"As much as I'll ever be," Miller answered softly.

Deke jumped right into it. "Murder six, yesterday, December twenty-second. Great Kills, Staten Island, Armstrong Avenue. Time of death around 7:00 or 8:00 P.M. Four victims. First victim, male white, age thirty-four, shot once in the chest and once in the stomach. Body was found on the living room floor right beside victims two and three. Victim two was a female white, age thirty-three, shot once, point-blank, in the face. Victim three, female white, four years old—"

"Jesus Christ," Miller mumbled, staring blankly ahead.

Deke paused a second, then continued. "Four years old, shot once in the back of the head. There was a high amount of trauma on this one; her face was almost completely blown out. This one might've been hollow-point."

"Changing bullets midstream?" Miller questioned. "Could've just been the angle it hit her."

"Maybe. Anyhow, her body was found directly on top of Mom's."

"This is friggin' unbelievable," he said. "Where was victim four found?"

"Victim four, male white, nine years old, shot once in the forehead. Body was discovered in his bedroom, under the bed."

"That's three kids in all now that this guy took out. I read a preliminary report about this just before I got on the plane. This bastard is ruthless."

"Heartless is the word we've been kickin' around. Anyhow, this family was tight-knit, no enemies, no outstandin' problems of any kind. They were about to leave for the airport on a trip to Florida when this bastard hit 'em. No forced entry, nothin' taken from the scene. This time, though, he may have left us somethin' we can work with."

"Let's hear," Miller said, leaning forward.

"He shot the victims at very close range and got his foot in the way of the blood spatter, leavin' what I call a reverse print on the carpet. We should have a rough idea by now of the size shoe he wears. From that we'll be able to estimate his height. With any luck, we'll come across that shoe somehow and pick up some of the victims' DNA on it. I don't think he'll be wearin' it around town lookin' the way it does. If he can't clean it, he's gonna have to toss it. Maybe we can find it. Even if he does clean it, I'm willin' to bet that we'll catch some DNA on it when we nail him."

Miller picked up the recorder from the desk and put his thumb on the STOP button. "Is that it? We up to date now?"

"For today. If we don't come up with somethin' quick, we'll be doin' this again tomorrow."

"Gonna make for *some* Christmas Eve. Damn! All right, let's get shaking, then." He took the talkie and chirped his guy at the ballistics office. "Where's that report?" he hollered.

"Just sent it, boss. Should be there any sec."

At that very moment the fax machine started ringing. Shortly thereafter, a sheet full of color photos of distorted bullets came sliding out. The three men took the one sheet and placed it on the desk where they all could see it. It was plain to see at a quick glance that the bullets used were the extremely common straight-lead variety. They would be impossible to track. The grooves left on the bullets by the barrel of the murder weapon were not well defined but still not hard to discern. It suggested that perhaps they came from a shorter-barrel revolver. Deke commented that if it was a revolver it would make sense that the killer was so careful when he fired not to waste bullets. A typical revolver holds only five or six bullets. Wasted shots mean time-consuming reloads. This guy was all about time conservation. Get in, get out.

It was still unclear whether he really was smart about all of this or just a lucky amateur. His bullet of choice was untraceable, but the gun he fired them with was pretty easy to trace, provided it had a history of being on the wrong side of the law. As a gun fires a bullet, grooves in the barrel help spin the bullet in an effort to keep it flying straight once it leaves the barrel. These grooves imprint themselves on the bullet and leave a fingerprint of that particular gun, making it easy to connect the two through ballistics. The grooves would be broken down into a grid and entered into a nationwide database to see if the weapon had been used in any other crimes. With luck, they'd get a match and then hope that the gun had been legally registered at some point in its life. That would give them a nice jumping-off point to start tracking the gun forward to the lunatic that currently owned it.

Captain Murray's desk phone began ringing, and he cringed as he saw Deke pick it up and answer for him. There was nothing like Deke's vocabulary on an important phone call. "Detective squad, Captain Murray's desk, Durgess speakin'."

Murray and Miller looked on quietly as Deke listened to what was being said to him through the phone. A few seconds later, the handset was back in its cradle.

"They need me upstairs. The first of the local workers from murder areas is here for questionin'. I want to be in on it." He took the photosheet of the bullets and handed it to the FBI assistant director. "You think you could get this run through your database? I'm sure it'll be a lot quicker if you do it."

Miller grabbed it happily. "That's what we're here for, Detective. Whatever you need."

"Anything else, Cap?" Deke said to Murray.

"No, go ahead, get up there. I'll help Dom brief his men."

"Call me if you get a hit on the gun," Deke said and rushed out the door.

Captain Murray motioned to the paper in Miller's hand. "How quick can you have that checked out?"

"We're already on it. My guy that sent this to me is having it run as we speak."

"I see you trained your men well."

"It's an elite unit, Captain, best of the best. They came to me that way."

Murray looked at his watch. "Quarter to ten. We better get something on this gun fast. Someone out there only has hours to live."

Chapter Three

Robert Russo stumbled through the front door at his usual time, which was pretty much any time he felt like it. He might have made it through the door a few minutes earlier had he not been sticking the wrong keys into the lock or clumsily dropping them every other second. His nearly frostbitten fingertips only added to his problem, the result of the loss of a forgotten pair of gloves, a pair that was thought of as necessity six hours earlier when he passed through this same door going the other way. At that point his wits were about him, his sobriety fairly intact after nearly eight hours of unconsciousness. He checked that sobriety at the door of his home away from home, a walking-distance bar that had a stool reserved for him. It was probably there that he lost his gloves. It was even more probable that they walked out covering someone else's hands, the new owner knowing when enough was enough. The limitations on Rob's alcohol consumption were only reached when the money in his pocket dwindled to nothing. For the most part, it was the only thing in his life that he had any control over. His Social Security check could only cover so much drinking, and Rob would actually budget this meager pittance into daily allotments, just enough to stretch out an entire month at the bar. The same amount went into his pocket at the start of each day, and the same empty pocket staggered home at the end. It lasted as long as it could in between.

The first sight his blurry eyes could make out after he slammed the door was his irritated wife, also in her usual position for this time of day. She was settled in nicely on the living room couch, surrounded by empty potato chip bags and candy wrappers. Certainly not the picture of health, she offset her lingering problem with diabetes by keeping her body full of the same poison that soused her husband. The more alcohol in, the less sugar produced by the liver. She believed in the concept of "an apple a day" but substituted a fifth of vodka instead. Where her husband took his straight with a few olives, she liked hers over ice with a splash of orange soda. They were a match made in hell. Neither had made it beyond an eleventh-grade education, and neither currently had any aspirations in life other than their daily dose of vitamin V. They were content to live off the fat of the U.S. government and let the chips fall where they may, so to speak.

Her eyes were red, and not just from drunkenness. "You were drinking outta my bottle again, weren't you, you piece of shit?" she asked in speech so slurred only another drunk could understand it.

"Bitch, shut your face!" Rob yelled. "I don't want to hear none of your crap."

"Stay out of my stuff, then. You got me falling short here," she yelled back as she held up the bottle and swished around a small amount of vodka barely above the bottom. "What'm I gonna do when this runs out?"

"Like I give a shit," answered Rob as he waved her off with his hand. He hobbled his way to the refrigerator, bouncing off walls and dilapidated furniture during the journey. He pulled on the fridge door and shut one eye to make focusing easier. "What the hell," he hollered, almost in disbelief. "You didn't make no dinner?"

"Sure I did," his wife answered, holding up and waving an empty potato chip bag. "Just the way I like it, too."

"Bitch! I'm hungry. Get up and make me something."

"You want something, you shoulda been home an hour ago. You coulda had some o' mine."

Rob looked around at the spinning room. "Where's Alexa? She'll cook for me."

"She's eight years old, you ass; she ain't cooking for you! Besides, she's been gone three days now. I knew you wouldn't notice until you needed her."

"Gone three days? Where?"

"My asshole sister. She said she'd call Children's Services if I didn't let her go. She says we got her in a bad environment."

"She's a bitch, too," Rob said in a mixture of English and burp. "You just let her do it?"

"Well, what else! I was already in the hole twice for this shit. I ain't goin' back for it again. Don't bother lookin' for Aidan. She took him, too."

Rob steadied himself by placing both hands on the kitchen counter. He let a string of 80 proof spit drip from his mouth into the sink as his diminished brain pondered the ramifications of two fewer mouths to feed. The equation kept coming back with the same answer—an answer that made complete sense in his selfish mind: There would now be more money in his pocket each day at the bar. He actually got butterflies in his stomach at the thought. "Eh, let her feed 'em, then," he said nonchalantly. "We could use a vacation."

"Screw the vacation. Gimme back my whisky instead." She stared at Rob with disdain as spit stretched from his mouth to the sink. "You might want to clean yourself up some. My sister's passing by with them tonight so they can wish us a merry Christmas, and I don't feel like hearing her with the 'I told you so.' "

"Christmas? They're probably just looking for presents."

"They're our kids, you schmuck. Of course they're looking for presents."

"Dopey bitch," Rob muttered. "What the hell do we have here that we could give them?"

"I'll find something when they get here. I'll rewrap one of their toys from last year in tinfoil. Christmas ain't for another two days, so by the time they open it—"

"Christmas," Rob said angrily. "What a happy time of year."

"Would be happier if you stayed out of my freakin' bottle, asswipe."

The growling in Rob's stomach was making him more irritable than usual. "Jesus, Cheryl, shut up already about the bottle! I ain't putting my mouth anywhere yours goes." More spit went into the sink. "Why you such a pain in the ass today?"

"Just giving what I get," she mumbled softly.

"Shut your fat self up already, bitch—or I'll come over there and give you what you get!"

Cheryl pushed and pulled and fought until she got her 250-pound frame into a sitting position. Gasping and breathing heavily from the struggle, she couldn't utter the words that Rob had inspired from her. Instead, the middle finger on her right hand was inserted into the air, and Rob did his best to focus on it.

"Think you're funny, bitch? I'll break that fat finger."

"You couldn't find my finger unless it was up your ass, dipshit," she responded, finger still in the air.

"Yeah, keep it up, idiot. Cops'll come in here and find you dead on that couch tonight."

"Only after I beat your ass to death first, you useless cripple."

Rob worked his way to the couch and parked himself next to

his wife. He rummaged through her empty chip bags and scavenged any crumbs he could find. Cheryl reached behind herself and handed him a bag that hadn't yet met its demise through her black hole of a mouth. Rob grabbed it happily and downed the chips as if he were drinking them.

"And you talk about me?" said Cheryl, hoping the walls and floor would stay still.

"I try not to," Rob answered, dealing with his own moving kaleidoscope of walls and furniture.

Uneclipsed love of the bottle was the only thing they had in common. It was the strongest bond that kept them together. It was also the biggest wedge that drove them apart. Neither had an inkling that this would be the finish line when they started out ten years earlier. Then, it was the sky's-the-limit mantra, and they packed tremendous energy and effort into building their future. Each worked and each saved, and within five years they had a house and a daughter and a real shot at life—but when an off-site injury took away the use of Rob's right leg, the job was gone, soon followed by the dwindling disability payments. The Social Security was only a fraction of what he earned. Cheryl's job didn't pay nearly enough to cover their mortgage or her increasing food bill. The house went into foreclosure, and they soon found themselves in a broken-down, rented trailer home. As their dignity eroded, each discovered a newfound confidence through the bottle. The more they drank, the more they liked themselves and the less they liked each other. They fought like cats and dogs, always threatening to beat the other into submission, but when it came down to it, neither would lay a finger on the other. Deep down inside, they knew they needed each other—if for no other reason, to make them feel good about themselves. To an extent it worked, but as the alcohol consumption increased, overall control of their lives disappeared. They were nomads in time, moving aimlessly from day to day, no discernible direction governing them. Basically, they were just plodding their way through life, dragging their two innocent children with them to wherever they'd wind up. No love, no responsibility, no chance.

"Any more chips?" Rob asked hopefully.

"Sure," Cheryl answered dryly. "Go hop over to the store and get them."

"Bitch," he answered.

Three short knocks alerted them that someone was at the front door. Rob pushed himself to his feet and limped toward the sound. He had begun to reach for the knob when Cheryl's shrill voice invaded his ears.

"Don't open the door, you ass! That might not be my sister. The lunatic that's killing people could be out there. Check the window first."

Rob looked at his wife with disdain. "If he is out there, I'm gonna let him in just so he can kill your fat ass."

Cheryl shook her head and whispered, "Shithead."

Rob pulled the bedsheet curtain to the side and had a look at who was at the door. It took a second or two, but then recognition hit his mind. "Hey, it's the guy I was drinking with at the bar today. He's got my gloves in his hand!"

Rob let go of the sheet and quickly opened the door. "Yo, man, you got my gloves. Where'd you find 'em?" he asked.

"Hey, what's up? You left them at the bar." He sniffled. "Can I come in a sec and warm up? I'm freezing my ass off out here."

"Yeah, I guess so. Just don't expect nothing to eat. My wife took the day off." Rob pulled the man in and closed the door behind him. "Sorry, dude, but I forgot your name."

"Dave," he said.

"Yeah, that's right. Dave, that's my wife, Cheryl, over there. Cheryl, this is Dave."

Dave nodded and put his hand up in a wave. Cheryl responded with a flick of the hand.

"So, where'd you say you found my gloves?" Rob asked.

"You left them right on top of the bar. You just walked out without them."

Cheryl chuckled to herself. "Stupid bastard," she mumbled.

"You say something, bitch?"

"Oh, go talk to your drinking buddy there."

Rob turned to Dave. "Sorry about her, man. She's useless."

"It happens," Dave replied.

"Hey, how'd you know where to find me?" Rob said while looking down at the gloves in his hand. "I don't remember telling you where I live."

"Yeah, I didn't think you'd remember, sot-boy. You didn't have to tell me. I already knew."

Rob had his hand on the wall to keep from falling. "Really? How's that?"

Dave turned the lock on the front door and tested it to make certain it was secure. "Because you two are the chosen ones."

Rob was still burping up alcohol. "Cool. Chosen for what?"

"Extinction," Dave said casually as he pulled a thick black gun from his waistband and pointed it at Rob's face.

"Whoa, what the fuck!" Rob yelled, suddenly more sober. "What the hell's this? Put that thing away!"

"Sorry, friend, no can do. Got a job to do here."

Cheryl's jaw dropped, and she pushed herself up a little straighter on the couch. "We didn't do nothing to you, mister. Just take what you want. We're not looking for trouble."

"Take what I want? That's very kind of you, dear. I think I'll start by taking your lives."

"That's not funny," Rob stammered. "Why don't you just turn and walk out before this goes too far?"

Dave shoved Rob backward, and he crashed over the coffee table onto the couch next to Cheryl. "You went pretty far there," he mused. Walking toward them, he caught a glimpse of a family portrait on the end table. "Nice-looking kiddies," he commented. "Would they be home now? Tell them to come out and play."

"We don't have them anymore," Cheryl said quickly. "Children's Services took them."

Dave pointed the gun menacingly at Cheryl's head. "You wouldn't be lying to Santa, now, would you?"

"No. Look around if you want. They haven't been here in a week."

"Oh, I'll look, trust me. Once I'm done chatting with you, I'll look. If they're not here, then I don't care where they are. If I do find them here, I promise you I'll make them die slow just for you lying to me."

Cheryl swallowed hard. "They're not here."

"Well," Dave said like it was time for work, "let's get to it."

"Come on, man," Rob said nervously, "you don't have to do this. Just walk away."

"Oh, I will walk away, buddy. Don't worry about that." A wry, evil smile came across his lips. "I don't think you will, though."

"Please," Cheryl said as her eyes welled up. "It's Christmas."

"Ho, ho, ho," Dave said demonically and then screamed, "I *hate* Christmas! This is what happens when you don't give your kid that train set he wanted when he was six."

"You stupid fuck!" Cheryl yelled at Rob, punching his arm, tears streaming down her face. "You hadda let him in!"

Dave held up the gun and slowly waved it back and forth between Rob and Cheryl. "Well? Who would like the first present?" The gun was aimed directly at Cheryl. "Would it be 'ladies first'?"

Her eyes shut tight, and her body trembled.

The barrel then shifted to Rob. "Or is chivalry not dead?"
Neither one answered the question.

Dave shrugged. "I guess I'll choose, then," he said, thinking
it over. The gun was then straightened into Rob's face. "Con-
grats, lout. For your admirable defense of your wife, you get to go
first."

Rob saw the hole in the black barrel in front of him, and his
eyes widened farther. A yell or a scream or something would
have probably escaped from his mouth at that moment, but his
vocal cords were paralyzed. His bladder wasn't, however, and it
released itself into the crotch of his trousers. The by-product of
all the alcohol he had drunk earlier at the bar seeped through his
pants and onto the couch cushions beneath him. The only move
he could make at the time was an instinctive one, to throw his
arms up into a cross position in front of his face in an attempt to
block the shot. That move turned out to be nothing more than a
microcosm of what his life had become—useless.

The gun was rapidly aimed lower, and a bullet ripped into
Rob's belly, causing both hands to instantly reposition over the
wound. It also caused Cheryl to start screaming hysterically. Another bullet then tore through his head, entering at the left eye
and blowing out the whole back of the skull. His body fell limp
against the couch and convulsed slightly as his nerves did their
thing.

Cheryl, splattered with blood and brain, stopped screaming
as soon as the gun was leveled at her head. She immediately realized that silencing herself was a better option than the killer doing it for her. She continued to sob and whimper quietly as the
killer sized up the situation. He was feeling particularly brutal
this night and decided to have a little fun with her. He moved directly in front of her and sat on the coffee table.

"You don't mind if I sit here, do you? I know some people

don't like feet on their coffee table. How do you feel about ass on it?"

Cheryl's hands were gripped tightly on the couch cushion as, wide-eyed and teary, she moved her head slowly back and forth. "It's OK."

"Thanks, that's nice of you." He motioned to Rob. "I didn't have the heart to tell him that Dave isn't even my real name." He leaned in close to Cheryl. "Would you like to know my real name?"

The question elicited no response.

"Cat's got your tongue, huh?" He looked again at Rob, whose face was a total mess of blood and hanging flesh. "I'm sorry. I just realized something. I didn't give you two a chance to say good-bye to each other, did I? We'll fix that now. Go ahead," he said, motioning to Rob with the gun. "Give him a kiss good-bye."

Cheryl wasn't moving, hopelessly thinking that the killer would somehow lose sight of her 250 pounds of motionless blubber. The gun was pushed up against her nose and then pulled back. "Did you hear me? I said kiss him good-bye."

Her head slowly turned to catch sight of her husband's bloodied corpse. She started crying uncontrollably again—some of it for him but more at the thought that she was facing the very same fate. Her thoughts went immediately to the kids and how she had to get this guy out of the house one way or the other before her sister showed up with them, especially after he had told her he would kill them if he found them. She thought of their reaction when they came in to wish her a merry Christmas and found bodies instead.

Make a move on him! she thought to herself. *At the very least, take a shot at it so it won't be so easy for him.* She took a deep breath and calmed herself as much as she could. She looked back to the killer and noted that he wasn't the biggest of chaps; if she could get him off his feet somehow she could probably just lie on top of him until help arrived. The main problem, though, was in getting that jiggly mass airborne from a seated position in order to land it atop her tormentor. That scenario was not a likely one.

"What are you waiting for?" the killer said in his trademark cold, gravelly voice. "I said kiss him good-bye."

"No!" Cheryl yelled and then made her move on the gunman. She threw everything she had into it, rocking and swaying back and forth on the couch, trying with all her might to get to the killer. She made little progress forward and gave the appearance of a turtle stuck on its back trying to get righted.

The killer slid himself and the coffee table back a few inches as he sat and enjoyed the sight of Cheryl trying to save herself. He couldn't help but smile at how ineffective she was at it. The happiness on his face only incensed her further, and whatever fear she had left was converted into anger. Her flabby arms took a couple of swings in his direction but never even came close to pushing a breeze onto his nose.

"Motherfucker," she grumbled to herself and began to do the old butt slide, using her cheeks to push herself along toward the front of the couch.

The gap between victim and tormentor had begun to narrow as Cheryl started inching her way along. The battle-and-war analogy popped into the killer's mind, and there was no doubt he planned to win both of them. The smile had been wiped clean from his face, and he was back into all-business mode as the bottom of his shoe impacted her face, sending her sprawling back into her original position next to her husband.

"I don't think so," the killer said icily.

Cheryl, breathing heavily, now realized that her only chance at this thing was gone, and the inevitable mercilessly sank into her consciousness. She hung her head and loathed herself for being too fat to even give herself a chance. She hated Rob also, for being too crippled and drunk to save her. The anger bubbled itself back into her belly but was now mixed with complete resignation and defeat.

The killer leaned into Cheryl. "Give up?" he asked coyly as he tried to antagonize her further. The gun was resting gently on his lap.

"Why are you doing this to us?" she cried. "What did we do to you?"

"You're just lucky, I guess," he growled. "Look at it on the bright side. From here on in, you'll only be losing weight."

She threw a pillow at him. "Bastard!" she screamed, then cried, "Just get it over with."

The killer tilted his head to one side and stared at her. There was something about her that he actually liked for some reason, something in her face, something that seemed familiar. He pulled himself in close to her again and put his hand on her knee. "I'll tell you what I'm gonna do—"

"What?" she said tartly. "I'm not kissing him."

"Maybe I don't want you to kiss him now," he said softly.

His fingers started tickling her knee, and a more sinister thought of what he wanted entered her mind. *Maybe,* she thought, *this could be a way out.*

"What is it you want me to do for you?" she asked as her eyes locked on his caressing fingertips.

"That depends. What *can* you do for me?"

She closed her eyes and shook her head slowly as she felt nausea emanating from her stomach. "Anything you want me to," she said submissively.

"Very good, then." The killer softly placed the gun down next to him on the table and began unzipping his coat in a very slow, purposeful manner, all the while staring into Cheryl's now open, apprehension-filled eyes. The left side of his mouth was curled up in a crooked half-smile that had gratification written all over it.

Cheryl stared back at his face, certainly nothing attractive, and pondered how close her kids could be to arriving at the door and what move could be made while this transaction was taking place that could possibly defuse the situation. It all depended on what he wanted her to do, what sick, filthy thought was carousing through his warped mind. As much as she was repulsed by him, she hoped that whatever was to be done would somehow involve physical contact between the two of them. That would at least give her the chance to get her belly on him and, potentially, a shot at survival. It all depended on him. He was completely in control of all that happened, as evidenced by his calm, condescending demeanor and reflected in her taut, trembling body.

The jacket fell open, and the killer took both hands and gently spread her knees apart, opening her legs as far as he could, enjoying the fact that her thighs never broke contact with each other. Cheryl, still sitting back on the couch, wasn't in a good enough position or condition to grab at him. She tried to entice him closer.

"How long are you gonna keep me waiting?" she said, attempting to sound sultry but sounding nervous instead.

"Why? You want it?" the killer said, running his tightly gloved hands up her thighs until they touched.

Cheryl swallowed down some vomit that had forced its way into her mouth. "Yes . . . please," she said, disgusted.

The killer pushed himself away from her and sat up straight again on the table. "OK, then, let's get right down to it." He reached into his left-hand pocket and pulled a folded piece of paper out. He then held it up in front of her face so she could read it clearly. "Tell me which of your bodies I should place this on when I leave."

"Better luck next time?" Cheryl said. "I don't want that on

me. What happened? I thought I was going to do something for you."

The gun was picked up. Stall tactics were over.

"You just did." The gun was raised to her face. "You think I'm stupid enough to fuck you, leave some DNA behind? Not today, honey."

"What about our deal?"

The killer was having none of it. "I do the dealin', baby. You just play the hand."

"Wait!" she shouted, hands straight out in front of her.

The bullet passed right between her outstretched thumbs and hit her square in the nose, traveling through her brain like a wrecking ball. It exited the back of her head and left a huge hole where her ponytail used to be. She was thrown farther back against the couch, and a gurgling sound came from her mouth as her last breath bubbled through a deluge of flowing blood and bone. Her eyes were wide, swollen, and reddened now by the explosion of their tiny blood vessels. Her left hand, ironically, came to rest in the right hand of her husband.

The note was placed carefully on Rob's lap so as not to have any of his blood saturate it. The killer stepped back, did a once-over on himself, and was delighted to see that he'd escaped spatter free for a change. He quickly checked all rooms and closets for the kids and then went back to the living room. He thanked both victims for their cooperation, callously blew each a kiss, and made his way to the front door. As he got there he heard the sound of footsteps coming up the wooden stairs just outside. He could hear the giggling anticipation of excited children. He pulled the gun from his pocket and pressed it against the door. Three loud raps then banged from the other side, followed by a woman's voice.

"Cheryl, open up. It's us."

The killer placed his ear to the door and listened as a man's voice followed the woman's.

"They're probably all drunk and passed out in there."

"Shh, be quiet. They'll hear you."

"Like I care."

"Relax. We're only going in and out."

A tiny voice then worked its way through the wood and into the killer's ear. "Mommy, hurry up, let us in."

There was more banging on the door. "Come on, Cheryl. Open the door. The kids are freezing out here."

"Yeah, I'm sure she hears you," the man's voice said. "Christmastime, the kids are out here, and those two are dead to the world in there. Come on, let's go. We'll do this another time."

The killer watched the doorknob jiggle as Cheryl's sister tried it from the other side. He thought about turning the lock and letting them gain entry, but without knowing exactly what was on the other side of the door, he couldn't take the chance. Besides, while they were still on the other side of the door they weren't marked for execution. A matter of a few inches was the only distance separating them from life and death.

"Unbelievable," he heard Cheryl's sister say from beyond the door. "Come on, kids. Mommy's probably out visiting Santa. We'll come back later."

Dejected cries and moans could be heard from the kids as they stomped away from the door. He felt the floor vibrating as the footsteps made their way back down the stairs and into the distance. His ear stayed glued to the door as the voices faded into nothingness. When he felt the coast was clear, he moved to the window and pulled the corner of the bedsheet gently to the side. Seeing the street was vacant of passersby, he stuffed the gun back into his pocket and zipped up his coat. He unlocked the door, grabbed Rob's gloves, and took one last glance back at his work. The door was pulled open and shut behind him. The cold winter air was like a slap in the face. He shook it off, had one last look around, and then sauntered off into the chilly darkness of night.

Chapter Four

The couch in Captain Murray's office was a standard-issue government-office piece of furniture made of wood, foam, and cheap cloth. There were a thousand just like it scattered throughout many New York City agencies across the five boroughs. The cushions were hard and lumpy; the material covering them was abrasive. They basically smelled like ass, a by-product of many years of many different people parking themselves on them.

None of this mattered to Deke. With his rolled-up jacket as a pillow and Captain Murray's jacket as a blanket, he had a makeshift bed that he could sneak an hour or two of sleep on. The interviews of potential suspects went on late into the night as five of them were grilled. The gasman and the three mailmen in the area at the time of the Nevalo killings were brought in and questioned. A flower delivery guy was interviewed by phone. It was time-consuming mumbo-jumbo, and Deke knew it was a waste of time and energy, but it had to be done. It was the only way to pare down a list that was way too long to comprehend. None of the suspects on any of the lists had overlapped from one murder scene to another. All of the detectives doing the interviews would compare notes to ensure that no suspect popped up more than once at any scene. Everybody so far was legitimately where he should be.

Deke did his increasingly frequent horizontal dance of tossing and turning on the couch, hoping to fall into some kind of restful sleep. He would fade a little bit, start to drift off, and then be wakened by a ringing phone or some detective shouting something across the office outside. He could have shot home earlier and grabbed a few hours in his own bed, but what was the point? The voices in his head would have kept him up, or he would've gotten another phone call demanding his return. This way was much easier. He got the same lack of sleep without the travel. The lunatic he was chasing, on the other hand, was probably out there somewhere sleeping like a baby. It pissed Deke off. His steel-trap mind was beginning to rust from exposure to this case, yet there was no laying off by the killer, no taking a day off from murdering so the police could catch up a bit. It was really hard to play this type of game as the pursuer. Running blind and tripping over mounting obstacles in front of you usually doesn't win the race. It's even harder when the guy in the lead is the one creating the course.

Deke flipped himself over on the couch and finally hit just the right sweet spot of comfort, coupled with a break in the action outside, that let him fall into a fairly decent sleep. Never one for snoring, he was more the drooling kind of sleeper, one that could create quite a puddle of saliva on a pillow and mattress when he got going. The puddle being created on Captain Murray's couch barely had time to soak in before the door flew open and Deke's forty-five minutes of restfulness were broken. He sat up quickly, wiped the wetness from his face with his hand, and dried it on the couch cushion. It was his gift to the next guy who thought of taking a nap on that couch, some poor slob with the unfortunate pleasure of falling asleep to the aroma of ass and spit.

As the blur cleared from his eyes, Deke could make out the hulking figure of Captain Charles Murray standing before him.

"Jesus, Deke, you really look like hell. Go to the locker room and take a shower."

"I'm all right."

"Bullshit, I can smell you from here. Go do what I tell you."

"I don't got nothin' in my locker to shower with."

"You got a change of clothes in it?"

"Yeah."

"Good. My locker's open. It has everything you need."

"Cap, I ain't got the time right now. I gotta get back on it."

"Deke, that wasn't a request. I'm ordering you to go and clean up. You really are starting to stink. Go. It'll do you good."

Deke slowly made his way to the men's locker room on the next floor up. He stopped frequently along the way to get progress reports from other detectives on the questioning of possible suspects. Nobody in particular stood out; no one could be linked from one murder scene to another. The dead ends kept piling up.

As the hot shower water flowed over his body, Deke felt a sense of relief from the tension building in his brain. The pressure to crack this case was intensifying by the day, and any new murders only added to that. He soaped, he lathered, he rinsed, and he tried to let the water wash away the memory of the little girl and boy he had seen at the last murder scene. Details always had a way of sticking in his head, but they were usually filed away as clues and particulars of a case. Rarely were they attached to his emotions the way the killings of Ginny and Tommy Nevalo were. Maybe it was the fact that Ginny was so young and tiny and the same age as his daughter. Or maybe it was the way Tommy was found hiding under that bed and how scared he must've been at that moment that resonated with Deke so much. Maybe it was just his fatherly instinct kicking in that zapped him so hard.

Whatever it was, it would have to be tucked away as just another one of those things an NYPD homicide detective had to end up living with and dealing with for the rest of his life.

As he worked his way through a final rinse-off, he stuck his finger in and around his mouth as a makeshift toothbrush. He sucked in a big mouthful of water, gargled, and spat it out into the drain. He reached for the faucets and then just stood there, head down, watching the water swirl down the drain. Thoughts began to wash into his head again as the water continued to wash over his body. The circling water in the drain was almost hypnotic, and Deke tried to get himself into the killer's mind, trying to come up with his own profile before the FBI gave him theirs.

The killer obviously had to be a loner. He couldn't be married or have kids because that wouldn't leave him much free time to be going around killing people at his leisure. Someone would notice him missing and become inquisitive. Then again, maybe that had already happened. Maybe that was how this all started, one guy going off the deep end and wiping out those close to him. Maybe he liked it and kept doing it. Family ties had been checked out initially at each murder scene but not cross-matched to any others. Deke made a mental note to go back and do that once he got downstairs.

Also, he thought, watching the water flow into the drain, the killer was almost assuredly a white male. Most women don't possess the callousness to murder at the rate these murders were taking place, especially randomly. Women were impulse killers, committing homicide out of strong emotion, usually killing a family member or some acquaintance that incurred their scorn. The same was usually true of people of color. The white male, 90 percent of the time, was the typical serial murderer. That wasn't a hunch for Deke; that was a flat-out statistic.

He spun the faucets, toweled off, dressed, and hurried back

downstairs. He stopped and discussed his mental notes with the detectives working under him and got them started checking out the new possible leads. He headed back to Captain Murray's office and, upon entering, was somewhat surprised to see the captain in conversation with another black-suited Fed. This one didn't fit the mold of the other stone-faced, rugged G-men. This guy had movie-star looks with deep, piercing brown eyes. He stood about 6'2" and didn't seem to have an ounce of fat on him. His tanned complexion immediately signaled to Deke that this guy was a California dude or down-South boy. Wherever he was from, it wasn't anywhere near icy New York. Deke took a fast peek at his watch. "I guess the Feds don't sleep much either, huh?" He smiled halfheartedly.

Captain Murray stood and moved away from his scratched-up wooden desk. "Much better," he said of Deke's appearance. "Come here, I want you to meet Agent Kurt Joseph. Agent Joseph, this Deke Durgess, detective in charge of the case."

The two men shook hands, with Deke speaking up first. "Agent Joseph, how are ya? That's some grip you got there."

"Ku-Jo," the agent replied. "I go by Ku-Jo."

"I hope that means you're dogged on a case," Deke said.

"That is my reputation, Detective."

"Good, we'll get along just fine, then. I go by Deke, by the way." He turned his attention to Captain Murray. "Where's Miller?"

"Gone. Flew back to Washington a few hours ago. Ku-Jo's gonna be our go-between now."

"You kiddin' me? I thought the guy was gonna be here for the long haul. How does he cut out just like that?"

"Relax, Deke," said Captain Murray. "He follows orders, too. Besides, Agent Joseph has some information for us here, if you'd just take a breath."

"G'head, I'm listenin'."

"OK," Joseph said, motioning with his hand. "If you gentlemen would please have a seat."

The two men grabbed chairs and gave their undivided attention to the Fed. He picked up a pristine laminated report from Captain Murray's desk and opened it for review. "Our profiling team finished their research. This is what we should be looking for with this guy."

Deke quickly pulled his notebook from his pocket and flipped it open to the first available page. With pen in hand, he began listening and taking notes.

"OK, you'd be looking for a Caucasian male, approximately twenty-five to forty-five years old. He'd be single, living alone, and most likely be somewhat extroverted. He'd hold a steady job, yearly salary somewhere around thirty thousand or less with access to all parts of the city. Am I going too fast here?"

"I'm with you," said Deke. "I'm only takin' notes in case the captain needs 'em."

"Go on," said Captain Murray as he threw a paper clip at Deke.

"OK. He would have no more than a high school education, would live mostly on junk food and takeout, and have little or no savings—"

Deke interrupted. "Most of this I can figure for myself, bud. Any way we can skip to the personality traits the psychologists came up with? I gotta start gettin' into this guy's mind."

Agent Joseph was a little miffed but didn't show it. He was trained to show anger only in life-and-death situations. It didn't always work. "Sure, Detective, let me jump down to it for you." His eyes scanned the page. "Here we go. It repeats about him being extroverted and the high school education part and the lack of a good diet. It also goes on to say that he would be very particular in certain aspects of his life, possibly clothing attire or hygiene, while other aspects would be carelessly disregarded, such as the cleanliness of his living space or the vehicle he drives. It says that he would have a very strong maternal attachment and a negative or nonexistent relationship with the father. There's a special note here that says that some type of incident may have happened in either one of these relationships that might have set him off. The mother may have died or changed her attitude toward him in some way, or the father could have come back into his life in some sort of negative way. More than likely, whatever happened was on the mother's side. He'd also be an only child or have no contact with any siblings." He placed his finger on the page. "It says down here that he's probably obsessive-compulsive, and although he may not want to kill his victims he feels that he *needs* to kill them. He'd have good verbal and social skills and could talk his way into or out of almost any situation."

Captain Murray looked at Deke and smiled. "That's *your* profile he just read. I should arrest you right here and now."

"I make more than thirty thousand, though," Deke responded, "and I can't talk a lick. Everything else you got a shot on." Deke stood up. "Is that it?"

"Where you headed?" Captain Murray asked.

"I wanna bump heads with the other detectives out there, inject some of this mumbo-jumbo into our possible suspects lists—see if anyone stands out. Could I get a copy of that?" he asked Joseph.

"Sure, take this one," Joseph responded, handing Deke the report. "I can get another if I need it."

"Thanks," Deke said as he ripped the paper from his hand. "Cap, I'm gonna get started on this list now."

"Go ahead—before this guy hits again. We may have gotten off lucky last night and our boy decided to stay home for the evening."

"What makes you think that?" Agent Joseph asked.

Captain Murray held out his wristwatch. "Nine thirty in the morning and all's well so far . . . hopefully."

Deke commented first. "He killed somewhere. We ain't heard about it 'cause no one probably found the bodies yet, but, trust me, we'll be hearin'."

"I agree," Joseph said.

"Deke, hold on," Captain Murray said as Deke began walking toward the door. "I want you to take Ku-Jo with you for the rest of this case. FBI says he's ours, so we may as well use him."

Deke turned around, disappointment all over his face. "What for, Cap? You know I work alone." He looked at Joseph. "Nothin' against you, guy."

Joseph shrugged.

"Listen, there's too much going on with this case right now. You're being run ragged, and Joseph here is fresh. Let him take some of this shit off your mind."

"That's bullshit, Cap. You know that, right? I don't need no one babysittin' me."

"Deke, it's done," Murray said as he shooed both men from his office.

Deke knew it was useless. The decision to partner him up again had to have come from upstairs. He begrudgingly accepted his new partner and trudged out of the office, Joseph in tow. They went over to where the other detectives were populating the persons-of-interest list that Deke had asked Captain Murray to get them started on the previous day.

"Whaddaya got for me, Ronnie?" he asked, yawning.

"This case boring you, Deke? I could try to make it more interesting."

"Nope, not gettin' bored on this one. Besides, borin' means it's too easy."

"Yeah, I know. Anything *but* this time around, eh?" Ronnie handed Deke a copy of the list they had so far. Deke took another copy and gave it to Joseph. The two men sat down facing each other and began reviewing the list.

"Let's see . . . OK, we got a UPS guy here, a FedEx guy, a phone guy. They all pretty much get around. They should be good to talk to."

Joseph jumped in. "What about all these letter carriers about midway down?"

"Letter carriers? I take it you ain't a native New Yorker, huh? Where you hail from?"

"Sunny California. Let me tell you, this weather out here makes me miss it all the more."

"California, huh?" Deke smiled condescendingly. "Never woulda got that one. By the way, around here we call 'em mailmen."

"Well, I think we should check them out, too," Joseph responded with a fake smile to hide his anger. Being made to look like a fool really irritated him. Back in the day before he completed the anger-management course the FBI forced on him, he might have ripped Deke right out of his chair and showed him the error of his ways, but those were his hothead days, when he'd fly off the handle at his convenience. Not many people would be able to stop him once that happened. Not many even tried to, lest they take the chance of incurring his wrath. Usually, anyone he was partnered with would look the other way when he would beat the daylights out of a suspect during an arrest. They deserved it, he said, for making him scuff his shoes or for putting a rip in his clothing.

That all changed, though, when during the arrest and street interrogation of a child-rape suspect, Joseph's gun "accidentally" went off in the man's mouth, blowing a hole through his right cheek and knocking out a few teeth. Everyone knew he did it purposely, that he had the gun at just the right angle to do damage without killing. Still, no investigation of the shooting ever took place, and the whole incident was ultimately swept under the rug. The FBI knew the suspect was guilty; they had DNA evidence on him in cases crossing five state lines. Things don't always go according to the book, especially when the suspect is a sleazebag and the agent isn't.

In exchange for his cooperation in the matter—namely, keeping his mouth shut as just to who blew his mouth out—the suspect was given a sweetheart plea deal that cut years off his sentence and even allowed him his choice of which federal prison to go to.

Agent Joseph was then offered a deal of his own: either go through a thirty-day anger-management course administered by the bureau or face a lengthy suspension for his actions. The choice was easy; he did his part and had walked the straight and narrow ever since. There were times, though, when he felt the suppressed temptation to lose his self-control, times when his volcano festered and he was ready to blow his top. He made sure to keep a lid on the eruption and let the steam escape safely.

This letter carrier/mailman thing with Deke was small potatoes in the grand scheme of things, but it was just the sort of thing that used to set Joseph off. Fortunately for Deke, the FBI had the check valve installed properly on their man.

Deke continued obliviously. "Don't worry, bud," he said casually. "We'll get to the mailmen, but before I do, I gotta see if they're the regular guys on the routes or not. If they're doin' the same routes every day, I doubt they'll be poppin' up at different murder scenes. Now, take the UPS guy and these other two, they have access to the whole city on different days. None of 'em has a steady route; that's why my guy Ronnie's got 'em on the list here." He continued poring over the list. "Whoa, whoa, whoa," he said excitedly, "check the guy out at number nine. Name's Coleman."

"Yeah, I see him," Joseph said, calm again. "Looks interesting."

"Interesting? A computer repair guy that gets his supplies from the same store two of the victims bought their computers at." He turned his head toward Ronnie. "Why didn't you come tell me this?"

"We just got it, Deke. No more than a few minutes ago. We're trying to cross the delivery guys and phone guy, but we haven't gotten anything back yet."

"Let me know when you do. You got my number."

"Will do."

Deke tapped Joseph on the leg. "Come on, let's go see this Coleman guy. He don't live far from here."

"Let's do it." Joseph took a small keychain-attached recording device from his pocket and said Coleman's name and address into it.

"What the hell is that?" Deke asked, squinting at it.

"It's one of those three-second recorders that you can speak into and play back stuff you might forget. The FBI gives them to us constantly."

Deke shook his head. "What ever happened to the days of pen and paper."

The ride uptown took only a few minutes as Deke used his portable emergency light but no siren to speed his way along Sixth Avenue. He pulled up in front of a fire hydrant and threw his OFFICIAL BUSINESS placard into the windshield. He called his location in to Central via radio and told Joseph to stay outside and watch the front of the building in case Coleman was there and made a break for it. "Keep your radio on. If he's up there and is willin' to talk, I'll call you. If you hear me shoutin', he's on his way to you."

"Got it. Just keep your eyes open in there, ya know?"

"Always."

Deke took the stairs up to the third floor, making sure to keep his eyes focused on everything in front of him. He didn't like using elevators when going to interview possible suspects because he always felt they were death traps with nowhere to go when push came to shove. If the suspect got wind that a detective was coming to see him, it would be real easy to wait on a floor, allow those doors to open, and then just fire away. The stairs left less room for someone to lie in ambush.

He arrived at Coleman's door and rang the bell. He put his ear to the door and could hear rustling inside; someone was moving about. He stepped to the side of the door just in case the answer was a bullet breezing through.

"Who is it?" came a voice from the other side of the door.

"William Coleman?" Deke asked forcefully.

"Yeah, who is it?"

"Detective Durgess, Manhattan Homicide. I'd like to talk to you. Can you open the door, please?"

"What's this in reference to?"

"I'd like to ask you some questions, sir. Open the door, please."

"Not unless you show me ID. Hold it in front of the peephole."

Deke pulled his badge and held it out in front of the small glass dot in the middle of the door.

"How do I know that's real?" said the muffled voice on the other side.

"Look at it closely, Mr. Coleman. You can see it's real."

"This glass distorts things. I can't see it clearly."

Deke was growing impatient. "Listen, buddy, if I wanted to rob you I woulda kicked the door in. This is official police business. Open the door right now!"

The lock was turned, and Deke could hear the door chain being slid across its track. The door opened as far as the chain would allow, and a slender face appeared in the crack.

"OK, let me see that badge again."

Deke held it as close as he could get it, and the door closed again.

"Give me a second," the man said.

A few moments later, the chain was slid back, and the door opened. Coleman backed into the apartment, giving way to Deke, keeping his eye on him all the way. In his hand was a cordless phone, and he was talking on it. "Yes . . . Says he's some detective from Manhattan Homicide . . . Yes, he showed me . . . I can't tell! It looks real enough . . . OK, thank you." He ended the call and tossed the phone onto the couch.

"Who was that?" demanded Deke.

"If you must know, I called 911 just in case you aren't who you say you are. They're sending someone over right now to check you out."

Deke smiled at the irony of the situation. It would be funny if each of them thought the other was the Daily Killer. Deke could only vouch for himself, though. He didn't know Coleman from a hole in the wall. He could either be what he seemed or just a very good actor.

"Have a seat, Mr. Coleman."

Coleman haltingly worked his way over to the couch, never taking his eyes off Deke, feeling very uncomfortable about cornering himself. The body language was telling Deke that the guy was for real, that his apprehension was no act. His cop's mind, though, told him not to believe everything he saw.

"I can see we got a lack of trust here, Mr. Coleman. Would it put you more at ease if I call my partner downstairs and get him up here?"

There was a change in Coleman's face. It was less tense. "It couldn't hurt."

Deke plucked the radio from his back pocket and called for Joseph while Coleman sat there watching his every move. Joseph answered Deke immediately and said he would be up in a flash. The verbal transaction between the two seemed to validate Deke's assertions that he was indeed a member of the NYPD. Coleman's nervous squirming on the couch continued, but the reasons for it had changed dramatically. It was now the questions that would be fired at him that worried him. Deke asked for permission to sit down. The request was granted, and Deke scribbled a few notes in his book.

He started slow with the questions in an effort to loosen Coleman up, touching on some basics like how long he had lived there and his background in the computer field. Once Deke felt the answers were flowing somewhat smoothly, he moved into the meat of the session.

"How tall would you be, sir?"

"Six three."

"You look to weigh about two thirty, two fifty. Is that about right?"

"Two fifty-five, but who's counting."

Deke gave a courtesy chuckle and snuck a peek at Coleman's feet. "Wow, those are nice shoes you got there. I always wanted a pair like that. Where'd you get 'em?"

"Right up on the corner here. They have more if you're interested."

"How comfortable are they?"

"I wear these things constantly. No problems so far."

"Nice, nice. Yours look kinda big. What size are they?"

Coleman was becoming exasperated. "Eleven wide. Do you want these or something? You can have them. They're brand-new."

Deke smiled. "I don't want your shoes, Mr. Coleman. I was just admirin' 'em. When did ya get 'em?"

"I bought them yesterday. My other ones were worn out, so I tossed them."

"I see," Deke said as he continued scribbling notes. He casually scanned the entire living room. "I don't see no pictures around, Mr. Coleman. You married?"

"No, sir."

"Really? No girlfriend, love interest, nothin'?"

"Not at the present time."

"Really."

"Why? Is that so hard to believe?"

"No, not necessarily. It's just that this apartment is pretty clean and well kept, that's all."

"I like it that way."

"Obviously." Deke made notations in his little book. A soft knock at the front door interrupted them. Deke threw his hand up hastily. "Stay seated, please, sir. I'll get that."

Deke walked over to the door and asked who it was. "It's us," said a voice that clearly belonged to Joseph. Deke pulled the door open to find his partner, accompanied by other members of the NYPD. "They felt the need to escort me," he said jokingly.

The police officers recognized Deke and vouched for him to Coleman. Deke pulled them aside and gave a few instructions that Coleman couldn't hear. The officers nodded to Deke and quickly made their way out the door. He returned to the couch and got right back into the questioning, Joseph standing off to the side.

"Mind if I have a look around, sir?" Joseph asked.

"Actually, I do," answered Coleman. "I do not know you, and I do have some personal possessions that are important to me."

"We don't steal, sir," Deke said sternly.

Coleman's reply was quick and curt. "I don't know that."

Deke gave him a hard stare. "Where do you get your computer supplies?"

"I get them from quite a few places in the city. It all depends on what I need and who's got it cheapest."

"You ever deal with a place called City Tech?"

"Here and there."

"When was the last time you visited them?"

Coleman thought a second. "A week or two, I guess."

"Do you have any access to their records, sales receipts, clientele?"

Impatience was beginning to surface. "I'm sorry, Detective, but what is all of this in reference to?"

Deke tried to put him at ease with a smile. "Just some stuff I gotta ask."

Coleman wasn't falling for the charm. "Why are you asking me?" he demanded.

"If you must know, we're investigatin' a murder."

"And you think I'm involved?" Coleman asked incredulously.

"Not at all. It's just that two customers that bought computers there since August have turned up dead. We're makin' the rounds of everyone that shops there, that's all."

"This doesn't have anything to do with the daily killings, does it?"

Deke ignored the question. "Do you own a gun, sir?"

"Wait, hold on a second. Answer me first. Does this have anything to do with the daily killings?"

"We don't know. Why?"

"Well, I think I'd be kind of interested to know if he's picking victims from a store that I shop at."

"We're not sayin' that, bud." Deke was getting pissed. "Listen, do me a favor. I'll ask the questions. You give the answers."

"Whatever," Coleman said with a wave of his hand.

"Again I ask you, do you own a gun?"

"Of course not! I am very against guns." Coleman could tell by the tone of Deke's voice that there was more to this than met the eye. "Do I need a lawyer here?"

"Do you think you do?"

"I think the better question is do *you* think I do?"

Deke was rapidly growing frustrated with the suspect's attitude and decided to take a break before he introduced his fist to Coleman's jaw. Joseph smiled as he saw the exasperation on Deke's face and recalled his own irritation when Deke made fun of him about the letter carriers.

"What goes around comes around," he said as Deke passed him by, not paying any attention. Joseph then pulled out his notepad and took over the questioning.

Deke stood in the background and paid very close attention to Coleman's body language and made further notes in his own book. The questions Joseph asked were almost identical to the ones in Deke's mind. The difference must have been in the way he delivered those questions, in that slow California style that obviously appealed to Coleman, because he seemed to loosen up a bit and was more forthcoming with his responses. There was nothing earth-shattering in those answers, and the questioning continued for another fifteen minutes or so before both men put their pads and pens away and took their leave of Coleman. On their way down to the car, Joseph attempted to discuss the findings with Deke. He was quickly stifled, Deke pointing out to him that the lobby had an intercom system that Coleman could listen in on. Any discussions held would have to wait until they got to the car.

When they reached the street, the two police officers Deke had sent out earlier were waiting by the car.

"You find anything?" Deke asked them.

"Nothing, Detective. We searched every garbage pail. No shoes. We even went and talked to the building super and looked in the waste disposal room. If he threw out the shoes you're looking for, he did it somewhere else."

Deke was disappointed but not surprised. "OK, good job. Thanks."

After the two police officers left, Joseph suggested that he and Deke go back upstairs and question Coleman about the missing shoes. There was no sense in doing that, and Deke knew it. With the amount of homeless people frequenting the area, it was entirely possible that that pair of shoes was now adorning a new set of feet. For the homeless, going through garbage pails was like window-shopping in Bloomingdale's, except the prices were way better.

"No," said Deke. "No need. It's cold out here. Let's get in the car."

Once the doors were closed and the key was shoved into the ignition, the analysis of Coleman's answers began.

"What do you think?" asked Joseph.

"You tell me. He does fit some of that profile you gave us."

"I was a little surprised you didn't ask him where he was last night. That's like the second thing you should have hit him with."

Deke fired the question right back. "Well, why didn't *you* ask him, then?"

"I figured that when you didn't bring it up, there must've been a reason. I laid back a bit."

Deke liked that answer. While the kid might have appeared to be young and rough around the edges, he did have a good grasp on how to conduct a question-and-answer session and a keen knack for reading his partner. "Very good," said Deke. "This thing might work after all."

"You gonna tell me?"

"I didn't wanna spook him. Let him think we're just tryin' to get information about the crime without makin' him feel like a prime suspect. Ask him the wrong question, and he starts to change his whole routine to throw us off. I don't want him stayin' home tonight if he's our guy."

"Sure." Joseph laughed. "It's much better to have him go out there and blow some people away."

Deke laughed, too. "Good one." He opened his cell phone and called Captain Murray's office. "Cap, it's Deke. Do me a favor, grab Ronnie and have him send someone right over to Coleman's place . . . Yeah, I want a stakeout on this guy. Uh-huh . . . No, not necessarily. I'm lookin' more to eliminate him than convict him . . . OK, we'll wait till they get here."

A stakeout was the easiest way for Deke to cut Coleman from the list without having to spend more of his time tracking him himself. Two other detectives would sit across the street and follow him anywhere he went.

When they arrived, Deke told them to figure some way to get to the guy's door and have a look at him so they knew who they'd be following. The way the killer was going about his business, Coleman would either be arrested by the end of the day or pushed to the back burner. The answer didn't matter much to Deke at the moment. Coleman was now considered old news. There was a new guy up on the radar screen who needed to be checked out. Deke tossed Joseph the keys to the car. "You're driving."

The ride to get to the new suspect was shockingly short, as Flatbush Avenue had so little traffic on it Deke would have sworn it was the middle of the night. He remarked to Joseph that everyone must already be where they wanted to be for Christmas Eve. They headed up to Kings Highway, took a left, took that to Foster Avenue, and took that straight up to East 105th Street, where they ended at a fairly large warehouse.

They jumped out and talked to the building supervisor, who explained that the driver they were looking for was still out making deliveries. They were welcome to wait in his office until the driver returned. That wait might have been all of ten minutes long, as a brown UPS truck pulled in shortly after noon to get reloaded with more Christmas packages needing to reach their destinations. As the driver stepped off the truck, his supervisor asked him to go immediately to his office. There, Deke and Joseph did their thing, asking their questions and taking notes. It became obvious early on that this guy could not be doing the killings. While he didn't have a steady route and bounced around the city to different depots from time to time, his logbook and GPS tracking systems only placed him near one scene—probably the reason Ronnie added him to the list. The FBI profile didn't seem to mirror him at all, either. He was black, to begin with, was married with two kids, and made more than thirty grand. There was no sense wasting time here. Deke looked the remaining list over.

"Let's go visit the phone guy. His HQ is only a few blocks from here."

As the car went into gear, Deke's cell phone did its thing, grabbing his attention from deep within his pocket. He looked at the face, and his stomach dropped. "Oh shit," he said quickly and turned his attention to Joseph. "Don't drive yet. I gotta take this call, and I don't need the car movin' and droppin' the signal."

Joseph put the car back in park and watched as Deke flipped the phone open and immediately told the person on the other end to hold on.

"Do me a favor," he said to Joseph. "Take a walk for a minute."

Joseph nodded and stepped from the vehicle to give Deke some privacy.

"Hello," Deke said again into the phone.

The response was quick, harsh, and to the point. "What time are you coming to get the kids tonight?"

"Come on, Frannie," Deke said angrily. "You know I'm runnin' an investigation here. You hadda see the news by now. I can't get away from this case right now."

"Yeah, par for the course," his ex-wife responded. "Everything else is always more important. That's OK. The kids are used to disappointment. Enjoy your Christmas. Good-bye."

"Frannie, wait."

"What?"

"Come on," he said softly. "You know how much I miss you and the kids. You don't think this is killin' me, not seein' my own kids on Christmas Eve? You know how much stuff I got for 'em at my apartment? It ain't wrapped, but it's there."

"Try telling that to Matthew and Lauren. They don't care about the reasons. They're looking forward to seeing Daddy tonight. You didn't even bother to call and tell them you couldn't come."

Deke's head was down. He hated that backed-into-a-corner feeling. "Frannie, why are you doin' this to me? I got a guy runnin' all over the city killin' people. I don't need this in my head right now throwin' me off."

"Deke, they want you. You're their father, and they want to see you for Christmas." Her voice was imperative and unwavering. "They're not going to understand that you have work to do. They're only seven and five, for Christ's sake."

"Frannie, please, I can't do this now. This case is too important. Tell the kids I'm sick or somethin' and that I'll see 'em soon."

"You see, Deke? It never, ever changes. Everything else before us."

Deke had no answer. She was right, hands down. It was time to get off the phone. "I gotta go. Just don't trash me to 'em, all right?"

"Deke, they're gonna make their own decisions about you. You just let them down again, as usual. Merry Christmas." The phone was hung up.

Deke thought about it for a second and actually hated Frannie for laying the guilt trip on him so thickly. He hated himself even more for allowing her to be right. Nothing she could say to him could be wrong. He had just put his own children at the back of the line on Christmas Eve. He had to somehow put it out of his head. It would cloud his judgment. The only way to do it was to jump right back into the pool.

He looked through the windshield and could see Joseph talking into his little recorder thing and placing it to his ear for playback. It was attached to a keychain that had about fifteen keys on it. They weren't large keys, but they must've made enough noise to interfere with any voice going into the recorder. It seemed kind of a dumb place to keep the thing. Deke didn't care. It was just an observation.

He reached over and tooted the horn to get Joseph back into

the car. Joseph shoved the keychain back into his pocket and eagerly jogged over and plopped into the driver's seat.

"Thank God," he said. "I was freezing out there."

"Sorry," Deke answered. "The ex was all over me about takin' the kids tonight."

"Didn't know you were divorced, man. Sorry to hear that."

"Me, too." Deke shook it off. "OK, let's get to the phone guy."

Joseph looked at his watch. "You mind if I make a call before we go? Mentioning your kids reminded me that I forgot to call mine."

"Go ahead. Family always comes first," Deke said and then paused at the irony of what he'd just said.

Joseph grabbed his government-issue, every-gadget-imaginable phone from his pocket and slid open the face. "This time difference thing between New York and California has me completely thrown off," he said to Deke.

"You're a young guy. How many kids ya got?"

"Just the one. My wife knew what she was getting into when I got accepted by the FBI. She told me there'll be no more kids until I get permanently assigned to the West Coast."

"What kinda kid is it?"

Joseph looked back quizzically. "What do you mean?"

Deke stared back, just as confused. "Is it a boy or a girl?"

Joseph laughed to himself. It was almost like talking to Yogi Berra. "She's most definitely a girl. Turned four years old a month ago. I was actually there for that one."

"Sounds good. My little girl is five. Maybe they could meet and play someday."

"That would be great."

Deke went to pull the door handle to get out of the car.

"Where are you going?" Joseph asked.

"I'm gonna go outside, give you some space so you can talk to your kid."

"No, no, no." Joseph waved him off. "It is really cold out there. Stay. There's nothing I can say to my daughter here that you haven't said to yours."

Joseph hit the speed dial and listened as the phone rang on the other end. "Hey, hon," he said happily when his wife answered. "How's everything going there?"

He listened carefully as his wife gave the rundown on all the happenings since the last phone call. It was the same old same old for the most part, but it was just the tonic a homesick Joseph needed to hear. A second dose of remedy was quickly administered when the phone was handed off to the brightest light in his life, little Samantha.

She went on for a few seconds about her pre-K class and the finger paintings she had for him when he got home. It was a bit tough to decipher what she was saying into the phone, but it was still a piece of cake when compared to trying to catch Deke's lingo, Joseph thought. He threw a short smile in Deke's direction, one that Deke didn't understand but one that made all the sense in the world to Joseph.

"Yeah, baby, I'm sorry," he responded into the phone as he punched his own knee in frustration. "I forgot all about it. I was on the plane last night." Some words came back to him. "Sure, I can do it now if you'd like," he answered as he reached into the backseat and unsnapped his briefcase. "Which one would you like to hear?"

He listened intently as the order came through from Samantha.

"OK, baby, I have it right here." He slid a colorful children's book from the briefcase and, in a voice full of meaning, read it to her right there over the phone. The book was only a few pages long, but it was part of the routine she had been accustomed to and simply would not do without.

Deke sat and listened to the one-sided conversation, hoping it would end soon so they could move on to the next destination. He was careful not to give his impatience away through body language or words. Some things in life should in no way be infringed upon. This was one of them.

Joseph reached the end of the story and asked Samantha if she liked it. "Good, I'm glad," he said. He looked at his watch again. "Sweetheart, I have to go now. I'll talk to you tonight, though, I promise . . . Yes, honey, and remember, Daddy loves you like the whole universe, and you? You are its prettiest star . . . Yep. Give Mommy a kiss for me. Bye." He somberly shut the phone off and slipped it back into his pocket. The children's book was placed back inside the briefcase, and its buttons were snapped back into place.

Deke sat still, steadfastly staring out the windshield at nothing in particular. He tried to give the impression of indifference.

Joseph fastened his seat belt and wriggled a bit in his seat to get more comfortable.

Deke could see that the phone call with Joseph's daughter had pained him. It was hard enough for Deke himself to be away from his own kids, and they were in the same city. He couldn't even imagine them being across the country. "That was a nice thing you said to the kid there, ya know, about the universe and the stars."

"I say that to her every night before she goes to sleep. I'm so pissed at myself for missing it last night."

"Don't worry about it. At least you know you'll be goin' back to her when this case is done. You wouldn't wanna be in my shoes."

Joseph gave a short nod of understanding.

"You ready?" Deke asked him.

"Yeah, I'm ready."

The car was thrown into gear, and the two men headed off to check the phone guy. When they arrived at his office, Deke and Joseph learned that he was somewhere out in the city working. They found his immediate supervisor barking orders all over the place, so they grabbed him instead and went to his office to get a little background information.

"Your name, sir?" Deke asked.

"Trebor. Izzot Trebor."

Deke rolled his eyes and jotted it down. He'd never heard that one before. "This guy we're lookin' for, Jesper, how long's he been a repairman with the phone company?"

"Myron's been with us a few months now. Can I ask what this is in reference to, please?"

"I'm sure it's nothin', sir. We're investigatin' a crime and tryin' to pare down our list a bit."

"You think Myron's involved? What kind of crime would this be?"

"We're not at liberty to say right now. Please, just a few more questions."

"I'm sorry, Detective, but we have hiring policies here. If one of my people snuck through the cracks on a background check, I'll need to make changes."

Deke looked him dead in the eye. "You can make them later. For now, you can answer my questions."

"Go ahead." Trebor was getting annoyed. He was usually the one in control and didn't like getting pushed around by anyone. "You know, I could get him back here for you if you'd like to talk to him yourselves."

Joseph jumped in. "You said he's up in the Bronx right now. We don't have the time to wait for him."

"Yeah," Deke agreed, "we'll talk to him later on today when we go back to Manhattan. You could have him meet us at headquarters. Now please, Mr. Trebor, I'd like some background here."

"Ask away." Trebor sighed.

"Do you know if Mr. Jesper is married?"

"No, he's not."

"Any kids?"

"Kids? Ha." Trebor laughed. "He's so scared of women he wouldn't be able to seal the deal."

"Really," Deke said with interest. "Would you know if he owns a gun?"

Trebor lowered his brow. This was turning out to be more serious than he'd initially thought. "I can't say for sure, but I would guess he does. He's pretty much into hunting, likes spending time out in the woods."

Deke added the notes to his book and put a star next to Jesper's name.

"You guys wouldn't mind if I lit up, would you?" Trebor asked, holding up a cigarette and motioning to the NO SMOKING sign posted on his wall. "I usually go outside."

"No," Deke said nonchalantly, "this is your place. Go right ahead."

Trebor puffed hard on the cancer stick, his pockmarked cheeks sucking in as far as they could. He inhaled the smoke with a deep breath and then let it slip slowly out. His eyes closed as he took another.

Deke and Joseph looked at each other. "You all right there, bud?" asked Deke.

Trebor opened his eyes and sat up straight. "Fine, fine. I just never thought Myron would be the type to get mixed up in anything illegal."

"We never said he was involved in nothin', Mr. Trebor. We

just want to question him to see if he saw anything." Deke stopped as he watched a cloud of smoke rise to the ceiling. "Exactly what is your relationship to Jesper, sir?"

Trebor looked back quizzically.

Deke clarified the question. "Is it strictly boss/subordinate, or are you guys friends off the job?"

"I'm just his boss. I don't like mingling around with the workers. They try to get too friendly with you, and then they start expecting special treatment."

"So then, I don't gotta worry 'bout you callin' him and tippin' him off that we wanna talk to him?"

"Not at all. I know the drill." Trebor leaned forward and dropped his cigarette in a stale, half-empty cup of coffee. "Come on, tell me, what did he do?"

"Not a thing. Right now, all we're lookin' to do is talk."

"Fine," said Trebor rather snippily. "Just keep in mind, please, that we have a code of conduct here that prohibits illegal activities. If he's involved in anything illegal, I will have to know."

"Not a prob, bud, not a prob. We'll work with you. 'Course, you gotta work with us, too."

"How?"

"When you talk to him later, don't tell him to come in and see us. I don't want him gettin' nervous. Give it to him as a phone problem he needs to check out. When he gets to my office, we'll take it from there. Here's my card with the address."

Trebor looked at the information on it. "Sounds easy enough."

"Good. Also, I need you to gimme some kinda list of the jobs he's been on for the last two weeks and whatever's on his slate for today. If you got an employee photo, I'll take that, too."

Trebor pulled some paperwork from his bottom drawer and then rolled his chair over to the file cabinet, where he took out Jesper's personnel folder. He put all the stuff together and handed it to Deke. "I will need this back, Detective, and don't be telling people where you got it. I just broke company policy by giving you his personal information."

"Done deal, bud," Deke answered.

"I'll tell you, though," Trebor said. "Sure seems like you're going through an awful lot of trouble just to ask a guy questions about something he's not involved in."

Deke looked over the paperwork while Joseph responded to the statement. "We'll make that determination, sir."

Deke chimed in. "Just have him there by five o'clock, OK?"

"Will do." He stood up. "Is that all?"

"For now. Remember, don't make him nervous about showin' up later. Make him think it's a service call." Deke put his hand out, and the two men shook. "If you don't mind me sayin', bro, you should try to cut down on those things." He nodded at the cigarette. "They sound like they're killin' your voice."

"Puberty did that to me," Trebor said scratchily and smiled.

"Well, Merry Christmas," Deke responded. "We'll be in touch."

"Same to both of you."

Joseph and Deke didn't wait for the car before discussing this one.

"We might have something with this. We need to put a tail on this guy now," Joseph observed.

Deke continued scanning the paperwork. "According to this, he has three more jobs in the Bronx today." He noticed a fax machine on the way out and grabbed somebody to ask if he could use it. He then sent a copy of all Jesper's information along with his picture to Captain Murray's office. He followed that with a phone call to Captain Murray to get the tail started.

On the way to the car, Deke yawned and tossed the keys back to Joseph. "Still feel like drivin', Ku-Jo? I'm friggin' tired."

"You're taking a chance putting a California guy in charge of navigation, you know."

"Keep usin' the GPS. You'll do fine."

The car was started, and Deke gave Joseph the next destination. Joseph wasn't done talking about Jesper yet. "I say we should go to the Bronx and tail this guy ourselves."

"No, let the cap give it to some other schmos. There's a couple other people on this list I wanna see. We ain't got no time to be goin' everywhere."

Joseph smiled at him. "Let me guess. You're from Brooklyn, aren't you?"

Deke looked back knowingly. "How'd ya guess?"

"Hey, I'm an FBI guy," Joseph said, laughing. He was growing accustomed to Deke's ways. "Now, who are these other people you want to see? I thought we were going to lock in on Jesper for a bit."

"Yeah, he sounds good, but if I learned anything on this job, it's not to settle in too hard on an early suspect, especially one we ain't even interviewed. Maybe this Trebor guy has it in for Jesper and would love to see us hassle him. The guy could be nothin' like what he said. We'll stick a tail on him for now and see what happens."

"Fair enough," concluded Joseph. "So, where to now?"

"A sanitation garage in the South Street Seaport. There's a garbageman there that likes to bounce all around the city." Deke punched the info into the GPS system. "He's got the seniority to stay put, but he's always the first one to volunteer to go out. Coincidentally, he just happened to be in all the same boroughs as the murders the days they took place. Let's go see why."

"Interesting. Let's do it." Joseph pulled his list out and looked it over. "You know, we can only do maybe one or two more interviews if you want to be back in time to talk to that Jesper guy."

"Yeah, I know. Let's see what the garbageman's got for us first."

Joseph folded the list and shoved it into his pocket. "Where'd your guy get all these names from?"

"Most of 'em are called in on tips. The guys in my office do some background checkin' and give me the ones that look like they might be somethin'." Deke reclined the passenger seat. "Onward and forward, Ku-Jo."

The car was put into drive and pulled away from the curb. Deke's head was back, and his eyes were closed. His head swayed gently from side to side as the car bounced and plodded over the pothole-filled streets. As always, different scenarios were flying through his head as he replayed the testimony from the first couple of interviews in his mind. Nothing really jumped out at him. They were what they were.

Joseph passed his time by paying attention to the GPS system directions and following them accordingly. Every once in a while he would glance over at Deke, wondering if he was sleeping, not wanting to say anything to wake him up in case he was. As they approached the Manhattan Bridge, Deke stuck his head up and had a look around to see how far they had gotten. "Good," he said, "almost there."

"Hey, welcome back," Joseph responded.

"Never left," Deke retorted. "I was just thinkin' to myself."

"Let me ask you a question."

"Go."

"Where'd you get Deke? Is that your given name, or is it short for something?"

"No, it's a nickname. Real name's Harlon." Deke looked him dead in the eye. "Laugh and I'll shoot you."

"Hey, I go by Ku-Jo," Joseph said. "Why would I laugh at you?" He entered the Manhattan Bridge off Flatbush Avenue and took to the right lane. "So, where'd Deke come from?"

"I picked it up in high school when I was a runnin' back. Our team had a crappy offensive line, and the other team's defense was constantly in the backfield whenever I got the ball. My guys used to say that I could deke and juke my way through all the tackles and actually gain some yardage. Some of 'em started callin' me Deke, and the name stuck. People on the job say I'm still doin' that today, dekin' my way in and out of trouble."

Deke's cell phone started buzzing. He saw the caller ID and opened it quickly. "What's up, Cap?"

"Where are you?"

"Just about to get off the Manhattan Bridge, why?"

"Well, turn around. I need you to go back to Brooklyn. We got another one."

"Jesus Christ," Deke said despondently. He pulled the phone away from his mouth and spoke to Joseph. "We got another one. Get off at the first exit and go back over the bridge." He then turned his attention back to Captain Murray. "Where?"

"Coney Island. Neptune Avenue and West Twenty-eighth Street. We just got it. There's a trailer home over there in a vacant lot. CSU's already on their way, if they're not there already."

The GPS system kept trying to reroute them to the Seaport, and the constant interruption was irritating Deke. "Can you kill that thing, please?" he asked Joseph.

The navigation was squelched, and the conversation resumed. "How many bodies?"

"Two that we know of so far. The woman that found them ran out of the house without looking around. She's in hysterics."

Deke grabbed his notebook. "Who's the woman that found 'em?"

"I'm not sure. Might be one of the victim's sisters. We don't know yet."

"This lady got a name?"

"Deke, this thing's two minutes old! It just came in. We got nothing yet."

"All right, I'll get back to you."

Deke shut off the phone and told Joseph to pull over so they could switch positions. With the lights and siren on, he easily navigated his way through his old neighborhood toward the crime scene. As they got closer, Joseph commented, "So this is Coney Island."

"Never been here?"

"Nope. Saw it on TV once in a show about the Cyclone."

"The Cyclone's only a few blocks from the scene. We're gonna pass it on the way back."

Joseph nodded his head. "Cool."

"If you got any stomach left after this, we'll take a stop at Nathan's and grab a couple of dogs for the ride back."

"What makes you think I won't have the stomach?"

Deke gave him a funny look.

"What?" said Joseph. "I've been at murder scenes before."

"Where, in California?"

"Yeah, why?"

"Please," Deke said begrudgingly, "murder scenes here are gunshots, knifin's, baseball bats clubbin' people, blood every-where. What do they do in California? Choke people, throw 'em in the ocean, poison their drinks. Those are wussy murders."

Joseph turned his head and looked out his window at the passing buildings. "Tell that to OJ," he mumbled.

Upon arriving at the scene, both men were greeted by a huge police contingent and a steadily growing throng of reporters. Deke flashed his badge and had the officer blocking off the street back his patrol car up so they could pull through. The reporters swarmed Deke's car, filming and asking questions as he passed. There were microphones in the window and strobe flashes going off in his face. He quickly rolled up the window and put an end to the craziness.

As they neared the trailer, Deke absorbed his surroundings, making note of how isolated the trailer was in that vacant lot. He commented to Joseph that nobody would have heard the gunshots. An ambulance was just outside the front of the lot with its rear doors open. In it, Deke could make out the figure of a woman surrounded by technicians trying to calm her. There was no doubt it was the woman who found the bodies. He flung the car door open, held his badge high, and yelled for anyone other than CSU and the ambulance guys to pull back from the scene and give them room. With Joseph in tow, he headed straight to the ambulance to get a quick statement. He threw a few of the techs out and stepped inside so he could sit with the lady. She was still shaken, taking very short breaths and crying as she spoke.

Deke knew to take it slow and spoke in a very soft, sympathetic voice. "Ma'am, I'm Detective Durgess. This is Agent Joseph. Can we talk to you a second, please?"

She nodded.

"You made the discovery in there?"

Another nod.

"Can I ask what your relationship is to the victims?"

The woman started sobbing again. "She was my sister."

Deke handed Joseph his pad and pen. He took the woman's hands and held them gently. "We're very sorry for your loss, ma'am." He checked for a reaction to see if his words were getting through. "I know this is a very difficult time, but I need to ask you a few questions."

She looked back at him through teary eyes and nodded again.

"Thank you. Can you tell me your sister's name, please?"

She started crying again. "It's Cheryl . . ." She completely broke down.

"Ma'am, I know this is hard, but I need for you to try to remain calm." He caressed her hands and waited for her to regain composure. "Can I have your name?"

"Susan Shafer."

"OK, Susan, just relax. This'll only be a couple more minutes. Was there anybody else in there with your sister?"

"Rob," she answered quietly. "My brother-in-law."

"Why were you here today?"

"We came by last night to wish them a merry Christmas. No one answered the door, so I came back to check on them today."

"Are you sure they were home at the time?"

"I don't know. They knew we were coming. They're not very reliable, though. They may not have been home. I mean, the door was locked, and I couldn't get in. Today I came with the key, and it was already open."

"The door was already open?"

"Well, it was unlocked."

Deke could see from the corner of his eye that Joseph was writing everything down. "I see. So, when was the last time you saw 'em?"

The tears started flowing again. "A few days ago when I picked up the kids."

Deke felt his stomach drop. "Yours or hers?"

"Hers."

Deke turned quickly to Joseph. "We might have kids in there. Go get me CSU—"

He was stopped by Susan. "The kids aren't in there. I have

them. I took them from her days ago. They're home with my husband now." She sniffled. "They don't even know yet." The tears really started rolling. "Tomorrow's Christmas. How do I tell them their parents are dead?"

Deke had no answer. The best he could do was to continue pumping questions. "Ma'am, what's your address?"

"Why?"

There was no time for explanations. "Ma'am, what is your address!" Deke demanded.

"One forty-two Stuart Street. It's in Marine Park."

Deke grabbed Joseph by the sleeve and locked eyes with him. Nothing needed to be said; Joseph knew what was on his mind.

He jumped out of the ambulance and grabbed the first two police officers he saw. He showed his badge, dropped Deke's name, and told them to get someone over to Susan's house as fast as they could. With the killer still out there, there was no telling if he would go after the kids to polish off his handiwork. The officers radioed ahead and ordered a squad car to the address on the highest priority. Once appeased, Joseph hurriedly returned to the ambulance.

Deke hopped out just as Joseph got there, and they both headed for the trailer.

"What's goin' on with the kids?" Deke asked urgently.

"There's a police cruiser headed there now."

Deke looked at him as they walked. "Squad car. This is New York, remember?"

Joseph let it go.

As they entered the house, both men were greeted by the strong smell of ammonia. It was an occasional practice of grizzled first-responding police officers to throw a rag soaked in ammonia into a murder scene to overcome the nasty stench of death. Decomposing bodies had a tendency to overpower even the strongest of stomachs. The rag would first be placed into an open plastic bag so as not to disturb any crime scene evidence and then would be tossed just inside the front door. The ammonia, as far as Deke was concerned, helped some but ultimately wasn't much of a bargain either.

The first sight they took in was the bodies. They weren't far from the front door at all, maybe ten or fifteen feet. No investigators were anywhere near them. All the CSU guys were dusting doors and windows for fingerprints and searching the ratty carpets for hairs and clothing fibers.

The condition of the bodies and the nature of the wounds left little doubt for Deke who the perpetrator was, especially once the infamous calling card came into view. Deke specifically pointed it out to Joseph.

"Better luck next time?" Joseph asked.

"He leaves it at every scene. Confirms right away for us who did it."

"Who's it written to?"

"I have no idea."

Deke leaned in close to the bodies in an effort to ascertain the entry direction of the bullets.

Joseph had a look around at the immediate area. "Doesn't seem to have been much of a struggle," he noticed.

"Never is," Deke answered. "Never no forced entry, and he don't leave a shred of hard evidence behind."

Joseph saw the empty bottle of vodka lying on the floor beneath the couch. He called one of the CSU guys over. "Dust that for prints for me, please." He turned to Deke. "You never know. Maybe they were doing a round-robin before it all went wrong."

"This guy wouldn't make that mistake." His cell phone started buzzing again. "G'head, Cap."

"What's it look like over there?"

"Same as the rest. A couple of bodies, nothin' else."

"He left the calling card?"

"Right on the male victim's lap."

"OK, listen. CSU just called me. They got some info back on that footprint from the Nevalo scene. They estimate it at about a nine and a half. That would make our guy anywhere from five six to six two."

"OK, good. Give that to Ronnie for me, and have him add it to the FBI profile."

"He's already got it."

"OK, understood. Let me get back to this here. If we find anything, I'll call ya."

"Go." The phone was hung up.

Joseph waited for the phone call to end and then grabbed Deke's attention. "Look," he said, pointing to the bodies, "they died holding hands."

"I know," Deke responded. "This must've been a pretty tight family."

Strobe flashes started going off like lightning strikes in the room as CSU continued processing the scene.

"Come on," Deke said. "Let's go. There ain't nothin' more we can do here. This guy didn't leave nothin' behind but the note. CSU can take it from here."

They walked outside and got a lungful of fresh air.

Joseph took a long, deep breath. "Where to?"

"Jesper," Deke answered. "I think it's time we meet him." He headed for the car. "Let's take a look at how tall he is."

Chapter Five

Myron Jesper's BlackBerry alerted him that a message was on the way through. With his little black tool case rolling behind him, he stepped underneath a sidewalk canopy to cut down the sun's glare on the message screen. He cupped its face with his hand.

> Myron, cancel all jobs.
> Report to 1 Police Plaza in Manhattan no later than 5PM.
> Go to detective office. Phones out.
> Emergency situation. Text me back to confirm.

He recognized the sender's number as his boss and quickly replied that he would be there on time. He checked his watch and headed for the subway to catch the downtown train. During the ride, nervousness bubbled in his belly. He was very trepidatious about going into the detective unit of a police station. He hoped he would handle it well. At the same time, he was awash in excitement and enthusiasm. He loved those Discovery Channel detective shows narrating true crimes. He was addicted to the prime-time cop dramas, detective dramas, courtroom dramas. He'd seen them all and studied them well, often wondering how he would do in a similar situation. He considered himself savvy to the many ploys of detective interrogation and steadfastly paid attention to the details of the crimes to see where the criminals would slip up. There were many times he bragged to friends that he could commit the perfect crime just on what he'd learned so far from TV. No one ever paid him any mind. Guys named Myron usually aren't taken very seriously.

When he rolled into the detective unit, everything stopped. All eyes went immediately to him, and all hands rested on their guns. The picture of him that came over the fax was only a head shot and did more to intimidate than the actual person would seem to. In the picture, his hair was not nearly as disheveled as it was in person. The face was clean shaven; stubble adorned the man who had just walked in. It was his size that surprised most. The guy couldn't make 5' 6" if he were standing on a milk crate. If he told you he weighed 150 pounds, you'd check his pockets for sand or lead.

Deke watched him come in as he sat in the confines of Captain Murray's office. He noticed the small size and nerdy look of Jesper and abruptly dismissed them. They meant nothing to him. He'd seen many times how a small, squirty nothing of a guy could add three feet to his height and demeanor just by carrying a gun. It was the greatest equalizer of all.

The other detectives pointed Jesper to Captain Murray's office. He opened the door pensively and stuck his head in. "Good afternoon, gentlemen. Phone company guy here."

"Hey, come on in," said Captain Murray. "We've been waiting for you."

"I'm not under arretht, am I?" he said facetiously.

The two cops gave a courtesy laugh. "Not yet," said Deke.

"What theems to be the problem?"

Deke and Captain Murray gave each other a cockeyed look. The guy seemed to be half a bubble off.

Captain Murray drew his attention to some phone wires that had recently been ripped out of the wall. "Think you can fix this?"

Jesper appeared surprised. "This wath the emergenthy they pulled me out of the Bronxth for?"

"Phone lines need to work," said Deke. "We're in the midst of a crisis out there. Don't you read the papers?"

"I read them constantly, Detective," Jesper snapped, insulted. "I might not look or thound like it, but thome people think I'm pretty smart."

Deke was having a hard time picking out whether the lisp was real or just a half-assed attempt at subterfuge. It didn't happen on every *S* sound, for some reason. "Why would we think otherwise, bud?"

Jesper stared at Deke quizzically. "Don't you hear the way I talk? I have a little thpeech impediment."

Deke nodded. "I wasn't quite sure. It doesn't seem to happen on every *S* word, though. A lisp is usually a constant thing."

"It's not a lisp," Jesper said angrily but calmly. "It'th a thpeech impediment."

"OK, but why doesn't it happen on every word?"

Jesper was caught off guard. "I don't know. My thpeech therapy muth be working. Really, I wathn't paying attenthion to mythelf."

"You seem to be paying attention now, though," said Captain Murray. "You're lisping on every *S*."

"I gueth I'm nervouth."

Deke had had enough with the charades. "You can cut the shit now, buddy. Just talk regular and fix the phone lines."

"What are you talking about?" The expressionless look on Deke's face signaled to Jesper that the gig was up. He let out nervous laughter. "All right, you got me," he blurted. "I wanted to see if I could fool you."

"Why would you wanna do that?"

"I don't know. It's just that I see so many detective shows on TV—"

"Ya know what it seems like to me?" Deke asked. "It seems like you were tryin' to test us."

"No," Jesper answered worriedly. "I was just having a little fun. Really."

Deke decided to let it go. He'd made his point. He needed Jesper relaxed and unaware. "So what about the phone lines?"

"It doesn't look so bad," replied Jesper. "Someone must've tripped over the wires and ripped them out of the wall." He was very happy to be away from the lisping talk. He pulled his telephone handset from his tool case and began testing wires. "I should have you up and running in no time."

"You got a name, bud?"

"Myron Jesper," he said while stripping and splicing wires.

"What's up, Myron? I'm Detective Durgess. This here is Captain Murray."

Jesper looked up and nodded to both men and then continued his work. His hands shook slightly as he twisted and connected wires. He always hated to be watched while he worked. It made him feel like he was on display. "You guys could go back to doing what you were doing if you want. I got this here."

Deke motioned with his head for Captain Murray to leave the office. He could see that Jesper was tight, and tight guys never give easy answers. He wanted Jesper to feel calm, unthreatened. The more at ease he was, the more likely he would be to answer questions without realizing he was being interrogated. Deke moved away from him and sat on the couch. "I'm at the end of a long day, Mr. Jesper. I'm just gonna sit here and unwind a bit, OK?"

"Mmm-hmm. I had a long day, too," Jesper answered from behind the desk. "It never ends sometimes."

"How long you been doin' this?"

"Almost ten years."

"You like it?"

"Eh, it pays the bills."

"Your wife don't complain that you get stuck sometimes?"

"Nooo," Jesper giggled sheepishly. "I'm not married."

"A good-lookin' guy like you?" Deke asked. "How's that?"

Jesper stuck his head up from behind the desk. "I'm not really good at talking to girls. Any one I meet my mother never likes for some reason. I get really nervous around them."

"Yeah, I had the mom problem, too, once. How old is your mom?"

He disappeared behind the desk again. "She died a few months ago," he said somberly.

"Oh, sorry to hear that, pal," Deke answered softly. "Must make the holidays tough for you, huh?"

"Yeah. I don't feel much like celebrating Christmas this year. I didn't even put any lights or a tree up."

Deke was making mental notes like crazy. He didn't want Jesper to see him writing anything down and get suspicious, but with every answered question a dozen scenarios blew through his mind. Maybe this thing had something to do with Christmas. The killings did start right before the holidays. It was just one more thing that would have to be checked out. "I lost my mom some time back also," he said. "Was real hard on me for a while. Nighttime used to be the worst."

"Yup," said Jesper. "I know what you mean."

"You, too, huh." Finally, his foot was in the door. "So, how do *you* pass the time at night? I did a lotta boozin' for a while myself."

"Not me. I can't drink. I watch a lot of TV. I really like the detective shows."

"Yeah, you mentioned that earlier. So, basically you stay home?"

"I used to. I did a lot of reading, some writing. Went on the computer here and there. Lately I've been doing a lot of walking, though. Really clears my head."

"Walkin' . . . I see. Could be a good way to calm down."

"For some people it is."

"Do you own a car?"

"Why?"

"I don't know. I figured maybe you like walkin' in different places, see different sights, different people. Don't you worry bein' out there alone with a killer on the loose?"

Jesper appeared confused by the question. "No, no. I stay in my own area." He paused a second. "Besides, he doesn't like killing people on the street anyway."

The line was delivered awkwardly, and Deke picked up on it. "How would you know something like that, Mr. Jesper? I don't recall that being in any reports."

"I follow this stuff very closely, Detective. So far, the only people who got killed have been indoors. No cars, no porches, no backyards, no streets."

It was an angle Deke hadn't even thought of but would now look into. "What if he decided to venture outside? What if you found yourself facing him?"

"Well, then, I guess that would be that."

"That would be that, huh? You almost sound as if you're not afraid of him. You gotta keep in mind that there's nowhere safe from him right now."

Up came the head again. "It's a big city, Detective. The odds are in my favor."

It was time for Deke to throw a little bait on the hook. "You come face-to-face with him and the odds'll be in his favor. You should try carryin' some kind of protection with you on your walks, ya know, like a knife or a billy club or somethin'."

Jesper stared blankly yet nervously. His lip quivered a bit.

Deke saw that he'd hit pay dirt. "What, you already do?"

Jesper stammered a little but said nothing.

Deke pressed the subject. "Whaddaya got, a gun?" He tried to play it like it was no big deal. "Makes no difference to me. You and half of the city probably have one. Look, honestly, I don't care if you're stickin' a gun in your sock when you go for your walks out there. I'd be doin' the same thing if I was you, but if you got one on you now, and you're in my buildin', you better tell me."

Jesper regained a bit of his composure. "I absolutely would not do that."

"What, wouldn't pack a gun? Or wouldn't tell me?"

"The former, Detective. The former."

"So you're not packin' right now?"

"No. Look, I really should finish this."

"Go right ahead." Deke started tapping the wooden arm of the couch and waited about ten or fifteen seconds. "So, between me and you, what kinda gun you got?"

It became clear to Jesper that Deke wasn't about to let the subject go without an answer. "Are we off the record here?" he asked hesitantly.

"Hey, we're just talkin'."

Jesper looked around and then whispered so only Deke could hear, "I own a few. I'm a hunter."

Deke realized that line could have been a double entendre. "I guess you could say I'm a hunter, too. Only I hunt down criminals. What do you go for?"

"It all depends on the season."

"I see. So, um, what season is it now?"

Jesper looked like a kid caught with his hand in the cookie jar. "I don't know. It's been a while since I've been out there."

"I see. So, why you whisperin'? Your guns legal?"

"Of course, of course." Jesper was stammering again. "I think I should finish these phones now."

Deke got up and walked over to the desk and sat on the edge. He looked down at Jesper, working feverishly on the wires. It was time to lie. "To tell you the truth, Mr. Jesper, I don't care if your guns are legal or not. I'm not here to arrest you. We were just talkin'. I have bigger problems out there right now than you. You can relax."

Jesper did just that. "Well, most of mine are legal. I only have one that's not registered."

"That's no big deal. What caliber is it?"

Jesper stared blankly again, pausing about five seconds, weighing if he should answer it truthfully or not. "Twenty-two," he said suspiciously.

"Pistol?"

"Yeah. I don't use it often. It's not very powerful."

Deke paid close attention to the body language as Jesper put the finishing touches on his work.

"There," he said. "That should do it."

"Phones are up?" Deke asked, putting a handset to his ear to verify. "Yes, they are. Good work."

"Thanks." Jesper opened his case and pulled out some paperwork. "I'll need you to sign this voucher, please. It just states that this was an emergency call. My boss said he'll take it from there."

"No problem," Deke answered as he inscribed the paper. "Hey, those are nice shoes you got there. Where'd you get 'em?"

"I get my stuff at Sears."

"You buy your hunting shoes there, too?"

"Usually, why?"

"Well, like I said, I do some huntin,' too, and I could use a new pair for myself. We look about the same size. What are you? Ten? Ten and a half?"

"I'm a nine. My mom always told me I'd grow into my feet. Never happened." He took the paperwork from Deke and placed it in a side pocket on his tool case. "Well, I'd better get going now. If you have any more problems with the phone lines, call my boss, and we'll send someone back."

"You got it," Deke answered. "So, where you off to now?"

"I'm done for the day," answered Jesper. "Time to go home."

"You goin' walkin' tonight?" Deke smiled.

"I don't know. Maybe."

"Well, if you'd like, we could try to hook you into some overtime tonight instead. There's a lot of other phone problems around here that could use fixin'. We'll call your boss—"

Deke was stopped right there by Jesper. "No, no, no," he said, wide-eyed. "I can't do it tonight. I have to get home."

"You sound a little desperate, bud. Everything OK?"

Jesper caught himself. "Yeah, sure. I just have cats that need to be fed and let out."

Deke took note of his apprehension. "Well, I guess you should get to it, then," he said, standing aside.

As Jesper passed, Deke sized him up skeptically. This guy really didn't look to be the killing type. He seemed to lack the coordination that would allow him to stealthily make his way into people's homes and lie in wait. He also didn't appear to have that confrontational mentality that a cold-blooded killer would need to possess. He was a loner, though, and he did own guns. Nothing, Deke knew, was ever out of the realm of possibility when it came to murder suspects.

Deke's mind kept bringing him back to the fact that a gun can change someone's whole demeanor. A gun in one's hand can triple one's size. Cowardice holding a gun can often appear to be bravery. If this guy was truly a hunter, then he was used to killing and probably enjoyed it. He certainly had the guts to do it. It was whether he could take that next sick step up to killing a human being that was the deal breaker. The only way to tell was to watch him closely.

Jesper, tools in tow, briskly walked through the hard stares of twenty or so police officers and detectives. His head was down, as usual, watching his feet, avoiding eye contact with anyone who might be looking his way. He buzzed past everyone and hit the stairs without breaking stride. On the street waiting for him were two detectives well blended in with the evening passersby, some on their way home from work, some on their way to Christmas Eve celebrations, some squeezing in some last-minute Christmas shopping. Jesper merged right in with all of them and headed for the subway.

The subway platform was packed with people trying to jam their way into sardine cans masquerading as trains. Jesper's small size and stature made him an unwilling participant in a game of platform pinball. It wasn't that people were being overly rude, it was just that they all had places to go but weren't paying attention to where they were going. He heard a train coming on his side of the platform and started working his way toward it. He heard the doors open, and the crowd on the platform seemed to part as the crowd on the train started making their way off. Jesper saw the perfect opportunity to weave his way through them and right onto the train's fourth car. He grabbed a corner seat, grinned victoriously to himself, and closed his eyes as he began yet another journey through the rat-filled labyrinth of New York City subway tunnels.

Chapter Six

Captain Murray had watched Jesper make his way past the detectives and out of the building. Like Deke, he wondered how such a diminutive guy would be able to pull off such heinous acts and get away unscathed. Also like Deke, he had learned never to underestimate the opposition. He returned to his office to find Deke sitting on the couch, head back, staring up at the ceiling.

"You get anything from him?"

"Yeah, a little. He's definitely worth keepin' the tail on, but the friggin' height thing really bothers me."

"Listen, Deke, you said it yourself a million times—"

"I know, I know, I know," Deke said abruptly. "Size ain't everything." His eyes were still locked on the ceiling. "This guy don't ring my bell for some reason."

"Well, what did he say? Did he give you anything?"

Deke closed his eyes and let the details of his and Jesper's conversation flood his mind. He passed along to the captain all of the pertinent information and any doubts or hesitations he had concerning Jesper. The height thing really was a major roadblock for Deke. Even though he knew that height, or lack of it, was perceived more by the person doing the looking than by the short person being looked at, it also occurred to him that in some ways Jesper's shortness seemed to be evident in his mentality as well. He didn't come across as being the sharpest knife in the drawer. Then again, a good, convincing actor usually isn't stupid.

Captain Murray sat there with the FBI profile in his hand. He mentioned to Deke all the items that fit Jesper. He was a white male in the age range from the report. He was single, only had a high school education, and did have access to all parts of the city. There was also the traumatic event of losing his mother. That could have set things in motion.

Deke retorted with the stuff that didn't fit. He was making way more than thirty grand, he didn't seem to be overly concerned with hygiene, and he gave the impression of wanting to keep to himself. The bottom line was that, either way, the search was in no way over.

"Where's Ku-Jo?" Deke asked.

"I think he's on a line with Washington. Miller wanted updates coming in."

"He better not take long. I wanna get over and talk to this garbage guy."

"Deke, relax." Captain Murray glanced at his watch. "It's six thirty on Christmas Eve. The sanitation guy's already been checked out. He's off the list."

"Who talked to him?"

"Ronnie. He pulled him in when you were with Jesper. I sat in on it for a little while. He's not our guy."

Deke was not happy. "Dammit! I needed to talk to that guy. What if Ronnie missed somethin'?"

The question irritated Captain Murray. "Hey, listen, Deke, I was doing interrogation when you were still a foot cop in Harlem. I've been around the block once or twice. Maybe I should repeat this since you didn't pay attention the first time. *I sat in on the ses-*

sion. Ronnie covered everything that needed asking. The garbage guy is not who we're looking for."

Deke relented. It was foolish of him to challenge Captain Murray to a battle of wills. The guy wasn't just a member of the homicide squad; he ran the thing, and had run it for a long time. The sanitation guy was now legitimately out of the mix. Deke had to accept the fact that other people could actually do the same job he could. Maybe not to the same level in some areas, but basic questioning was still basic questioning. Ronnie had done the right thing. Deke knew to just let it lie.

He apologized to Captain Murray for the slight, and the two resumed conversation as if nothing had happened. They covered more of the ins and outs of Jesper and even threw some of Coleman in as well. There were currently fourteen people on the list of hopefuls, and all either were being checked out or had a two-detective team tailing them. Deke and Captain Murray knew it wasn't enough.

"He's probably gonna hit again, Cap, and all this crap'll be for nothin'," Deke noted, holding up the suspect list. "We'll be right back to square one."

"I know," Captain Murray responded. "Deke"—his fingers tapped the desk lightly—"we might have to start thinking about the unthinkable here."

Deke realized exactly what the captain was hinting at. The thought had been in his mind for a while now but was one that sickened him to even consider. "You really think it could be one of us?"

Captain Murray's answer was quick and concise. "The guy's using a .38, and he sure does seem to know his way around a crime scene, or at least what we'd be looking for at one. He seems to know exactly what *not* to leave behind."

"True, but how the hell are we gonna check all these guys

out? There's about forty thousand cops on the job now. Half of 'em use .38s."

"Well, there ya go. You just narrowed the list down by half."

"Funny," Deke said sarcastically. "Where would we even start?"

"How about ballistics?" Captain Murray offered. "Every cop has to register his gun through ballistics, right? We can run the ballistics from the bullets through the system and see if they match up to anyone's service or off-duty weapons."

"Come on, Cap," Deke answered dryly. "How many cops out there you think really only got two guns? They might register two, but they really got three or four. I got five myself. The job only thinks I got two. You really think that if it was one of us he would use a registered piece?"

It was a valid argument, and Captain Murray knew Deke was right. A rookie just starting out on the job might only have his allotted two weapons, but the seasoned veterans and even the in-betweens all had numerous guns in their collections. Some were acquired legitimately, but many more were grabbed under the table. Many times there were busts where the arresting officer would come across an illegal gun or two, and once in a while one of those guns would find its way into the officer's private collection, especially if it was a gun with its serial number filed off. Those were the cream of the crop, the ones most desired. Guns without serial numbers were often tucked into a sock or into a different holster as an insurance policy. If a cop shot a perpetrator without just cause or even accidentally, the illegal gun could be pulled and placed in the perp's hand so it would look like the cop was defending himself. It was even more handy in getting information from guys reluctant to give any. The cop would threaten to say the gun belonged to the bad guy, which meant he'd be looking at a weapons rap. That, often enough, got the perp to spill his guts. Weapons charges almost always carried jail time, especially if the officer testified that the gun was used in a criminal act. The dirty-cop angle was going to be a difficult path to follow but would have to be considered in pursuit of this particular killer.

Deke suggested that if the killings continued and all the present suspects were exonerated, then they should form a secret task force that would look into and check the backgrounds of all the members of the NYPD. They could start by using the FBI profile sheet to pare down the list as much as possible. They could then look at the yearly performance evaluations of all the officers remaining on the list to see if any had strayed off the beaten path around the time of the killings. Deke volunteered to be the first on the list to be checked out, guns and all.

Captain Murray dismissed the idea. "Get the hell out of here, Deke. I know you're not the killer. We can't be wasting time on something like that."

"I just don't want nothin' comin' back to you, Cap, if guys get pissed off and wanna know why I wasn't checked out, too."

"Don't worry. I'll handle that." Captain Murray walked over and sat next to Deke on the couch. "I need to talk to you about something more important anyhow."

"What?"

"I saw you a couple of times on the news today. The reporters are everywhere, and they're starting to put two and two together that you're the lead on this case. Your name is already out there."

"So what about it?"

"I'm sure the killer is keeping tabs on this thing, too. If he also puts two and two together, he might go after Frannie and the kids."

A cold chill went down Deke's spine. He was so consumed

by the hunt for the killer that he hadn't even given a thought to the danger his wife and children could be in. He immediately shifted on the couch and reached for the phone.

Captain Murray stopped him. "Relax, relax. I already took care of it."

Deke put the phone down. "How?"

"I sent a car over about an hour ago. The guys called in just before Jesper left. They're in the house. Everything's OK."

"Who'd ya send?" Deke asked worriedly, the earlier conversation about dirty cops still fresh in his mind.

"Don't worry," Captain Murray smiled. "It's Jimmy and Larry. Everything's cool."

Deke felt a tremendous weight lift from his mind. Jimmy and Larry had been his good friends and co-workers on the detective squad for many years. Frannie was very familiar with them, as they had been over to the house quite a few times for poker games and parties. Their kids even played together at the NYPD Family Day barbecues held every summer at the Randall's Island training center. The fact that they were willing to give up Christmas Eve with their own families in order to protect Deke's family said a lot about their own dedication not only to the job but to him as well. Deke took some solace in the thought that, hopefully, Frannie would see that there was more than one cop on the job that had to give up his personal life occasionally in order to nail down a case. It might make it a little easier to smooth things out later with the kids.

A loud knock on Captain Murray's door was followed by Ronnie barging his way in.

"We have problems, Cap," he said urgently.

Captain Murray stood up quickly. "What's the matter?"

"The two schleps following Jesper . . . they lost him in the subway."

"Jesus Christ Almighty!" Deke yelled. "How the hell did they lose him so quick? We put the tail on him two minutes ago!"

"Easy, Deke," the captain said. "Relax a minute."

"Bullshit relax! The guy's at the top of our list right now. I gotta know where he is at all times!"

Captain Murray let the rant fly right by. "Ronnie, where does this guy live?"

"What, you couldn't ask me that?" Deke asked loudly.

"Go away," Captain Murray dismissed him. "You're too hyper right now."

Ronnie answered the question put to him. "His residence is in Old Mill Basin, Brooklyn. I have the address on my desk. I'll go get it."

Deke took a couple of steps around the room and shook off the anger. "It's 6240 East Fifty-third Street," he said, much more calm.

"Oh, back so soon?" Captain Murray asked. "That was quick."

"Whatever," Deke answered. "We gotta get a car over to his house ASAP."

"No shit. What do you think I'm doing?"

"I know, Cap. Sorry. Just tell them to put cops on the stake-out that actually know how to follow someone." Deke thought a second. "Ya know, we're screwed if this guy don't go straight home."

Captain Murray paid no attention to the comment. He was busy on the phone with the Brooklyn South detective bureau setting up a stakeout across the street from Jesper's place. After a couple of minutes, he placed the call on hold and got Deke's attention. "Hey, listen, this guy's familiar with the area Jesper lives in. He says that area has a bunch of three- and four-family homes right across the street from the place."

Deke was all over it. "I still have some doubts about the guy,

Cap, but if you wanna set up a plant there, g'head. Can't hurt. Might even be better than a stakeout."

"Good idea." Captain Murray returned to the call. He told the detective in charge to get a plant going as soon as they possibly could, time being of the essence. It would do even more to incriminate or exonerate Jesper than just a tail would. The plant would set himself up in a residence across the street from Jesper and watch all facets of his home life. He would almost become a new neighbor, coming out and even interacting with Jesper if the situation allowed. It was a relatively drawn-out process, but in a situation such as this, if Jesper did turn out to be the killer, it would be the perfect way to find out if he worked with accomplices. Captain Murray hung up the phone and gave Deke the details.

"OK, once they get the tail going on Jesper again, they can set up the plant. Should be a day or so."

"Good luck findin' a family that wants to get displaced on Christmas," said Deke.

"We'll set them up in a nice hotel, room service and all. Someone will go for it."

"You know you're gonna have to find a judge willin' to sign the order to get the plant goin'?"

"Whaddaya think, I'm an idiot? I know that! Listen, you worry about your job, I'll worry about mine."

Joseph knocked on the door and entered the office. "Sorry about that, guys. My boss is very hands-on with this case. He needs to know every last detail."

Deke smiled an angry smile. "I got a real good detail for you."

Joseph felt uneasy. "I'm listening," he said pensively.

"We lost Jesper."

"What? How?"

"I don't know, but I would guess that ineptness had a lot to do with it."

"Well, let's grab his boss and have him page Jesper and tell us where he is."

"No, I thought of that," Deke said, "but there's no way Trebor is still workin' this late on Christmas Eve. He ain't gonna have Jesper's number on him. Besides, it might tip Jesper off that we're lookin' for him."

"Are all the other tails in place?"

"Yup, as far as I know. All the other possibles are bein' followed."

The intercom on Captain Murray's phone beeped, and the little red light flashed. He picked it up quickly and listened as orders came flying through the line. He hung it up just as quickly and began straightening his tie. "Come on, Deke. We gotta go upstairs. The commissioner wants to see us for a briefing." He gave Deke a fast look-over. "Thank God I had you go clean up this morning."

"Doesn't anyone take off for Christmas around here?" Joseph said with a chuckle.

"The only person we need to take a night off right now is probably out there scopin' out his next victim." Deke got up and grabbed Joseph gently by the shirt. "You're comin' upstairs, too. You could be our fall guy if we need one," he kidded. Before leaving the office, he turned back to Ronnie. "If they pick Jesper up again, come up and get me out of that meeting. I want regular updates on all the other tails, too."

"You got it, Deke."

The three men headed for their meeting with the Big Man. He certainly couldn't be pleased with the progress of the case, or the lack of it. The pressure would almost assuredly be turned up to the highest level until the lunatic out there was caught. Deke couldn't care less about what was coming from above. It didn't bother him. The only person he was concerned with was the one destroying lives every day. He wondered to himself as he entered the meeting how many people would be dead by the time he came back out.

As they came into the commissioner's office, it was plain to see that the man wasn't happy. In fact, he was downright pissed. He was on the phone taking his daily chewing-out by the mayor, who was also no bucket of joy. The commissioner just sat there and listened, knowing that was the easiest way to end the onslaught. Deke, Captain Murray, and Joseph stood by in front of his desk and could hear the mayor's voice in the phone but couldn't make out his words. The commissioner said only that he understood the mayor's message and would see to it that it was carried out. He slammed down the phone and glared at all three men. Joseph was the only one who didn't feel the stare. The commissioner had no control over him and no say-so in his jurisdiction. He did feel slightly uneasy for the two men to his left.

"Murray," the commissioner barked, "I sent for you and Detective Durgess. Who's this?"

"I'm sorry, Commissioner, this is FBI Agent Joseph. He's working with Detective Durgess in connection with the FBI profiling team."

"Pleased to meet you, Commissioner," Joseph said, hand out.

"Yeah," the commissioner huffed, giving a quick shake of Joseph's hand. "Go have a seat over there."

Joseph moved to a sofa and sat down quietly. Captain Murray waited for his invitation to sit, which came with a growl by the boss. He and Deke took the hot seats positioned directly in front of the commissioner's huge mahogany desk. The desk seemed designed almost as much to intimidate as to impress, and to an extent it worked that way on Captain Murray. It was no secret he was to be the fall guy here. Sure, Deke was calling most of the shots, but the sword always falls on the neck of the guy in charge, and Captain Murray did run the Homicide Unit.

The commissioner looked at both men angrily. "I don't suppose you need me to tell you who that was."

Deke had no reaction. Captain Murray shook his head slowly.

"I'm sick of these goddam phone calls. The mayor calls me a hundred times a day looking for progress. You guys better be here with something for me to give him."

Captain Murray cleared his throat. "Well, Commissioner, we do have a person of interest that we're looking at right now. Detective Durgess just finished a Q&A with him." It was all the captain could think of at the moment. Jesper might not be the guy they were looking for, but at the very least he was a stall tactic that could give the commissioner something to focus on.

"Who's this person of interest? Where is he now?"

Captain Murray spat out the details of the Jesper interview and threw in as much of his background as he could remember. Then he turned it over to Deke for some insight into the gist of their conversation and any thoughts or feelings he had on the subject. The smoke screen actually worked to a degree, and the commissioner felt a little better about having something that might temporarily pacify the mayor. That easy feeling didn't last long once he found out the tail had lost Jesper.

"What! How the hell could your guys lose him?" he asked harshly. "I want whoever was tailing him reassigned immediately!"

"Yes, sir," Captain Murray responded with no intention of carrying out the order. The commissioner was blowing steam, and everyone in the room knew it.

"Jesus Christ!" he yelled, shoving his chair back and walking to the window. "Look at the streets out there. I haven't seen it this dead since Son of Sam."

"Well, it *is* seven o'clock on Christmas Eve, sir," said Captain Murray futilely.

The commissioner spun quickly. "Bullshit!" He glared at the captain. "You think I started this job yesterday? I've spent thirty-five years on these streets. Not everyone is Catholic, and not everyone celebrates Christmas Eve. I've only seen the streets this empty twice. Summer of 'seventy-seven with Berkowitz, and now." He made sure to lock eyes with all three men. "I want this stopped now!"

Deke was getting pissed and squirming in his chair.

Captain Murray caught it from the side of his eye and gave him a little foot-to-foot kick. "We're doing our best, sir."

"Get better," the commissioner growled. "Or I'll find someone that will."

That pretty much did it for Deke. Brooklyn-born guys only take so much. "What more you want us to do?" he said forcefully.

The commissioner spoke his answer slowly and clearly. "I want you to fucking catch the guy."

Deke stood up in a flash. "No shit, Commissioner. I'm glad you cleared that up for me, 'cause I thought we were just supposed to keep lettin' him go. Fuckin' asshole!"

"Deke, shut up!" hollered Captain Murray. "Commissioner, let me apologize for Detective Durgess's outburst. This has been a very difficult case, and he hasn't slept in days."

Joseph hurried over and pulled Deke away. He walked him to the doorway and held him there while he took a couple of breaths to calm down. The commissioner and Captain Murray continued talking, but the other two men couldn't make out what they were saying. When cooler heads prevailed, the commissioner called both men back to their places.

"Listen, Detective," he said, "I've been in your shoes before. I know what it's like to have a demanding boss. It's just the way things go. I'm going to give you a pass this time." He looked hard into Deke's eyes for effect. "This one time."

Deke nodded knowingly but didn't speak.

Captain Murray jumped in again. "The detective and I appreciate your understanding, Commissioner, and we thank you for it."

The commissioner shrugged off the incident. "Let's move on," he said.

The commissioner and Captain Murray discussed the contingency plans for the police response in the event the killer struck again and was unable to make a clean getaway. The plans were almost identical to the ones made when Son of Sam terrorized the city thirty years earlier. The call would be routed into the commissioner's office, and all other city agencies would be notified to implement the plan. Whatever borough the murder took place in, all bridges leading in and out of it would be shut down so a check of all cars could be made. The same would be done for the trains. Wherever they were within the borough, they would be stopped on the tracks so no one could get on or off. Two transit cops that were already placed on each and every train could then do a search of all passengers on board and see what they might come up with. The ferries, airports, and bus terminals all would be shut down and thoroughly combed for the suspect if they were within a certain radius of the killings. The borough would effectively be held on lockdown until the hunt was deemed either successful or futile.

There were more cops, detectives, and private eyes working this case than any other before, including the case of '77. Most of them did their regular tours of duty and then looked for the killer on their own time, often putting in eighteen or more hours a day. It was mostly a sense of duty that made them do it, although many of the private eyes were focused on the combined reward of a hundred thousand dollars offered by public and corporate interests. The problem in the whole thing was that New York City was a really big place, and everyone was looking for one needle in about ten million haystacks.

Deke sat there and listened to the plans that he'd already heard a hundred times before. He looked up at the clock and mumbled to himself, "Quarter past seven." He knew it was paradox time: witching hour for the good guys, happy hour for the bad one. Seven o'clock was about the time he usually started doing his thing. Deke mentioned this to the commissioner and suggested that all city agencies be immediately notified to stay on high alert in case the call came in to implement the plan. The commissioner agreed and had one of his deputies set things in motion.

Deke, Joseph, and Captain Murray were then dismissed to get themselves back into the hunt. On the way down to the detective unit, Deke tapped Joseph on the shoulder. "That was fun, wasn't it?"

"Loads," came Joseph's sarcastic answer. "You have some set of balls."

"C'mon, let's hit the street."

"Let's go."

"Where you headed?" Captain Murray asked.

"I don't know yet, but we sure ain't gonna find what the hell we're lookin' for in here."

"OK. Watch your asses."

"We'll try, Dad. Let me know right away if the tail picks Jesper up again. Same for any of the other ones."

"Will do. Go on, get out of here."

"Yeah, yeah, yeah. We're goin'," Deke said. "Ku-Jo, it's time to take this city back."

"We'd better hurry, then," Joseph said, smiling. "Santa will be here soon. We can't have him run into this guy."

Deke actually laughed. "Imagine the negative publicity on that one, huh?"

When the two men got out to the street, Deke took in a deep breath of cold air. "He's out there somewhere in the same conditions we are. He's breathin' the same cold air and dealin' with the same dark streets. We gotta get in his head somehow."

"You think he's out there right now?"

"I'm *sure* he is. It's the guy that doesn't know he's out there that I feel bad for, you know, the guy that don't know he's comin'." He stared up at the bright stars shining in the night sky. "Someone out there right now is about to have a last Christmas."

Chapter Seven

Mike Davis raised a plastic cup of cheap red wine and toasted his hardworking employees. All five of them clicked cups and downed their little mouthfuls of Christmas cheer.

"I just want to thank all of you again for making our first year a semisuccessful one." There was some light applause from the poker-game-sized bunch. "Next year will be far more profitable. The video game market is really exploding right now." He looked at the bored faces of his people. "I guess you all don't need me to tell you that, huh?"

"Whatever you want, boss," one of the guys said.

"Always sucking up, eh, Jimmy?"

"Gotta get that raise somehow." He laughed.

"Well, again, I thank you all for giving up your Christmas Eves so we could knock out this last-minute inventory stuff and have our first and hopefully annual Christmas party."

The hot, catered food was opened, and they all had their fill. The two bottles of wine went quickly, and once that light buzz had set in, more wine was greatly needed.

Davis grabbed his chair again and stood atop it. "I need a volunteer to go on a liquor run. I'll buy, you fly."

"I'll go, Mike," said Vanessa, a sweet-faced girl who worked the register. She had always been a little bit of a wild child, gaining a taste for booze by stealing sips from her father's liquor cabinet when she was younger. She knew exactly where the liquor store was and, since Mike was buying, could grab herself a nice half pint of So-Co. "Besides, I could use a walk after that food."

Mike set her up with a C-note and a list of what to get and sent her on her way. When she turned the inside lock and opened the door, the icy air made her almost regret the decision to volunteer for the assignment. She trudged down the sidewalk, making sure to keep her eyes peeled for any patches of ice that could take her feet out from under her. The street was eerily empty, and fears of the Daily Killer swept through her head, especially as a darkly dressed figure walked toward her and then passed on her left side. She felt relief as she turned quickly to see him continuing on his way, not giving her the second thought she had given him.

On the next block was the liquor store, and she threw caution to the wind and started running as she saw the gates being pulled down to close the store.

"Wait!" she yelled to the man, waving her arms frantically. Her effort was successful, and the man stopped pulling the gates, although he was pissed that she had gotten him before he was officially closed.

"What do you need, sweetheart? Make it quick, please. I'm trying to get to a party."

"I will. I only need a couple of bottles."

"OK, come on." The man pushed the gate back up and allowed Vanessa into the store. She ran as quickly as she could up and down the aisles filling Davis's request list.

Jimmy had stuck his head out the door and watched her as she walked, then ran to the next block to beat the gates coming down. He stepped a foot onto the sidewalk and was ready to play the hero as he watched the man approach her and then pass her by. When he saw her disappear into the store, he returned to the party, making the bell above the door jingle as the top smacked it.

"She's in, boss. I'll give her five minutes and then watch her as she comes back."

"What a guy," Mike said, smiling. "You sure there's nothing going on between you two?"

"Not yet," Jimmy answered, grinning. "I'm working on it, though."

Mike handed out Christmas cards with coupons for five paid "anytime" days off during the upcoming year. It was easier than giving bonuses with money he didn't have and would be more appreciated during the summer months when someone wanted to spend a day in the sun. He understood the dedication of his employees and tried to be as much a friend to them as he was a boss. He mingled with them as they ate more of the food and eagerly awaited Vanessa's return with the booze.

A couple of minutes later, the bell above the door jingled again, causing Jimmy to spin quickly on his heel. "That was quick—"

It wasn't Vanessa.

"Oh, I'm sorry, sir," he said nicely. "We're closed for the night."

"Yes, you are," the man said as he locked the door behind him and pulled the shade down so no one could see in.

"Excuse me," Jimmy said more forcefully. "I said we're closed for the night."

The man ripped a gun from his pocket and pointed it at everyone in the room. "Do I look deaf to you?"

Everyone stood frozen in shock, eyes fixed on the gun. No one answered his question, no one screamed. A couple of the women did let out gasps, though, short but audible. They all had a hard time processing the information. Here it was, Christmas Eve, and their night had just gone from complete merriment to utter horror in one second flat.

The man with the gun had a sinister grin on his face, and no one dared flinch while the gun was pointed in his or her direction. There was a lifeless look in his eyes, making him appear almost zombie-like. The scariest thing of all was that he was in complete control of his senses and the situation. He wasn't as far out there as he seemed. He was merely wearing his game face.

"What do you want, mister?" Mike asked, voice trembling slightly.

"I'm here to crash the party." The grin got wider. "Actually, I'm really here to end it." The gun was raised to eye level and straightened.

"Whoa, there's no need for that!" Mike shouted. "Take anything you want. Just don't hurt anybody."

The man looked confused. "I guess you don't read the papers much, do you?"

Everyone stood still and pensive as the gun was slowly waved around the room, stopping just long enough on each person to cause some wet pants. "I have a present here for each of you. Who would like to open theirs first?"

"Look, sir," Mike said, voice quivering more heavily now. "We all have families here. Please don't hurt anyone. It's Christmas," he said in a last-ditch effort.

The man's voice was cold, callous, and unfeeling. "If only I had a nickel for every time someone said that to me this week."

"Then let them go. I'll be your hostage, for God's sake!"

A loud muzzle blast blew a hot lead bullet directly through Mike's face. His head snapped back, and his body fell immediately to the floor among the screams and the shrieks of his remaining employees. Jimmy shook in panic, as some of Mike's blood had splattered onto his hands and clothing.

The killer was no longer smiling. "There is no God," he said angrily. He looked at the faces of his captives. He had them both physically and mentally. "Which of you would like to leave?" he asked coldly.

No one answered.

The killer's eyebrows lowered. "Are you all stupid? Who would like to leave?"

Still no one answered.

"OK, so none of you wants out, huh? Good." The gun was cocked.

"I'll go," a lady named Helen said impulsively. She was the bookkeeper for the new business, supplementing her retirement income.

"Atta girl," the killer said condescendingly. "I like someone gutsy enough to take a shot. You're out!"

The gun was quickly aimed toward her face, and another bullet left the chamber. When it found its destination, more screaming could be heard, and another body lay crumpled on the floor.

"What is happening here!" Jimmy screamed in panic, garnering all of the killer's attention.

"I think you know, my friend. It's pretty simple. You are the chosen ones."

"You didn't have to fucking do that," he said, now sobbing softly. "You said you'd let her out."

The killer was angry. He took a step toward Jimmy. "Are you calling me a liar?" He pointed to Helen's body with the gun. "She's out, all right. I told her to take a shot, and she did." He smiled. "Took it right in the face."

The next two shots from the gun went fairly rapidly. First it was Jimmy who took a blast in the forehead, ending his hysteria. The next bullet found its way into Janet, a twenty-six-year-old married mother of two, in charge of inventory and ordering. She took one in the back as she turned and bolted for the rear exit in Mike's office. The last man standing, so to speak, was an old fellow named Frank, who was known as the Disco King for his 1970s outfits, a guy who hung around the store so much that Mike finally put him on the payroll for the heck of it. He was there, oddly enough, for security reasons, to make sure no kids came in and stole games or accessories. His frail eighty-two-year-old body didn't allow him any opportunity to rush the killer and save the day, as he would have fifty years earlier when he was a spry, fleet-footed naval reserve officer. Back then he would have turned the tables on this guy and kicked his ass, but on this day he could be nothing more than a victim.

"You really shouldn't be doing these things," he said, trying to reason with the killer. "This is the time of the birth of Christ."

The killer stood and listened as Frank spoke, taking the scolding for what it was worth. He looked at his watch. "Are you finished now, old man? I'm on a schedule here."

Frank started saying the Hail Mary prayer. The killer lowered his gun and slapped it against his hip in frustration. He cursed under his breath as he allowed Frank to finish. The old man took notice of this and, when done with the Hail Mary, began reciting the Act of Contrition.

This time the killer would have none of it. The gun was brought back up and emptied into Frank's chest, sending him sprawling backward into a glass showcase filled with the video games he was hired to protect.

"Sorry, Pops," the killer said quietly. "I'll give you the Hail Mary thing, but that second one is way too long." He noticed the pans of hot food sitting above the burners and stuck his finger into one to have a taste. With his still gloved left hand, he reached into his pocket and pulled out his calling card. He placed it neatly on Davis's body and gave him a little wink.

The front door began banging and shaking, startling the killer for a moment, and a voice could be heard yelling from the other side.

"Guys, open up, it's me."

The killer stood still and slowly opened the gun's chamber and poured the empty shell casings into his hand. He shoved them into his pocket and inserted a fresh new set of bullets with a slick speedloader. The door continued to shake, and then loud knocking began as Vanessa tried to gain reentry.

"Come on, it's freezing out here. If you don't want the liquor, I'll take it home with me," she teased.

When no answer came from inside, she placed the bags down on the sidewalk and reached into her pocket for the key. The killer heard it slip into the lock and took aim at the doorway. As the door began to push open, the killer threw his hand in front of his face and allowed his eyes to peek between the fingers. Vanessa picked up the bags and threw the door all the way open. The first thing she saw was the bloodied bodies on the floor, and then she took notice of the man aiming at her. She let out a loud shriek and dropped the bagful of alcohol on the ground and took off running. The killer darted after her and stepped out onto the sidewalk to see her running down the street about fifteen or twenty feet away. He raised the gun for an easy shot but did not fire. It would have been against the rules. She was outside the four walls and therefore not in the jurisdiction of death.

The killer stepped on the broken glass and had a quick peek back inside to see if anything was left behind. He stuck the gun back into his pocket and beelined it down the street in the opposite direction that Vanessa was running. Her screams were beginning to rouse people, and the liquor store guy heard her coming as he once again tried to close his store.

This time the tone of her yelps was different, and he picked up on the severity of the situation right away. He ran toward her and met her a half block from his store. She was screaming hysterically and crying and pointing back to where her store was. As the liquor store owner looked to where she was pointing, he noticed a shadowy figure hurriedly walking down the sidewalk way down on the next block. When the figure reached the corner, it made a quick left on the avenue and moved out of sight.

The liquor store guy brought Vanessa back to his store and locked the door behind them. He sat her on a chair and dialed 911. The operator picked up just as Vanessa passed out from hyperventilating and hit the floor.

Deke and Agent Joseph were on their way up toward Harlem when the emergency call came over the two-way radio.

"Central on a 10-9, Central on a 10-9. All units stop transmitting, K." Then there was a pause that only made the moment seem that much more chilling. "Central on a 10-9. All units in the area of 445 West Thirty-seventh Street, report there immediately. Repeat, all units in the area of 445 West Thirty-seventh Street, report there immediately. Multiple shooting, possibly the serial killer. Suspect wearing dark clothing and headed north up Eighth Avenue, K."

Deke and Joseph looked at each other with urgency in their eyes. They were only blocks away, up around West Forty-fifth Street. Deke threw the car into a violent U-turn and headed the wrong way down Eighth Avenue toward the murder scene. He took a big chance by turning off the headlights and not driving with lights or siren, but he didn't want the killer to see him coming if he was still headed toward them. Deke scanned the left side of the street while Joseph had the right, looking for anything that moved that fit the description they were looking for. As they passed Forty-second Street, Deke noticed the train stations and cursed. "He's gotta have at least a five- or ten-minute head start by the time the call went out. He coulda hopped a taxi, train, or bus."

"Or he could still be around," Joseph added.

The radio continued to blare the orders coming from Central. "All units be advised that there will be plainclothes on the scene. All units be advised that the COD is number three, the COD is number three, K."

Joseph spoke quickly to Deke. "What the heck is COD?"

"Color of the day," Deke answered in the same rapid style. "Headquarters sends out a specific color over the teletype every day that our plainclothes will wear as wristbands. The colors are numbered from one to five—blue, green, red, yellow, black. If a uniform cop comes up on a plainclothes at a scene, the only way he's gonna know the guy's a cop is if he sees that wristband. It keeps guys from gettin' shot."

Deke's cell phone started buzzing. He pulled it out and flipped the front. "Durgess," he said quickly.

"Deke, you got it? He may have hit on West Thirty-seventh Street. Get your ass over there."

"I got it, Cap. We're a few blocks away. He should be headed right toward us."

"Watch your ass and let me know what happens."

"Yeah, OK. Listen, anyone pick Jesper up yet?"

"Not yet, that was my first call. He's still MIA."

"OK, I'll get back to you."

The psychedelic aurora of squad car lights came into view in the distance. Almost immediately the sound of sirens penetrated the ears. One after the other they turned onto the avenue and proceeded in a zigzag pattern toward Deke's car.

"Look at these idiots," Deke said. "Can they make it any more obvious?"

Suddenly a dark figure came running up the sidewalk on Deke's right-hand side. Joseph was the first to see him, Deke a half second behind. It was hard to see if he fit the description they were looking for, but he was clearly running away from the direction of the police cars, and at the moment that was good enough for Deke. The car skidded to a halt, and both men jumped out and ran to intercept the guy. Deke ignored departmental protocol and had his gun pulled out the second he left the car. He and Joseph headed the guy off perfectly, Deke getting in front of him and Joseph backing him up, a little behind the suspect and just off to the side. The detective shield hung by a chain from Deke's neck glimmered smartly from the light of the streetlamp, and the barrel of his gun was trained ominously on the face of the running man. There was absolutely no doubt that this man's odyssey would be ending in a few more inches.

"Police! Down on the ground!" Deke screamed as the man got near him. "Get down on the fuckin' ground now!" His voice was overly forceful in hopes of impressing upon the man's mind that there was no doubt who was in control of the situation. It didn't work.

The man lowered his shoulder and, with a full head of steam, bowled into Deke, taking them both down onto the frozen, dirty sidewalk. A struggle for Deke's gun immediately ensued, and the barrel was ominously spun into Deke's face.

As two sets of fingers fought over possession of the trigger, Joseph sprang upon the guy like a cat, flipping him over hard onto his stomach and putting a knee in the back of his neck, pinning his face to the sidewalk. Deke rolled out to the side and regained control of his gun. He kept it square on the guy and tossed Joseph a pair of handcuffs to slap on his wrists.

"What's going on?" the man yelled. "What is this?"

"Shut up!" Deke hollered. "Stay still or I'll blow your fuckin' head off!"

"What'd I do?"

"How 'bout we start with assault and attempted murder of a police officer!"

Deke got on his walkie-talkie and called for backup. He made sure not to put it out there as a 10-13, officer in need of assistance. A call like that would have brought every squad car in the area to his location. There was no need for that. The suspect was secured, and in case he wasn't the killer, it was a good idea to have the other cars still searching around out there. In no time at all there were two additional cars at Deke's location, and he left it to those officers to search the man for weapons and ID. Nothing was found on the guy, and he was placed into the backseat of one of the squad cars.

"Were any of you guys at the murder scene yet?" Deke asked in a blanket question to all the cops.

"We were, Detective," one of them answered.

Deke walked over to him. "What's it lookin' like?"

"Multiple shooting. Five people down, one survivor."

"What's the condition of the survivor? Is he conscious?"

"It's a female, Detective, and she was untouched. Supposedly, she ran out to the store a few minutes before the whole thing went down. When she got back, she came face-to-face with the guy and took off."

"She get a good look at him?"

"No. She said she only saw him for a second. According to her, he had his hand in front of his face giving her the finger. All she gave us was that he had dark clothes on."

"Tall or short?"

"She wasn't sure. She said he was about average. We tried

to get what we could from her, but she was freaking out too much."

"I gotta talk to her," he said emphatically. "They're definitely gonna take her to a hospital for a look-over. Find out for me which one." He looked at the guy in the backseat. "I'm gonna go talk to this guy for a few."

Deke sat in the front passenger seat and turned to face the guy. "Looks like you got a real fuckin' problem here, bud. Attempted murder of a cop'll run you a hard stint in Rikers. What's your name, and why were you runnin'?"

The man sat there and said nothing, peering out the window into the distance. He was petrified, and Deke picked up on it right away. He used that fear to his advantage.

"Listen, buddy, I'm tellin' you right now, don't screw with me. I'll take you into an alley and beat the livin' shit outta you if you don't start tellin' me what I wanna hear. You won't get lucky twice with me. I'll even bring my partner along for laughs. We clear on all this?"

The man looked at Deke's face and could plainly see that there was no mistaking his intentions. In his mind, there was an ass-whooping coming if he didn't start dropping some answers, and dropping them pretty fast.

"Name's Murphy. Johnny Murphy," he said, swallowing hard.

"Where's your ID?"

"It got stolen two days ago."

"It got stolen, huh?"

"Yeah."

"So, I guess I should be able to read a police report on that then?"

"There's no police report. I didn't tell the cops."

"Oh yeah? And why not?"

The man was getting more nervous. "Look, man, I can't be

having contact with the cops. My probation officer says I gotta stay clean."

"Probation? That's why you were runnin' away from us?"

"I didn't know what else to do. I heard the sirens and saw the lights and didn't want to get caught up in anyone else's mess."

"What are you on probation for?"

"I was caught dealing pot."

"Why didn't you get down when I told you to? Attacking a cop was a stupid-ass move."

"I didn't even hear you, man. I was just trying to get far away from whatever the cops were chasing. I look up and there's a guy in my face with a gun, yelling something. I didn't know who you were. I just wanted to go right through you and keep going."

Deke looked at him skeptically. "Where were you runnin' to?"

"The halfway house on Forty-third Street. I gotta be back there by nine or my probation agreement's busted."

"Where you comin' from?"

The man was hesitant.

Deke threw his elbow over the seat and repeated the question. "Where you comin' from, bud?"

"I, I was at a bar about four blocks from here."

"A bar," Deke said with a smile, "and you're worryin' about the time?" He shifted his position on the seat to be able to stare at the man more directly. "Let me tell you somethin'. I'd be more worried about bein' at the bar and gettin' into it with me than gettin' back to the joint on time."

"Look, I know I wasn't supposed to be there, but really, I wasn't doing nothing wrong. I just had a couple of beers, that's all. I wasn't bothering anybody. Please, just let me get back to the house."

Deke glanced at his watch. "It's twenty to nine right now. I don't think you're gonna make it back in time, bud."

"Come on, man," the suspect pleaded, "I'm sorry about knocking you over. I really didn't know you were a cop, and believe me, whatever you guys were chasing out there, I ain't who you're looking for."

"I guess we're gonna find out about that." Deke stepped out of the patrol car and called one of the officers over. "Listen, take this guy over to Thirty-seventh Street and see if the girl recognizes him. Shine some headlights in his eyes so she can see him clearly and he can't see her. Make sure she gets a good look at what he's wearin'. Pull him outta the car if you need to."

"Understood," the officer replied and immediately headed around the car to the driver's side.

Deke knocked on the roof. "When you get an answer, get me over the radio. I'm on your channel. My call sign is Car 509."

"Understood," the cop said again. He yelled for his partner, and both cops slipped into the car, one in the front driving and the other in the back watching the suspect.

Deke had the officer roll down the back window, and he stuck his head in. "Listen," he said to the suspect, "if you ain't who we're lookin' for, we'll smooth it over with your probation officer. The bar thing'll never be mentioned. I'll even let the assault thing go. I ain't got the time to be doin' paperwork on you tonight. If you are who we're lookin' for . . ." He pointed a finger menacingly at the man. "You'll be goin' down in a big way." He backed away from the car and let the cops pull away. He walked back to the sidewalk and grabbed the other two officers. "I want you two guys to trace back from here all the way to Thirty-seventh Street and look for the gun. If this guy's the guy we been huntin' for, he dumped it somewhere between here and there. Check all the garbage pails for clothin', too, just in case he got rid of stuff."

"You got it, Detective. Where are you going to be when we're ready to give you the report?"

"Get me on the radio, your channel, Car 509."

"OK."

The two officers pulled their flashlights and started off down the street. Deke and Joseph headed for their still running car. When they got back inside, the heat was a much needed respite.

"God damn!" said Deke. "Next time we do that, make sure I put my coat on, will ya?"

Joseph was blowing into his hands. "Yeah, right after I remember to put on mine."

"Aw, shit," Deke said, annoyed. He looked over at Joseph. "That guy's got my cuffs. I never switched with the cop."

"You need them? We could take a ride there and get them."

"Naa, I got another set. I'll get 'em back somehow." There was a pause. "Listen," Deke said, "I really appreciate you jumpin' in like that back there. That was gettin' a little hairy."

Joseph gave him a wave of the hand. "Don't worry about it. You'd have been right in there if the situation was reversed and I was the one on the ground."

"I know," answered Deke, "but a lot of guys tend to freeze up in that intitial second or two when it matters most. You were right on it with no hesitation. That's an important thing for a cop, to know that his partner's got his back like that when the chips are down. I owe you."

"Wow, thanks. Nice compliment—but did I hear you say 'partner'? I thought you didn't want one of those."

Deke looked at him long and hard. "You just earned the job."

The two men began driving up and down blocks in a sweeping pattern searching for other suspects to question. Deke took a peek at the LED clock on the dashboard. It was at least forty minutes since the murders took place. He pulled the car over, parked it, and reclined his seat a touch. "Break time," he said.

Joseph knew all too well what Deke meant. There was no sense in looking for the killer any further. If the guy in the car wasn't the one, then the real one was long gone. There were buses and taxis that could've been hopped by now. Even if he took a train from Forty-second Street, he could have gotten off after one or two stops before the shutdown plan was thrown into effect. Deke resigned himself to the fact that the guy was good or, at the very least, resourceful. Still, he wasn't infallible.

"He messed up a little tonight," he said, head back, eyes closed.

"How's that?" Joseph asked.

"The girl. This guy don't leave no witnesses. Now, accordin' to the cops at the scene, the girl was sent out to the store a couple of minutes before the whole thing went down."

"So?"

"So it tells me the guy ain't casin' the place before he hits it. If he does, he knows the girl went out and don't get surprised by her comin' back."

Joseph nodded approvingly. "It might mean that he's not doing too much planning before making his move. These things could be totally random."

"They ain't random. He got some kinda selection process, I'm sure of it. I don't think he's plannin' far off. I think he's comin' up with 'em by the day."

"Sure does make it hard to get a bead on him, ya know?"

"Until we figure how he's pickin' 'em. If he don't got no plan goin' in, though, I don't think he got a plan goin' out. Sooner or later he's either gonna walk into a guy that's got a gun of his own or he's gonna get stuck out in the middle of nowhere when we're closin' in. Nothin' lasts forever. Definitely not his luck."

The radio mounted under the dashboard called out to Deke. "Car 716 to Car 509, K."

He grabbed the handheld mike and pushed the button. "509 to last unit, go."

"Detective, this is Car 716, be advised we're back at the scene. It's a negative on the ID from the woman, K."

"Negative how? Negative she couldn't ID him or negative it definitely ain't him, K?"

"She said it's not him, K."

Deke was disappointed but certainly not surprised. "10-4, 509 clear."

"716 to 509, Detective, what do you want us to do with this guy, K?"

"Take him back to his shelter and smooth it over with the people runnin' the show, K."

"10-4, Detective, 716 clear."

Deke turned to Joseph. "Well, so much for that."

"You're letting him go on the assault rap?"

"Yeah, he was tellin' the truth. He wasn't thinkin' of nothin' but gettin' away. We ain't got time for that nonsense right now."

"So now what?"

Deke threw his hands up. "I'm open for suggestions."

Both men sat silently and stared blankly through the windshield for a few minutes. The cold winter air outside and the hot, steamy breath inside began to cause the windows to fog over. Deke quickly put the defroster on to clear them.

"Ain't that just what we need. Some beat cop to come knockin' on the window thinkin' we're in here makin' out. I'll never live it down."

Joseph got a little chuckle out of that. "Let me ask you a question," he said. "Why is it you work alone? You seem to be a pretty good guy, have a lot of knowledge about the job. Why the hesitance to take on a partner?"

" 'Seem to be a pretty good guy'? What the hell is that?"

"Come on, you know what I mean. Why would you work alone when there are probably dozens of people looking to work with you?"

"I'll tell ya why," Deke began. "Because it's one more thing to worry about that I don't need. I had lots of partners on this job. Partners come and go, but it's that one guy that gets hurt *because* of you that stays with you forever."

Joseph knew immediately that he had treaded onto a touchy subject. "What happened?"

"Eh, it was a few years ago. I had a partner—my last partner, as a matter of fact—his name was Leo Dorsey. We were partners for a pretty long time. He'd go to my house, I'd go to his, ya know, we were pretty tight." Deke thought a moment and then laughed. "He was a real son of a bitch, too, that bastard. He would always be gettin' on me about my weight. Not that I was huge or nothin'. I just had a little bit of a belly, and he knew it annoyed me. Anyhow, I come into the squad one day, and I'm pissed off because nothin' I was doin' was helpin' me lose the stomach. Finally, after listenin' to me complain about it for an hour or so, he gets up and yells at me in front of the whole room. He's like, 'You want to lose weight?' and I'm like, 'Yeah.' So he repeats the question again, 'You want to lose weight?' and again, I'm like, 'Yeah.' So he looks me dead in the eye and yells out in front of everyone, 'Don't eat, fat pig!'" Deke laughed again. "The son of a bitch. To this day, every time Ronnie sees me with a sandwich he reminds me of that. I been laughin' about it for years, too."

"Sounds like a funny guy," Joseph said, smiling. "What happened to him?"

Deke took a deep breath and started knocking gently on the driver's side window. "We were sittin' in the car one night, and a domestic call comes over the radio, ya know, a guy smackin' his wife around. We happened to be right there, and we were bored, so we figured we'd take the call so a squad car wouldn't have to roll. Soon as we show up on the scene, a guy comes runnin' up to the car and tells us he was the one that called, that he's been hearin' the husband and wife fightin' it out inside. Leo tells me he's gonna go around the back of the house to cover things in case the guy makes a break for it. So I give him a couple of seconds to get there and then, ya know, he finally chirps me on the radio and tells me he's in position. Soon as I got to the front door and was about to knock, I hear four shots ring out from the back, real quick, pop, pop, pop, pop. I friggin' pull my gun and radio and start headin' for the back, screamin' into the radio that we got shots fired at the location. Now I come runnin' around the side of the house, and here comes this guy runnin' right toward me, gun in hand and lookin' behind him as he goes. When he got about fifteen feet from me, I identified myself and told him to drop it. I knew he wasn't gonna let it go. Soon as I saw that gun start comin' up in my direction, I squeezed off two rounds on him. Caught him once in the chest and once in the shoulder. He went right down. When I got near him, I could see he wasn't movin', but he was still holdin' the gun."

"You kick it away?"

"No. I stepped on it. I had no faith that the guy was dead. I tell ya, though, if I felt any movement from him I woulda popped him again right there."

"What happened to your partner?"

Deke grabbed the steering wheel and held it tightly. The events were just as clear in memory as they were on the night they happened.

"He took four shots in the chest and stomach. He wasn't wearin' a vest, of course. Ya know, we're detectives, who needs a vest? When you're a detective, you never think anyone's gonna shoot at you. Anyhow, there he was, squirmin' around in the yard. I could see him in the dark, but at least he was movin', so I knew he was alive. A couple of seconds later I heard the sirens comin'. I knew those cops were gonna take me for the suspect. So I get back on the radio and call it in as officer down, suspect down, detective on scene, and then I held my badge up as high as I could. Idiots got there and *still* had their guns on me thinkin' I was the perp. It all got straightened out once they saw the badge. A little while later the ambulance came, the ME came, it was a pretty screwed-up night."

"Did your partner make it?"

"Yeah, he made it. It was touch and go for a while, but he pulled through. Knocked him off the force, though. We wound up gettin' promoted from third-grade detectives to first-grade detectives off that bust. Leo couldn't stick it out, though. They wanted to give him light duty, but he didn't want to stay on the job if he couldn't work the street. I go see him every once in a while. He still ain't right."

"It doesn't sound to me like what happened to him was your fault, though. Why are you blaming yourself?"

"He was my partner. My health was his responsibility, and his was mine. I came out OK, he did his job. He got shot, I didn't do mine." Another deep breath. "It was right after that I said I wasn't takin' on no more partners. Things change too fast on this job. One minute you're sittin' in the car bullshittin', and the next minute you're in a life-and-death struggle." He shook his head slowly. "Changes way too fast. Soon as you think you feel comfortable, somethin' comes down the pike. They set you up for that at the Police Academy. They pump your head full of nonsense that no one out there can beat you. They whip you into a frenzy, and you come out like a lunatic ready to take on every bad guy, like no matter what, you'll never lose." He looked over at Joseph. "Trust me, you come up against the wrong guy, you'll lose. I almost did back there. All that shit they tell you goes right out the window. I saw it with Leo. That night was enough for me. I'll never have another partner get shot on me. Clouds my mind worryin' about it."

"Still, it doesn't sound like your fault. Anyhow, don't go clouding your mind worrying about me. I can hold my own."

"Yeah, that's what my old partner used to think. If we get into another situation, you better make sure you keep your head on a swivel stick. Don't take nothin' for granted. Remember, things change fast!"

"That, Deke, is a promise." Joseph gave it about thirty seconds to let the memory play its way out of Deke's head. "Listen," he said, glancing at the dashboard clock. "Is it OK if I give my daughter a quick call and read her a story before she goes to sleep? I can't miss it again."

"Yeah, no prob. We got a little time."

Deke sat and listened to the story while Joseph recited it to little Samantha over the phone. He could imagine her tiny face on the other end as she lay there on her pillow and let her dad's voice carry her off to dreamland. The call didn't last long, and Joseph signed off the same way he had on the last call.

"Remember, baby. Daddy loves you like the whole universe, and you? You are its prettiest star."

When the call was ended, Deke asked Joseph if he had a picture of Samantha with him. Joseph pulled out his wallet and let a plastic insert unfold itself to reveal about ten small photos of his daughter in various poses and situations. Deke turned on the car's interior light and held the pictures to his face.

"Wow, cute kid," he said meaningfully as he quickly scanned the pictures. "She's got happy eyes." He handed the pictures back.

"She's great," Joseph answered. "No matter what kind of day I'm having, she always makes it better with that little smile. I don't know if you heard, but I tend to fly off the handle some-times. The thought of her face brings my mind back into focus."

"You don't seem the type."

"Trust me." Joseph smiled. "My daughter's got one of those faces that can brighten anything."

"Yeah, I know what you mean," Deke said softly. "My kids are like that, too, but I don't get to see it too much no more."

"That's gotta be tough."

"It is. Especially around this time of year. Well, whaddaya gonna do. I dug my own grave . . ."

"Got any pictures?"

"Not with me. I don't like keepin' info on my family with me, you know, just in case somethin' bad happens. Don't need no bad guys seein' who they are and where they live."

"I never really thought about that," Joseph responded. "It's a good point."

"I'm supposed to be with my kids right now, as a matter of fact. Can't get away now, though. Too much goin' on."

"I thought you said earlier that family comes first."

"I know," Deke said, shaking his head. "I really don't know what the hell's wrong with me."

"You still have tomorrow. There's magic in Christmas Day, you know."

Deke pushed the cobwebs out. There was work to be done. "If there's magic, maybe we can make this guy disappear then."

Joseph knew the moment had passed. "OK," he conceded. "Let's go find him. You should give some thought to getting with your kids, though."

"I can't right now. I need my mind clear."

"Understood," Joseph said somberly. "So, you want to get out of here?"

Deke sat up and put the car in drive. "Yeah, why not." He

sighed. "Let's go over to the murder scene and see what's goin' on. CSU should have it all screwed up by now."

Joseph let out a small laugh. "We'd better get over there and stop 'em, then."

The two men headed down Ninth Ave. to the murder scene. As they approached Thirty-seventh Street, the flashing multicolored lights in the distance seemed to multiply more and more the closer they got. The entire street was clogged up by emergency service vehicles. Deke and Joseph left the car running at the corner, told a cop to watch it, and walked their way in. When they got to the front of the store, they had a good look around at the activity on the street. There were investigators across the way looking at building facades, windows, and doors. There were photographers taking pictures of everything from the bodies inside to the broken glass outside.

Deke and Joseph stepped over the glass, careful not to disturb it. When they got inside, they had to work themselves past a wall of CSU guys to get near the bodies. All of them seemed to have fallen right near each other. Deke had seen similar scenes many times where multiple murders were carried out execution style. The victims get lined up and down they go like dominoes. The killer had to have caught them all off guard. The element of surprise was unquestionably this guy's best friend—but how, in a city gripped by its throat with fear over the guy, did he keep managing to sneak up on people? It was without doubt an eerie situation of history repeating itself. Son of Sam had this same streak of murderous fortune during his spree. Even at the height of his stranglehold on the city, there still were people out there stupid enough to take their chances by playing the odds he wouldn't be where they were. For his last few victims, it was a foolhardy strategy.

Deke, as always, grabbed the lead CSU guy. "Talk to me. You got anything?"

"It's a store, Detective. There's a million fingerprints here, hair samples all over the place, and no real way to find who left them behind."

"What about sales receipts?"

"Fine, but that's if they bought something. What if they just came in and looked?"

"Yeah, good point. What about a note?"

"He left it on the male over there."

"Any prints on it?"

"We haven't dusted around the bodies yet. We're still waiting on the medical examiner to get here and do his thing."

"What's with all your guys snoopin' around across the street there? Killer took a shot at the female, or are they lookin' for a stray shot?"

"We're trying to find that out now. The lady said she heard a pop when she hightailed it. We're looking for any impact zones or stray slugs."

"OK, good enough. Look, here's my card. Anything comes up here, gimme a buzz."

"You got it, Detective."

Deke and Joseph headed out of the store and back over the broken glass. Deke pointed back to it as he and Joseph walked up the block to their car. "I guarantee that's the pop she heard when she thought the guy took a shot at her; when the bottles hit the sidewalk and broke."

"Makes sense. You know, Deke, this is the first nonresidential killing by this guy."

"I know. He's fuckin' pickin' 'em somehow. It's really pissin' me off not bein' able to figure out how he's doin' it."

"When I was doing my training in California, we were given the Zodiac case as a study course. There was some speculation that he was choosing victims from specific points on a map. Maybe that's what this guy is doing. Maybe we should plot all the victim's locations on a map and see if any patterns become visible."

It was as good an idea as any, and one Deke had not thought of. It gave him hope that this could be the angle they had not come up with yet.

"Tell me more. Did you grid the locations out or use a city-wide map to show 'em?"

"We used a citywide map. We marked the locations with a red marker and checked for patterns or diagrams. We even made straight lines between the points and logged the mileage from one scene to another to see if it was a linear thing."

"You come up with anything?"

"Nothing conclusive, obviously. The guy was never found. Still, it was an interesting study."

"Well, ya feel like doin' all that again?" Deke asked as they reached the car.

"Absolutely. Get me to a citywide map, and let's see what we come up with." Both men returned to headquarters, where Deke set Joseph up with everything he needed to plot the murders on the map. They went though every scenario they could think of to come up with patterns the killer might follow. They separated the murders by day and night in certain cases to see if anything stood out. They tried separating by gender, financial status, age, ethnicity, marital status, and even education. Nothing came of it except about three hours' worth of wasted time. It was close to midnight when Captain Murray came into the room.

"Forget about the girl tonight, Deke. They got her sedated at the hospital, and her family is insisting on no visitors."

"We got cops guardin' her?"

"Of course."

"Good. Maybe tomorrow I'll switch with one of 'em and sneak in to ask her a couple of questions."

Captain Murray smiled. "Do what you want, but I didn't just hear that, OK?"

"Hear what?" Deke asked smartly.

"Very good. Listen, why don't you get out of here and get some sleep? You really look like you need it."

"Too far to drive," Deke said, yawning. "I think I'll crash on your couch again."

"You could come back to my hotel, if you'd like," Joseph said. "There's plenty of room."

"Yeah," Deke said as he caught a glimpse of the smile on Captain Murray's face, "that wouldn't get the guys talkin' too much, now would it? Deke and the Fed sleepin' together."

Joseph stared at Deke disgustedly. "I'm not talking about in my bed. The FBI took out a whole floor for the time we need it. There are still three or four rooms unused. You could come with me and take one."

"Horse of a different color," Deke answered. "Let's do it."

"Turn your phone off when you get there, Deke. You're under orders not to take any calls. Your brain is a step slow right now with all the lack of sleep."

"No prob. I gotta recharge it anyway."

"Your brain or the phone?"

"Both."

"OK, get out of here. Hey," Captain Murray shouted to the two men as they were leaving the office, "it's after midnight. Merry Christmas."

Deke glanced at his watch, walked back over to the captain, and shook his hand. "Same to you, boss."

Joseph walked back and did the same. It was the first semi-normal moment any of them had had in days.

"Let's hope Santa leaves this guy as a present under my tree," Deke said.

"Beat it," said the captain.

Joseph drove Deke over to the hotel and made sure he was checked into his own room, complete with a room service tab for anything he'd like. Deke left a do-not-disturb order with the front desk and a wake-up call for 7:00 A.M. The two men then headed up to their floor, where their rooms were only a few doors apart. Deke was actually excited at the prospect of having a free ride at a top-flight hotel. For Joseph, it was nothing more than the same old tired thing, just on a different day.

"I am really getting sick of these places," Joseph told Deke. "There is nothing here that gives me the feeling of comfort like I have at home."

"Whaddaya expect? It ain't home."

"I know, but this is all . . . just so impersonal."

"So here, then," Deke said while pulling keys from his pocket. "Go sleep at my place if ya want. I'll switch with ya in the blink of an eye."

Joseph looked at Deke's keys and actually thought about it for a second. If it hadn't been so late and Deke's place so far, he might just have gone for it. Then again, he wasn't entirely sure Deke was being genuine.

"Not tonight," he answered, "but I will definitely keep the offer in the back of my mind for future reference."

"Whatever you want. I'll see ya in the mornin'."

Once in his room, Deke groggily slipped out of his clothes and hung them neatly over the back of a chair. He pulled the bedcovers down and eagerly slid under them. The mattress was more comfortable than he anticipated, and it almost invited him into a deep sleep. His last thoughts before drifting off were, of course, about the killer and what more he could be doing to catch him. The absence of sleep he'd experienced over the last week had finally caught up to him, and he fell into utter unconsciousness where not even a dream was to be had. Even the puddle of spit on the pillow could not stir him from this slumber. For six and a half hours, Deke would leave the world behind and enter a realm he had not known in a while, a realm of peace and quiet where no one was killed, a realm that, if he had his druthers, he would remain in for eternity.

Chapter Eight

Agent Joseph was awakened at 5:45 A.M. by the soft beeping from his alarm watch. It didn't matter that he could have slept another four hours; Assistant Director Miller wanted his report by phone at precisely 6:00 A.M. There were about thirty agents scattered all about the city working the case, and each of them had his specific time to call in. Joseph, being something of a rookie, got the earliest and most inconvenient time. That was OK with him. It was all part of earning his stripes and doing his time as the bottom guy. He made his phone call and updated Miller on all that had happened since they last talked. He covered the meeting with the commissioner and the capture of a potential suspect, which ultimately proved to be nothing. Basically it was all fodder, as he had nothing productive to offer. The phone call ended, and he tossed his cell onto the night table. He pondered getting back into bed but was now too awake to fall back to sleep. He took a hot shower and pulled a fresh suit from the closet. He grabbed his little travel grooming kit from his satchel and fixed his hair, shaved, and brushed his teeth.

Four doors down in a similar room, Deke was out like the proverbial light. Just slightly less than an hour after Joseph's morning phone call ended, Deke's was set to come courtesy of the front desk. When it arrived, his morning would start like Joseph's with an early hot shower. That was pretty much where the similarities ended. The previous day's clothing went back on, the fingers were wetted and brushed through the hair like a makeshift comb, and the index finger rubbed on some soap doubled as a toothbrush. Not once did it dawn on him that he could just call the front desk and have proper toiletries sent up or that the hotel had laundry service. He was completely inexperienced; he never, ever stayed at hotels.

Deke took his watch from the night table and slipped it on his wrist. He saw that it was a little after seven thirty and knew that the kids had probably been up at the crack of dawn bugging Frannie to let them go open what Santa brought them. The conversation he'd had with Joseph the previous day played through his mind, especially the "Family comes first" mantra. There was a lot of truth to it, and Deke really did mean it when he said it to other people. Perhaps it all stemmed from his own failings as a husband and a father. Maybe he was just trying to save others from his own fate. Either way, it all brought him right back to another saying he had heard many times over the course of his lifetime, "Practice what you preach." It was high time for him to drink from the cup of tonic he had served others again and again when in the same situation.

He sat on the bed, grabbed the phone, and spent about five minutes trying to figure out how to get an outside line. When the dial tone finally came through he started to dial, then hung up, started to dial again, then hung up again. Finally, he just took a deep breath, pressed the buttons, and waited for the call to connect.

"Hello," Frannie said happily.

"Hey, it's me."

"Oh," she said, now not so happy. "Where are you calling from? I didn't recognize the number in the caller ID."

"I'm at a hotel in midtown. The FBI hooked me up so I didn't have to go all the way home."

"That was nice of them," she said distantly. "How's the case going?" she asked as a formality.

"He hit again last night, took out five people. Had a witness this time, might be somethin'."

For about thirty seconds, neither said anything.

"Anyway, Frannie, merry Christmas."

"Yeah, you, too. You want the kids?"

"Yeah, but listen . . ."

"What?"

"When I'm done with them I wanna talk to you again."

"About what? I have a lot to do here. Your cop friends are still guarding the place, and I invited their families to come spend Christmas here, too."

"Good, that was nice of you to do that. Besides, the more people that are there the safer you'll be. What I wanna talk to you about will only take a couple minutes. Let me talk to the kids first, though."

Deke heard Frannie muffle the phone with her hand to shout for the kids. Both took their turns on the phone with Dad, asking when he would see them and bring the gifts he had. Their time on the phone didn't last too long, as Deke could see he was losing their interest to the many toys that were probably laid out in front of them. He didn't feel right about being in a hotel on a case while his family was celebrating the most important holiday of the year. The holidays usually made him more melancholy about the kids, and this one bothered him more than the others because this one was supposed to be spent with them. To miss it for exactly the reason Frannie left him was the thing that hurt most. It was so preventable.

He sat there waiting for Frannie, looking around at the room and wishing he could rewind the clock eight months before their falling-out took place. It didn't take long for Frannie's voice to bring reality back to the situation.

"What?" she said harshly.

"Whaddaya mean *what*? What kinda way is that to come back on the line?"

"Deke, I really don't have time for this. I have people coming today."

He took another breath and gave it his best shot. "You got room for one more?"

"Who now?"

"Me."

"Yeah, right. What happened? You said you didn't catch the killer yet."

"I know. I wanna take the afternoon off so I can see you guys."

Frannie was somewhat angered. "All of a sudden, now you want to come? What makes today any different than last night when they were waiting for you? You know, Deke, you can't keep playing these games."

"I know, I know. I'm not playin' games here. I shoulda been there last night. I didn't sleep in days; I was runnin' on fumes, Frannie, I wasn't thinkin' right. My head's in the right place now. I made a mistake yesterday."

"Deke, it's the same mistake you've been making for years with us. We always had to take a backseat to you. What's the matter now? You don't like taking a backseat to us?"

"No, Frannie, it's not that. I know I'm wrong in the thing. I just wanna come see you guys, that's all."

There was silence on the other end, and Deke knew she was mulling it over. He figured he would throw one more pitch in there. "Come on, Frannie, it's Christmas, and I'm all alone."

It was a fastball, and Frannie took it right down the pipe. "You know, Deke, I hate it when you do this." Another pause. "Be here at three o'clock." She then took a late swing. "But I swear to God, if I tell them you're coming and you don't show—"

"I'll be there. I promise."

"I've heard this before. You know what's gonna happen, Deke. You're gonna get here, and your phone will ring, and you'll be gone again."

"My phone will be off. I'll even give it to you at the door."

Frannie smiled at that one. She was like the designated driver for his phone. "Be here at three."

"Will do." He gave a little fist pump to the ceiling. "Frannie . . ."

"What?"

"Thank you."

"I'll see you at three."

The phone was hung up, and a feeling washed over Deke that he hadn't known in a while. It was almost as if a sense of normalcy returned to him in that for the first time in a long time he would actually be exactly where he was supposed to be on a holiday, with his family. Even though he and Frannie had been divorced for months, he never stopped considering her part of his family. Spending all his holidays staring at the four walls of his apartment and eating frozen dinners by himself only made his loneliness seem that much more unbearable.

He took his cell phone from his pocket and turned it on. When it connected to the network, his first call was to Captain Murray. His game face was back on.

"Yo, Cap, it's me. Anything happen since last night?"

"The girl is off the sedation. We can talk to her now."

"What about Jesper? Did he turn up?"

"Yeah, he showed up at his place about 1:00 A.M. He was grilled by Brooklyn Homicide for hours."

"Where was he?"

"He said he stopped in at a movie house where a buddy of his runs a projector. He got to sit in and watch a couple of films."

"Did anyone talk to the projector guy?"

"He was called. Said Jesper was there, but who knows, he could have been lying to protect him."

"No weapon found on Jesper when they picked him up?"

"Nothing. Just his little rolling tool case. The Brooklyn DA even had a portable forensics kit sent to the interrogation. No gunpowder residue found on his hands or clothing."

"Really. What about all the other tails?"

"All good. No one else got lost. They're all in the clear. It's pretty much just Jesper on the list now."

"Ya know, Cap, we gotta start lookin' somewhere else. This Jesper guy really don't hit me."

"Right now he's all we got, Deke. I'm not dropping him on your whim. I took another major chewing-out from the commissioner after losing Jesper and having those killings last night. Until you get me someone else, Jesper is prime. What makes you think it's not him, anyway?"

"Just a hunch. He don't come across to me as the type that could pull this kinda thing off."

"Well, if that's all you got, I'm not dropping him. You want him off the list, then clear him."

Deke knew it was useless pushing the captain. Jesper made the most sense, even if he made none at all. It would only take another day of tailing him to clear him, providing someone else got killed while Jesper was in sight. The cops wouldn't let him get lost again. Even the tail had a tail.

Deke went in a different direction. "Listen, Cap, between three and eight tonight I am off the clock. I got somewhere I need to be."

"That's a hell of a time to take off, Deke. This guy does his business at that time. What do you have to do?"

"I'm gonna spend Christmas with my family."

Captain Murray was at a loss. He could hear in Deke's voice that he was serious. "First time for everything, huh?"

"Cap, I gotta be there. I wanna see my wife and kids on Christmas. I promised 'em I'd be there, and I'm gonna."

"What's going on, Deke? Is it this case that's getting to you?"

"Maybe it opened my eyes a little, Cap, yeah. Ya never know how fast it could all be gone. Well, I ain't waitin'."

"All right, Deke. Do what you gotta do. Keep your phone on in case I need you."

"Phone's gonna be off, Cap. I made the deal when I got invited. If it's really an emergency, and I mean a *real* emergency, call the cell of one of the detectives guardin' my place. Tell 'em to pull me to the side."

"What are you doing in the meantime?"

"I'm gonna grab Joseph and talk to the woman at the hospital, find out what she saw."

"OK, fine. You get anything, you call me, and I better be the last call you make at two fifty-nine before that phone goes off."

"OK."

The captain's tone of voice changed. "Hey, Deke."

"Go."

"You gonna try to patch it up with Frannie? Is that what all this is about?"

"I don't know if she'd be willin'. I'm just takin' this a step at a time."

"All right, Deke. Good luck. Go get your head cleared and be back for me at eight."

"Thanks, Cap."

Deke met up with Joseph, and they went downstairs and grabbed some breakfast. They discussed the day's plan of what they were going to do and who they were going to see. Deke told Joseph of his plans with Frannie and invited him to come along. Joseph politely declined, saying he would continue to follow up on the leads they were looking at in hopes of minimizing Deke's absence.

"You sure? I'm sure Frannie still puts out a good spread. You look like you could use some good home cookin'."

"Thanks, but no. You're trying to put things back together. The fewer people there, the better. Besides, the killer doesn't seem to be taking any time off. One of us needs to stay on him."

"OK, Ku-Jo. Thanks."

"You just make sure you get that girl alone somewhere and say your piece. You might not get another crack at this, you know."

"Already on that." Deke smiled.

"I figured that. Good luck with it, and I want a full report when you get back."

"Come on, let's get outta here."

They hopped in the car and headed for the hospital. When they entered the lobby, they were nearly overwhelmed by a huge group of reporters trying to get an interview with Vanessa. Most of the reporters immediately recognized Deke and set upon him and Joseph for comment. The two men forced their way through the crowd and into a private elevator used by the doctors. They arrived at Vanessa's floor, and a nurse directed them to her room. Standing around her bed like watchdogs were her parents and two of her brothers.

Deke walked over to the father and introduced himself. "If

it's OK with you, sir, I'd like to ask your daughter a few questions in private."

"She's not feeling up to it right now, Detective. I don't want her remembering this whole thing."

"It's OK, Daddy," Vanessa said groggily. "I'll talk to him."

Her father rubbed her forehead gently. "You sure, baby?"

"Yeah. They need to talk to me."

Her father turned to Deke. "I'd like to be here while you speak with her."

Deke was straight as an arrow. "Stand outside, sir. I don't need the interruptions."

The room was cleared except for Deke, Joseph, and the girl. Deke started to fire questions at her, and every once in a while he would glance at his watch for a time check. Joseph got the impression that Deke's mind was more focused on his Christmas plans than on the interview, so he threw a couple of questions in there, too, some of his own, some following up one of Deke's. It didn't matter either way, as the whole interview turned out to be a colossal waste of time. The girl had absolutely no pertinent information to offer. She wasn't sure of the killer's height, weight, or facial features. She said she only saw him for a second and he was giving her the finger. She reiterated her belief that the killer took a shot at her as she fled. Deke brought up the possibility that the killer never fired at her by informing her that no forensic evidence had been found. He suggested his theory of the dropped liquor bottles popping and simulating the sound of a fired gun. Vanessa lay there, propped up on her pillow, and offered a blank look as her answer to Deke's theory.

The two men realized the uselessness of the interview and thanked Vanessa for her time and wished her well. Deke handed her his card and told her to call him if she remembered anything. They made their way out of the building the same way they came in, right through the throng of reporters. Deke kept his head down and strolled past everybody while Joseph repeatedly yelled that they had no comment at the current time.

Once back in the car, Deke told Joseph that he would drop him off at headquarters and that he was headed home to Brooklyn for a change of clothing and another shower before going to Frannie's place. They discussed a dual plan of things for Joseph to do if the killer hit again or if he didn't. Either way, Deke was to be left out of the loop until at least eight o'clock. There were still hundreds of cops, detectives, and Feds working on the case tracking down leads, so Deke's five-hour absence would not be a problem. Anyway, if an extreme emergency arose he could still be reached as a last resort.

Deke left Joseph in front of headquarters and took the city car home with him. It was a standing order from Captain Murray that he have access to the car at all times during this case so as to cut down on the travel time if he had to report directly to a crime scene. It was far better than his having to go all the way to HQ with his own car to pick up the city car to travel in. Deke didn't mind, either. An official police car with official plates gave him immunity when trying to park the thing anywhere near his building. If there were no legit spots to be found, he would just pull right in front of the fire hydrant a few feet from the front door. No meter maid or NYPD officer would ticket an official license plate. Being the Man sure did have its perks.

Deke stopped at a grocery store near his apartment and picked up some cake to bring to Frannie's. It was embedded in his brain from when he was a child that you never show up to dinner at someone's house with just an appetite. Empty hands equaled an empty head, he was taught.

He dressed casual, a nice pair of black slacks and a red and white wool sweater. He slapped a light splash of Frannie's favorite aftershave on his face and even threw some spray on the hair to keep it in check. As he slid the comb through his hair on a final touch-up, he felt a bubbling of nervous excitement rumble through his belly. He felt good about the prospect of spending the holiday with his family, even if those feelings were somewhat diminished by the lunatic patrolling the streets of New York. The case still hung over his head like a black cloud ready to let loose, but this was Deke's one last chance to choose right from not right, and he knew it. Always being available to the job and not to his family was certainly not right in many ways, and with all the crap that was currently clouding his brain, the biggest clarity came from hearing Frannie's and the kids' voices a few hours earlier. For a moment, he almost didn't care about the killer and whether he ever got caught or not. All he could think about was leaving the job and going back to his family. Deke looked at himself hard in the mirror and felt terror. Distancing himself from the NYPD was a land he had never found himself in. If he was going to start this new journey, though, he felt that Frannie and the kids were the perfect trail guides.

He arrived at the front of his old house, which was now hers, with the kids' presents and the cake. He quickly made his obligatory call to Captain Murray and, after being assured that nothing of note had happened with the case, shut the phone down and slipped it into his hip pocket.

He rang the bell and could hear his kids anxiously yelling to Frannie that Daddy was outside. The door opened and, aside from Frannie's smiling and genuinely joyous face, Deke was greeted by her outstretched hand looking for the cell phone before he would be admitted.

"Can I at least put this stuff down inside first?" He laughed. "Where is it?"

Deke motioned with his head. "Front right pocket."

Frannie reached in with two fingers and slid the phone from his pocket. "You'll get this back later."

Deke had almost forgotten what Frannie's happy face looked like. In the eight months since they had broken up, her gleaming white smile had been replaced by a nasty scowl whenever he would come to pick up Matthew and Lauren or drop them back off. Her once bright and captivating blue eyes had turned all red and tired. The dyed yet authentic-looking blond hair that was always primped and perfect had been allowed to go black. He knew it was all the result of her being thrust into the life of a single mom. He also knew it was all his fault.

Deke was allowed in and was immediately set upon by his two kids. They hugged him briefly and then went automatically to the presents and what was there for them. Jimmy and Larry came over and gave Deke a big hug also. They were glad to see him back in the presence of his family, too. It was almost like the old days.

Deke thanked the guys for watching over his family but made no attempt to discuss the case with them as Frannie playfully stood there to keep him honest. They all had a drink and waited eagerly for the Christmas dinner to finish cooking.

When it came out, Deke saw that Frannie had given him his old seat at the head of the table. To him, it seemed a sign of respect that he thought she had long since lost for him. For her, it seemed nothing more than a fond remembrance of the way things had been. To the rest of the people at the table, it went by with hardly a notice.

The food was cooked to perfection, and they all had their fill. Deke was still on his third helping as Frannie cleared the table around him and put out a new set of plates and cups in preparation for the dessert and coffee. As everyone sat around and enjoyed the cake, Deke nudged Frannie and asked if he could talk to her alone.

She looked begrudgingly into Deke's eyes and sighed. "I guess I could use a walk after all that food," she said.

"Cool, let's do it."

They grabbed their coats and told everyone they'd be back shortly. Frannie noticed Deke's off-duty revolver stuffed into his waistband. She mentioned it to him but also said she had no problem with him carrying it considering the current circumstances going on in the city.

They walked up the block just short of the corner and Frannie stopped them there. "OK, what is it you want now, Deke?"

"This is as far as you go on your walks?" he asked jokingly.

"I don't want to go that far if I'm just gonna get pissed off and walk back home."

"C'mon, Frannie. Can't you keep an open mind here?"

"Deke, you're stalling. Whatever it is, just say it, please. I'm freezing."

"All right, it's like this." Deke was actually nervous. "I think we should try to put this thing back together."

"Oh boy," Frannie said harshly and started walking back to the house. "Not again with this, Deke."

He took hold of her coat at the shoulder as she passed. "Really, Frannie, c'mon, just hear me out."

"Deke, we've been through this a thousand times already. I'm not competing with your damned job anymore."

"You won't have to," Deke conceded. "I'm gonna give it up . . . for you."

She turned and looked at him skeptically. "I heard that one, too. Let go of me, please. I have a party to host."

Deke held firm. "I ain't kiddin', Frannie."

"Really, Deke? How are you going to give the job up? What, you'll cut your work hours down to a hundred a week, maybe?" she said sarcastically.

"Frannie, I'm serious. Gimme another chance, and I'll walk from the job. I'll put my papers in."

"You know, Deke, while that sounds all well and good, I don't want to hear you telling me that I was the reason you had to give up the job and what a mistake that was."

He placed his hand gently on her flushed cheek and stared deeply into those beautiful blue eyes. "I already made the biggest mistake of my life, Frannie, and that was eight months ago when I watched you walk away. Trust me, my heart and head are in this."

She took his hand in hers. "Deke, I wish I could believe you, but I can't. I won't do this to the kids again. They don't deserve it."

"I'll make you a deal, then. I gotta finish this last case off. Nothin' I can do about that. I started it, and I'm gonna catch this guy. Soon as I do, I'm gonna walk away. I'll put my papers in that day and never look back. I'll officially retire, I promise."

Frannie looked back into his eyes. She knew them very well and could always tell if they were lying to her. This time she saw nothing but sincerity. "I need some time to think about this, Deke."

"While you're thinkin', could I give you the present I got ya?"

"Present? You didn't have to get me anything."

"Well, I did. It's right here," he said as he pulled a platinum, diamond-encrusted wedding band from his left-hand pocket. "Maybe you could look at this while you're thinkin'."

Frannie's eyes teared up at the sight of her old ring. "You still have it? You told me you sold it after I threw it at you that day."

Deke laughed. "I lied."

Frannie took the ring and stared at it closely. "You had it cleaned?"

"I did it in the sink. Soap and water."

"You're giving this to me?"

"Under one condition. I get you in return."

Frannie hugged him. This embrace felt completely different from the one he'd received when he first got to her house. "I'll think about it," she said.

They returned to the house, and Deke could see a big difference in Frannie's attitude and mannerisms since their talk. She was downright giddy and light on her feet. She was like a school-girl who just got asked out on her first date.

Eight o'clock came, and Deke said his good-byes to the kids and the guests. Frannie walked him to the door and, once outside, handed him back his phone. Before he could say good-bye, she leaned in and gave him a huge kiss on the lips.

"What was that for?" he asked, surprised yet happy.

Her answer was direct. "Incentive," she said. "Retire from the job, and we'll have a deal."

Deke grabbed her and hugged her. "Really?"

"Really. It's all up to you now."

He kissed her forehead. "Then let me go get this guy quick. He's screwin' up the works here."

Frannie giggled.

"What's so funny?"

"You once told me no man would ever come between us," she mused.

"It definitely ain't gonna be this one. Let me go do my thing."

Deke hopped in the car, and Frannie watched him drive away. When he got around the corner, he turned on the phone. The first call was to Captain Murray.

"What's up, Cap? Anything doin'?"

"Hey, Deke, nothing much other than Jesper. He went and got himself a lawyer today. He filed some papers to get us to drop the tail on him, said it was harassment without probable cause."

"Did we?"

"Yeah, for now."

"What about the plant across the street?"

"Pulled them out. If there's another killing, his house will be the first we hit."

"OK, that's not a prob. We gotta start lookin' elsewhere anyhow."

"Hey, what happened with Frannie?"

"It was good. Everyone had a good time."

"You guys gonna put it back together?"

"Maybe. All depends on how long it takes for me to catch this guy."

"OK, come back here and get Joseph. He's looking through the FBI database now for potential suspects."

"How'd he get access to that through our computers?"

"He didn't. Miller sent him up a laptop with the code chips. Ku-Jo's been on it for hours."

"All right, I'm on the move. Gimme an hour or so."

When Deke hooked back up with Joseph, he already had a list of five solid leads to check out in regard to rap sheets and the FBI profile list. That was all deemed temporarily unimportant. There was a more pressing issue.

"Well?" asked Joseph.

"Well what?" Deke responded.

"Come on. What happened with your wife?"

"I said what I hadda say. It's lookin' good, as long as we catch this guy soon." It was back-to-business time. "I hear you got somethin'."

"Right here," answered Joseph, holding up a few sheets of paper.

Deke took the list and ran it through the NYPD database. Four of the leads were currently in prison on sentences of fifteen to life or better and had been there long before the murders started. The fifth was six feet under after a drug deal went bad.

Joseph, angry, took the list, crumpled it up, and forcefully threw it into the garbage pail. "This is friggin' ridiculous. I'm really starting to get frustrated here."

Deke had been there before. He was there now. He just didn't show it like Joseph did. The less people can read into you, the less they can use against you, he always felt.

Joseph pulled his little electronic device from his pocket and spoke into it. "Five leads, no good. Square one."

"Again with that thing?" Deke asked.

"Hey, it makes life easy."

"You wanna make life easy, you should get one that transmits, too. A good FBI guy woulda had that." Deke smiled.

"Trust me, they don't make them yet. When they do—"

"You'll be all over it, eh?"

"What can I tell you, I love gadgets."

"Don't take this the wrong way, but that's somethin' that a kid would play with. Mine would love it. They would play with it left and right."

"You want one? I'll get you one. I have tons of these. My daughter has six of them."

"Really? Cool, yeah, definitely get me one. Next time I see the kids they'll go nuts."

"Here, take this one," Joseph said, slipping the circle ring off his key chain and tossing the device to Deke. "I'll get another one when I go back to the hotel."

Deke looked at it. "Whattaya gotta do with it? Just hit the side button here?"

"Yeah, hold the button while you talk. It'll record for three seconds. Let the button go when you're done. The button on the other side is for playback."

"Excellent," Deke said as he attached it to his key chain. "I'll make sure I tell 'em where I got it when I show it to 'em. Thanks."

"You're welcome. Are you coming back to the hotel again tonight?"

"It's up to you. If you can fit me into a room again, I'm in."

"Sure, that's not a problem. Remind me when we get there about these recording things. I'll give you a few new ones so your kids can give them to their friends if they want."

"Good man, Ku-Jo. I appreciate that." Deke pushed his button on the device. "Testing, testing, one, two, three." He then pushed the button on the other side and heard his voice in playback. "Wow, is that what I really sound like?"

"Pretty much."

"Hmmph, not good."

"No one ever likes the way they sound, Deke. It's weird."

"Well, how 'bout you?"

"How about me what?"

"You goin' back to the hotel, or are you gonna use my place?"

"I wasn't sure if you were serious or not about that."

"Why wouldn't I be serious? I trust ya. Ain't got nothin' to steal there anyway. You want that homey feeling, it's all yours. Besides, how could I say no after you gave me this top-notch recorder thing."

"OK, then. Maybe tomorrow, though," Joseph answered. "I would have to go to the hotel, pack, and then go all the way to Brooklyn. I'll be too tired to do that later."

"Hey, whatever," Deke said. "It's there when you want it. Come on, let's get outta here."

"Where are we going now?"

"I wanna check out the last murder scene again. You play the part of the killer, and I'll be the girl in the doorway. She hadda see somethin'. There's gotta be a way to shake her memory."

"Didn't you think that scene was overcrowded with crime scene guys yesterday?"

"Some of 'em were crime scene guys. The guys in the tan overcoats were our dopey friggin' inspectors. They're just lookin' to show their faces so the higher-ups'll think they're doin' somethin'."

"Yeah, we have those in the bureau also."

When they arrived at the murder scene, there were still a couple of CSU guys looking for anything they could find. Deke worked his way under the yellow police tape to where they believed the killer to have been according to the witness statement. Joseph hung by the front door on the other side of the tape to see what kind of view the girl would have had of the killer.

Upon hearing Deke's shout, Joseph would open the front door as the girl had, get a glimpse of the killer, and turn and run. They did it a few times, and each of those times Joseph was convinced that he got a good enough look to at least give a description. Deke wasn't so sure. He asked Joseph questions about things that were on the periphery of his line of sight, things on the floor or on the table where the food was. Joseph had no idea; all he saw was Deke. Deke mentioned to him that the girl might have indeed been telling the truth about not getting a good enough look if the first thing she had noticed was the bodies on the floor. Most anyone would tend to look at the gory scene on the floor before getting a peek at the cause of it.

Deke had a talk with one of the CSU guys. "Any chance of a surveillance tape here, maybe?"

"No, Detective. That was the first thing we looked for. This place wasn't up and running very long. Judging from the receipts they have in the back office, it appears they've been in business only about a year."

"OK. We get anything from the scene here?"

"We got lots of stuff, but all stuff common to a business. Fingerprints, hairs, scuff marks from shoes and stuff. Nothing major to make us think we found something."

"Let me know if you get a hit on any of the prints."

"Will do."

Deke and Joseph drove around Manhattan for an hour or so listening to the police radio in case there was another hit. It was so quiet that both men thought the radio was broken and tested it with a call to Central. Nothing was doing anywhere. The Christmas spirit seemed to have suffused everyone.

At midnight, Deke and Joseph called it a day and headed for the hotel. As they walked down the hallway to their rooms, Joseph asked Deke if he had a clue where in the city the killer might have struck this time.

"I ain't sure, but he definitely hit somewhere. This don't seem to be the type of guy to take a day off."

"Yeah, I guess we'll find out soon enough. Hopefully, Christmas infected him."

"Never," Deke said emphatically. "This guy's got no conscience."

"Unfortunately, I agree, but I can hope."

"I'll bang on your door at eight o'clock. We'll get an early start again."

"See you in the morning."

Deke went into his room and performed the same before-bed ritual that he had the night before. Never known as the praying type, he looked up to the heavens and gave a little fist pump to God as if to say, *Help me catch this guy quick so I can get on with my life.* That was the extent of it. Just as quickly, he was back to being on his own again.

He rolled into bed and pulled the covers over himself. They felt different tonight. Everything had a different feeling for him this night. It was Frannie and their little deal that had changed everything. The future was a future again for Deke. No longer would he be trapped in the day-to-day saga with no looking forward to tomorrow. All he had to do was catch one more bad guy to make it all happen. He felt reenergized, empowered. It was high time for Detective Deke Durgess to throw it into overdrive.

Chapter Nine

Deke was up at the crack of dawn, almost an hour before Joseph's alarm went off. He did the shower thing and the finger toothbrush thing. Somewhere along the line, he thought, he had to stop at a store and pick up a toothbrush and toothpaste if he was going to keep this hotel gig going. Then again, maybe it would just be better to have Joseph use his place for a couple of nights. At least then he could have some of his stuff brought back to the hotel.

He bounced around the room with an energy he hadn't felt in years. It surprised him, considering he was up numerous times during the night after being woken by dreams about Frannie. Maybe the energy came from the fact that she had replaced the killer as the center of his unconscious thoughts. Maybe it was from the fact that he had finally made a life-changing decision that had eluded him for what seemed like eons. It didn't matter to him. He was ready to tear into it again. The killer's time was fast coming to a close. Deke felt it. The clues were there. He just had to find them.

He rapped on Joseph's door at 7:00 A.M. and told him he'd see him downstairs at the breakfast buffet. Deke got himself a cup of strong coffee and some high-sugar cereal. He took out his phone and laid it on the table. It was coming, he knew it. It was just a matter of time. Captain Murray would be calling soon to punch his time card.

Deke sat there and sipped his coffee, replaying facts that had been taken from all the murder scenes. He revisited the interviews with Coleman and Jesper, as well as the UPS guy and the gas man, in his head. He processed their words with what had so far transpired in all the killings. There was nothing from any of them that could really be considered incriminating.

There was one thought in Deke's head that kept resounding, kept trying to kick him in the rear and into action. It was the girl. She was the whole kit and caboodle at the moment. She had been the only one to see the killer and live to tell about it, at least a little. Deke saw her as the key. There had to be a way to get the killer out of her mind and into reality. Maybe a hypnotist could do it. If she could be put under and relive the night, maybe she could give an accurate description while her mind was at ease. Maybe her memory could be jogged a little clearer so a set of photos and mug shots could be placed in front of her. It was worth a shot. Deke knew it was going to be a tough sell to the father. His main goal was trying to get Vanessa to forget as much as possible. She was of age, though, so it would be her decision to make. It all depended on who was more persuasive to her.

Deke sat there and pondered scenario after scenario, all to no avail. If the answer was somewhere in there, it was cleverly hidden. Or maybe it was just that he needed more food. He went back to the breakfast bar and loaded up on fresh waffles, bacon, and eggs. He stopped at the muffin display and grabbed a blueberry and a cranberry. On the way back he found the bagels. With an overloaded plate, he headed back to his table and began devouring all he could. The food tasted great. It always tasted great when someone else was buying. The FBI was footing the bill, and Deke made sure to get his money's worth for all the tax dollars he paid.

Joseph came down and was taken aback by the size of the spread of food on the table. "Any of that for me?" he asked.

Deke's mouth was stuffed. "You're on your own," he muttered.

"All I need is that muffin there," Joseph said, pointing at the blueberry.

Deke picked up his knife and held it tightly in his hand. "Go for it," he said menacingly.

Joseph thought about making a grab for it. The look in Deke's eyes stopped him. "Would you really stab me if I tried?"

The reply was instant. "Maybe. I got a gun, too. Don't know which way I'd go yet."

"Be right back," Joseph answered with a laugh as he headed for his own supply of food. As soon as he walked away, Deke's phone started doing its thing.

He picked it up and flipped the front. "What's up, Cap?"

"You guys coming in?"

"Yeah, we're grabbin' some breakfast. Why, somethin' happen?"

"No, not yet, but we're expecting the call, you know."

"OK, gimme 'bout a half hour. We're just finishin' up."

Joseph came back to the table with a large plate of hot and cold food. Deke was standing up.

"You gotta eat that on the run. Let's go."

"What happened? Another hit came in?"

"Cap needs us, told me to shake it. C'mon."

"Shit!" Joseph said as he took a couple of the muffins off the plate and left the hot food behind. "How is it you get to eat and I don't?"

"It's all in the timin', buddy. Besides, a big FBI guy like you coulda got room service."

"That's only for the twenty-year men," Joseph joked. "I'll meet you at the car. I gotta run back up to the room for a minute."

"There's a bathroom down here," Deke deadpanned.

"Funny. I packed a bag for myself so I could hit your place tonight, if it's still OK."

"Fine with me. I really don't know how you could not like stayin' in a place like this, though."

"It's not my thing. I feel like I'm constantly at work when I go back to a hotel every night. Would you have food at your place, I hope?"

"Sure, Italian, Chinese, Mexican, all kinds. Just grab a menu from the kitchen drawer."

"I see."

Deke brought the car around front and waited patiently for a couple of minutes while Joseph got his stuff. His calm demeanor was somewhat surprising for him, as normally he would be beeping the horn and tapping the steering wheel until finally being appeased by the sight of the person he was waiting for. He was in a different frame of mind since his encounter with Frannie the previous night. He was more relaxed, not just physically but mentally also, and he figured it was just another fringe benefit of sharing his life with the only woman he ever cared to share it with. As long as Frannie didn't call him up and rescind the offer, Deke felt he wouldn't be distracted from the task at hand.

From the corner of his eye, Deke saw Joseph come running out the front door of the hotel, suitcase in hand. The suitcase was thrown into the backseat, and the Fed hopped into the front. They quickly shot over to detective headquarters and burst into Captain Murray's office like men on a mission.

"Why the hell are you barging in here like that?" the captain yelled.

"Sorry, Cap," Deke answered. "I hadda make it look good for the Fed, or he woulda been pissed that I made him miss breakfast."

"What? We didn't have to leave like that?" Joseph asked in a huff.

"Sorry, bud, I was done, and I hate sittin' there and watchin' someone else eat. Gets borin'." His attention turned to Captain Murray. "Anything?"

"Nope. Don't worry. When I get the call, you'll be the first to know. By the way, Ronnie wants to see you. He's got a new list of potentials to go over."

"Let's do it," Deke said as he slapped Joseph on the shoulder and headed quickly out the door.

Ronnie had only two possibles for Deke to check out, but at least it was something. One was a limousine driver whose GPS system had shown him in or around every crime scene at some point either right before or right after each murder. The other was a dishonorably discharged sergeant from the Marine Corps who did odd jobs as a carpenter in three of the neighborhoods where murders were committed.

"Where'd you get the marine guy from? Guy seems like a vagabond," Deke asked.

"He came up on a list of disgruntled former military people. We're looking now at *anyone* with access to a gun. It's getting that bad."

"You get a background report on him from the Corps?"

"We're trying. The marines are kind of reluctant to give any info out on past or present soldiers. The higher-ups in our department are working on it now."

"You run his name through BCI yet?"

"BCI?" asked Joseph.

"Bureau of Criminal Identification," Deke answered.

Joseph was amazed. "Man, you guys have more letters for things than you can shake a stick at."

Yeah," Deke said sarcastically, "this comin' from a guy that works for the FBI." He turned his attention back to Ronnie. "Well, did ya?"

"Yeah, came back clean."

"OK, I don't wanna bother with him, then, till I see that marine report. When you get it, call me."

"Understood."

"Where's this limo guy?"

"Two detectives just picked him up a few minutes ago. They're bringing him in as we speak."

"Freakin' Ronnie," Deke said happily as they exchanged high fives. "Way to be right on top of this shit."

"Thank you," Ronnie answered.

"Set him up in Interview Room Three. I'll be there in a few. I gotta go drop a load," Deke said as he headed for the bathroom with a newspaper.

"Not the most eloquent sort, is he now?" Joseph said quietly to Ronnie.

"Not since I've known him, but if you need a tough case solved, that's your boy, and all the bosses know it, all the way to the top. That's why he gets away with all the crap he does. I'm surprised it's taking him this long to catch up with this guy."

"Well, he's not leaving us a lot to work with. Not a whole bunch of evidence to look at, you know."

"Evidence?" Ronnie chuckled. "Shoot, I've seen Deke catch guys just by sense of smell." He shot Joseph a sideways glance. "Truthfully."

Joseph stared back skeptically. "Yeah, right."

"I'm not kidding, really. There was this one time me and my partner were chasing a perp through Chinatown. He was a gang-banger, ya know, a real penny-ante thug. Anyhow, we're running after him up Canal Street toward the diamond jewelry district, and he breaks off onto Mott Street."

Joseph shrugged at the mention of the area. He had no real clue about New York streets. Ronnie noticed this.

"It's basically at the foot of the Manhattan Bridge," he said with a wave of his hand. "Anyhow, we lose him up near one of the sweatshops, but we know he didn't get far because we had a unit on the other side of the block to make sure he didn't come out. Plus, we found the kid's shirt on the sidewalk when we came up. It was all sweaty and crap. We recognized it right away 'cause we were chasing it so long. He probably tossed it so he'd be harder to ID. Anyway, we're standing out there trying to figure out what building he went into when Deke shows up."

Ronnie put up his right hand and swore to Joseph that what he was about to say was true. "He takes the shirt and takes three small whiffs of it. Then he comes up to me and sniffs me and my partner. 'OK,' he says to me. 'This guy's wearing English Leather.' I had no idea if he was kidding or not, but, son of a bitch he is, he leads us into a building two doors away, and sure enough there's the kid hiding behind some boxes in a hallway. How he found him I have no idea. Maybe he really did smell him, I can't say for sure, but he did find him."

Joseph had a smile on his face. "English Leather?" He laughed.

"I don't know. Ask him. He found the kid, that's all I know."

The intraoffice phone line rang, and Ronnie picked it up. "Hello . . . yeah . . . where you got him? OK, put him in Room Three. Durgess will be there in a few."

"Where's Interview Room Three?" Joseph asked.

"Down the hall and to the right. You can't miss it."

"Does it have a two-way mirror in it?"

"Of course. You're not waiting for Deke?"

"I'm not going in. I just want to look through the mirror at his mannerisms, see if I can pick anything up. All part of the profiling."

Ronnie held his hand out in the direction of the room. "All yours."

Joseph studied the man for almost ten minutes while waiting for Deke to arrive. He was nervous and fidgeted in his chair incessantly. He looked all around, sometimes directly at Joseph through the mirror, although he had no clue he was there. He had a blank expression on his gaunt face; his eyes were dark-ringed and worried. His thin lips trembled in anticipation of the unknown that was coming his way. He found a loose paper clip on the desk in front of him and started fiddling with it, bending and straightening it until it broke. He was a complete wreck, and it was clear to Joseph that this guy was worried about something big. Whatever the case, murderer or not, this guy was no angel wrongly taken in for questioning. This guy came with baggage.

"That's our boy, huh?" Deke said, startling Joseph. "Easy there, cowboy. No need to jump like that."

"You caught me off guard. I was so focused on this guy."

"You pick anything up?"

"I'll tell you one thing, that guy right there is definitely guilty of something. Look at him. He's scared to death. I think you can roll him."

"Let's find out."

Deke walked into the room and had a seat across from the man. "Good morning. I'm Detective Durgess of Manhattan Homicide. Can I get your name, please?"

The man stammered. "P-Pete Stewart."

"Don't be nervous, Mr. Stewart. I'm just here to ask you a couple of questions. Just relax."

Stewart took a deep breath. "Why am I here?"

"I just told you. I got a couple of questions to ask you. Is that OK with you?"

"I guess."

"Very good. What is it that you do for a livin'?"

"I drive a limousine."

"You work for someone, or you freelance?"

"I work for myself. I put my cards in all the airports and bus terminals, and sometimes people call."

"Do you keep a list of all these people?"

"I'm not sure I know what you mean."

Stewart's hands were shaking, and he couldn't even make eye contact. Deke picked right up on it.

"Whaddaya mean you're not sure? Don't you got any kinda list that'll tell me who you picked up and who you dropped off?"

Stewart's eyes were darting back and forth. "It's not with me."

"But it does exist."

"Yes."

"OK, I'm gonna need to see that. Now, when you drop these people off, do you walk 'em to the house? Or do you just leave them and their suitcases on the curb? Whaddaya do?"

"It depends on what they want me to do."

"Then do you hang around the neighborhood, or do you have other stuff lined up?"

"I don't know. It all depends on what time it is and where I am. If I'm around an airport, I'll go there and try to pick up a fare."

"What if you're not?"

"I'll go home, I'll go to a bar, I don't know. What is this all about?"

"I think you're a little confused, bud. I ask the questions in this room."

"Just tell me what this is all about."

"OK," Deke said, "I'm sure you've heard about this guy goin' around killin' people all over the city—"

"What about him?"

"Well, your car just happened to turn up near every one of

the murder scenes before or after a killin'. Why do you suppose that is?"

Stewart's mannerisms changed. The question was one he hadn't expected. He seemed less uptight. Joseph noticed it right away.

His answers were more forthcoming, too. "I don't know, Detective. I would say it's a coincidence. I go where the people tell me to take them."

Deke slammed his hand on the table. "Not good enough! A coincidence puts you at two or three of the murder scenes. Not all of 'em."

"I am not a killer, sir. Think what you want. I drop off my fares where they tell me to."

"Do you own a gun?"

"Own one? I won't even hold one."

"How is that, bud? Most livery guys would give anything to be able to carry a piece. What's the deal? Nothin' out there scares you?"

"A lot scares me, Detective. Right now, it's you."

"Listen, dude, you don't start giving me the answers I'm lookin' for, I'm gonna beat the shit out of you. Look around. It's just me and you. No one to help you."

"What do you want me to tell you? I killed those people?" He leaned in and placed his elbows on the table. "Well, I didn't."

"Then you wouldn't mind if I searched your car, would ya?"

Stewart was adamant. "You're not going through my car without a search warrant. I have many personal things in there."

Deke put his foot up on the chair next to Stewart and scrunched down into his face. "I won't take nothin'. You can stay there and watch me search it if it'll make you feel any better."

"Listen, Detective, I am telling you the truth. I didn't kill anybody. Can't we just leave it at that?"

A soft knock on the door captured Deke's attention. He looked over and saw Joseph's face in the glass, calling him over.

"What?" Deke asked as he pushed the door open.

"I'd like to talk to you for a second."

Deke gave Stewart a don't-even-think-about-moving-from-that-chair look and stepped through the doorway. He stood with his foot against the bottom of the door, making sure he still had a clear view of Stewart through the small, rectangular-shaped door glass.

"OK, g'head."

"I've been looking at this guy real closely while you talked to him. He's not the killer."

"How the hell do you know that? I just started talkin' to him."

"Come on, Deke. You had to notice that he loosened up when you started talking to him about the killings. Whatever he's hiding, it's not about being a murderer."

Deke took a look back into the room while Joseph kept talking.

"He was all antsy when you brought up the passenger lists. I thought he was going to explode. As soon as you moved to the murders, it was like the weight of the world was off his shoulders. He's not our guy."

Deke played it back in his head and realized that Joseph might be right. It dawned on him that the Frannie incentive of getting the case over with as soon as possible might have been clouding his judgment and had him looking for a suspect where there was none. One thing was for certain, though, the guy *was* hiding something. He might not be the killer, but it was possible that he knew who was.

Deke gave Joseph a tap on the shoulder in appreciation for getting his head back in the game. The Frannie thing, while giving him a sense of euphoria he hadn't known in many years, was taking him off the beaten path, so to speak. Normally on the straight and narrow, he was now finding himself occasionally detoured to roads he had no business being on.

He burst back into the room and slammed a clipboard down on the table next to Stewart. "I wanna know right now why you were in the same areas where the murders went down."

"I already told you. I go where the passengers tell me."

Deke grabbed him and forcefully lifted him from his seat. He threw him up against the door.

"What are you doing?" Stewart yelled. "I'm telling you the truth."

"We're goin' on a little field trip."

"What are you talking about?"

"We're takin' a ride to get your passenger lists and receipts. I wanna know where you picked 'em up, where you dropped 'em off, and anything else I can find."

The nervousness was back in Stewart's voice. "I told you, I'm not sure where the lists are."

"That's OK. I'll look through your car for 'em myself."

"Wait, hold on a second . . ."

Deke had him by the scruff of his neck. "What?"

"What would happen if you found the list and there was a problem with it?"

Deke threw him back toward his chair and told him to sit. "What kinda problem?" he said angrily.

"Can I talk to you off the record for a minute?"

"You better start talkin' to me any way you can," he answered forcefully.

"OK, listen." His head was down and his voice soft. "A lot of my passengers pay straight cash. Some of them pay a little extra for me to forget who they were and where I dropped them."

"Like who?"

"Like the kind of people that aren't supposed to be here to begin with."

"What are you talkin' about, illegals?"

"As far as I can guess, they are. I don't ask questions. They're willing to pay me extra to get them to Brighton Beach. I figure, if they're smart enough to get past customs at the airports, who's gonna care if they get past me."

"Russians?"

Stewart looked up. "Who else goes to Brighton Beach, Detective?"

Deke scanned his face closely. "No, no, no. I'm not buyin' this shit. You're not goin' through all of this just to hide some under-the-table cash."

Stewart didn't say anything.

"Anyway, how is it the TLC didn't pick up on the fare discrepancies?"

Stewart shut his eyes tight and slowly shook his head back and forth. Deke knew he had something.

"Why is that, bud?"

"Because the Taxi and Limousine Commission doesn't know I exist."

Suddenly it all came together for Deke. The guy was driving around out there picking up passengers without a medallion, without a hack license. He was just a regular guy with a nice car who made money by illegally driving people around town. It wasn't a serious offense, but it was jail time for sure. It was time for Deke to put on the old squeeze.

"You stealin' money from the TLC, bud? They don't go for that shit. I think you're lookin' at some time in the can here."

"No, come on, Detective. Please don't do that! I had no other way to support my family."

"Then tell me what you were doin' in all those neighborhoods."

"I swear to God I was just dropping people off. I had no idea about the murders."

"Were any of your passengers repeat performers?"

"Huh?"

"Did anyone like your services and use you more than once?"

"Sometimes."

"Take a look at this sheet of paper here," Deke said, handing over a list of the areas where the killings took place. "I wanna know if anyone used you more than once to get into any of these neighborhoods."

"I would have to look at my lists, Detective. I drive a lot of people."

"Where are they?"

Again, Stewart was nervously silent.

"Listen," Deke said, "you help me out, and I'll help you out. Deal?"

"How would you help me?"

"By lettin' you walk out the door."

"I could just go? You won't report me?"

"Report what? I hate the TLC. You're small potatoes compared to what I'm lookin' for. Gimme the list, and we'll call it even."

"Can I get that in writing?"

Deke gave a look of disbelief to the mirror Joseph was standing behind. Joseph stood back there shaking his head. How stupid was this guy? Put in writing a deal that incriminates both the police and the criminal?

Deke ignored the question. "Where is the list?"

Stewart resigned himself to the situation. "It's in my car."

"Where is the car?"

"At my house. Your guys picked me up there."

"OK, listen. I'm gonna have a couple of detectives drive you there, and you're gonna get that list and bring it back to me. We're gonna go over it bit by bit. Clear?"

"Then you'll let me go?"

Deke looked him square in the eye. "As long as you don't lie to me. One time I feel you're lyin', the deal's off. Understood?"

"Yes, sir."

Deke walked out of the room and grabbed two detectives for the job. He then went back to Murray's office, where Ronnie and the captain were having a conversation.

"Sorry, Cap," Deke said as he interrupted their talk. "Can I borrow Ronnie for a sec?"

"What do you need, Deke?" Ronnie asked.

"Anything goin' on with the marine guy? We find him yet?"

"I was just talking to the cap about that. The guy hasn't been seen in ten days. Last one saw him was his landlord on rent day."

"Ten days? He has no family?"

"None that we can find, and, get this, the landlord said he was showing off a new gun he bought on the street."

Deke's heart jumped. "Did the landlord describe the gun?"

"Only that it was a revolver and that it was big. He didn't get a real good look. Landlord said the guy makes him nervous."

"We gotta find this guy," Deke said emphatically. "Get a picture of him somehow and put an APB out on him."

"Whoa, hold on, Deke," Captain Murray said. "You put out an all points bulletin on this guy, and some rookie cop out there is gonna wind up shooting him."

"Gimme an alternative, Cap."

"I don't have one." He gave Deke a wry look from the corner of his eye. "You know, you really piss me off sometimes. OK, go with the APB. Make sure you put it out there that he is *not* a suspect, understood? *Not a suspect.* He's only wanted for questioning."

"Got it," Ronnie answered and headed out the door.

Deke and Captain Murray followed him out and went to the desk where all the information on the suspects was laid out. Joseph was already sitting there, feet up, circling some names, crossing off others.

"We might have somethin' with this marine guy, Ku-Jo. He's got a gun, and he's runnin' around out there somewhere unknown."

Joseph's feet hit the floor. "Let's go find him."

"Relax," Deke said. "We got an APB out on him. Someone'll pick him up."

Everyone stopped as a story about the killer came on a newscast playing on the office television. It was just an update, one that stated that no killings had yet been reported for the day and that as soon as some info came in, it would be passed along.

Deke stared at the screen for a few seconds. "Ya know, maybe the guy *did* take the day off yesterday. Maybe he's some kinda religious fanatic and couldn't kill on Christmas."

"It's possible," Joseph responded.

Deke rethought it. "Possible, but not likely. All of a sudden the guy would get a conscience? He killed. We just didn't hear yet."

"Maybe."

The news went to commercial, and Deke asked Captain Murray to shut off the TV. Just before he hit the button, the lottery came on with its daily number drawing. Joseph yelled for Captain Murray to leave it on.

"Hold on. I got Deke's car number played in the midday. A dollar straight two times."

"You played five oh nine?"

"Sure, why not? I hit the number in California all the time."

The first number popped up. It was a five. Everyone was transfixed by the screen.

The second number came in. It was another five.

"Dammit," Joseph said. "There goes that."

For good measure, the last number was also a five.

"Five five five?" Deke muttered. "You guys hadda give me five oh nine. I coulda been eatin' good tonight."

The four-digit number came rolling in, 0-8-7-0. Deke looked at Joseph. "Did you have that one?" he asked sarcastically.

"Nope."

"So what the hell is this you-hit-all-the-time shit? That was thirty seconds out of my day that I'll never get back. Shut that thing off, please."

All three men sat around for a couple of hours poring over names, faces, and what little evidence there was, which they had already gone over numerous times before. Basically it was a waiting game, and while none of them wanted to admit it, they were waiting for news of the next killing to come in or for anything to surface on the marine guy. It was a shitty detail, and no one liked being part of it, but it came with the territory. Detective work wasn't always what was seen on TV. A lot of the time it was a hurry-up-and-wait sort of thing where events would need to progress to a point where action could be taken. This was one of those times. Unless something dropped into their laps from above, they were going to have to wait for the killer to make his next move.

Dinnertime rolled around, and all was still eerily quiet. No news of any killings had come in.

Captain Murray was very matter-of-fact. "We're gonna have to start looking at this like maybe he did take a day off. The Christmas angle might play into it."

Deke wasn't buying it. "Why would he decide to have a heart now? The guy blew away children without even a second thought."

Joseph chimed in. "Captain Murray could be right. A lot of

these religious wackos think they're doing God's work when they kill people. We might be dealing with one of them here. At the very least it's worth looking into."

"What are you gonna do? Get every Catholic in the city to come in for questioning? It's not a Christmas thing."

"Then why would he take the day off?"

A thought hit Deke. "Maybe he didn't take the day off," he said. "Maybe he didn't kill because he *couldn't* kill." He rose to his feet quickly and yelled for Ronnie to hurry over. Ronnie wasn't coming fast enough, so Deke walked toward him to meet him halfway. Joseph and Captain Murray followed close behind.

"What's going through your mind, Deke?" Captain Murray asked.

"Maybe somehow he was stopped from killing yesterday. Maybe he planned to but the opportunity was taken away."

Ronnie stood and waited for Deke's instructions.

"Listen, get on the line with all the other precincts and get a list of everyone that was brought in and detained yesterday. Anyone who was put in lockup goes right to the top of the list. I also want you to call all the hospitals and get a list of anyone that was admitted yesterday and still hasn't been released."

Captain Murray was impressed. It wasn't an angle he had even thought of. It was still a long shot, but at least it was one that made sense. It was certainly worth checking.

"Let's go," Deke said hurriedly to Joseph.

"Where to?"

"Central Bookin'. Anyone taken in yesterday will probably be passin' through there now. Let's go see what we got."

When they hopped in the car for the trip, Deke had the wheel, and Joseph rode shotgun. Joseph had a sheepish smile on his face. Deke noticed it.

"What?" he asked.

"I have to know something. I was talking to Ronnie back in the interrogation area . . ."

"And?"

"Did you really once catch a guy just by smelling him out?"

Deke looked puzzled for a second, and then it hit him. "Whaddaya talkin' about? The gangbangin' kid in Chinatown?"

"Yeah. You tracked him by smell?"

Deke let out a hearty laugh.

"What, you didn't?"

Deke laughed some more. "Ronnie is supposedly one of our better detectives, too," he said, wiping a tear from his eye. "No, I didn't catch the kid by smellin' for him."

"Then what? How'd you find him?"

"I knew who he was!" Deke said emphatically. "The kid they were chasin' is one of my street informants. Soon as I saw the shirt with his colors on it, I knew who it was and where he'd be runnin' to. I knew the kid's name, address, even his shoe size."

"His cologne, too? Ronnie said you told him it was English Leather."

Deke had another good laugh. "I didn't smell nothin' in the shirt except stink. I threw the English Leather thing in there just to piss Ronnie off when I went lookin' for the kid. I never thought he'd fall for it."

Joseph started laughing also. "That's pretty funny. I think he really does believe that you sniffed the kid out."

"Don't ever tell him," Deke warned. "I wanna keep that one goin'."

"Not a worry, partner. I feel happier just being in on it."

"OK, we done with this? Time to get outta here. We got work to do."

They flew over to Central Booking and sat in on all the arraignments, taking names and notes. Some guys stood out like sore thumbs and had asterisks placed next to their names, while others were callously disregarded. Deke hoped they might get the old grand slam by finding out the marine guy had been picked up; he even dropped his name around the building to different judges and lawyers. No one had ever heard of him, and after a few phone calls it was determined that he had never been there at all.

Deke tried talking to all the guys with asterisks, but all of them had either a court-appointed lawyer or a high-priced mouthpiece and wouldn't even give him the time of day. He did have names, though, and with that info he could track down their latest movements to see where they fit into the puzzle, if at all.

He and Joseph headed back to headquarters with all the names on the list and assigned the tracking down of those names to a squad of waiting detectives. Joseph decided to call it a night and asked Deke if it was still OK for him to use the apartment.

"Sure," Deke responded. "Someone's gotta feed the roaches."

Joseph stared back blankly.

"I'm kiddin'," Deke said as he pulled the key from his ring. "It's all yours." He handed the key over and playfully wished Joseph luck. He wrote down the address so it could be programmed into the navigation system in the car.

Joseph drove Deke back to the hotel and said he'd be back in the morning to pick him up. Deke asked Joseph to grab a fresh set of his clothes and certain toiletries that he needed and bring them back with him. Joseph then informed him that the hotel had a concierge that would see to it that the clothing he was wearing was cleaned and pressed and delivered to him bright and early the next morning, but that a new set would be brought back anyway. Deke headed upstairs and settled into his room.

An hour or so after Deke's head hit the pillow, the hotel phone rang. He answered it groggily. "Hello?"

"Yeah, it's me, dude," Joseph said. "Nice place you have here."

"You coulda told me that in the morning."

"I know. I just thought maybe you'd be up."

"What, you didn't get enough of me today?"

Joseph laughed. "Believe me, I did. I just wanted to comment on your team of detectives working with you. They really seem to be good."

"That's 'cause they *are* good," Deke answered quickly.

"I know. That guy Ronnie is all over things. He's on top of everything."

Deke could tell that this wasn't just a comment being made by Joseph. This was something more. It woke him up a bit.

"Whaddaya tryin' to say? You ain't thinkin' Ronnie's involved in this thing, I hope."

"No, never. He's a good guy. He just seems to be way, way ahead of everything with all the tips he gives us. It's almost like he's leading us places."

"Listen, I know what you're tryin' to do here. Ronnie ain't involved, so get him outta your head. Just because the guy got great instincts ain't enough to put him on the radar. I've known him a long time, and he never steered me wrong. I trust the guy."

"All right, Deke. I wasn't casting suspicion on him. I'm just trying to cover every base."

"Well, you ain't even in the right ballpark with this one." Deke looked at the clock and noticed that it was still thirty-five minutes until midnight. He knew Frannie always watched the late news, so he figured he'd take a shot and give her a ring. "Listen, man, let me go. Now that you got me up, I think I'm gonna make another call."

"OK, talk to you in the A.M."

"You call your kid and read her her story?"

"Yeah, I snuck it in a couple of hours ago. Thanks for reminding me, though."

"No prob. I'll catch ya in the morning. Hey!" Deke said with emphasis as the cool wetness from his pillow touched his cheek. "Don't use the pillow on my bed. Grab one from the closet."

"Will do. Good night."

"Later."

Deke called the front desk and got himself an outside line. He dialed Frannie, and she picked up on the second ring. They spoke mostly about the kids and how happy they were to have Deke there on Christmas. They talked a little about the case and the progress he hoped he was making on solving it. Before they hung up they discussed their deal, and Frannie repeated the leave-the-job-or-nothing credo. They shared a laugh, said they'd see each other soon, and said good night.

Deke lay on his back and stared up into the darkness. As always, the day's events played through his head like a recurring movie, all the while he was searching for clues. Even Ronnie passed through his head, only to be quickly shaken off with a no-way thought. He ultimately drifted off into unconsciousness, only to be woken again by the same circumstances that had plagued him days earlier. The murders were pushing themselves back into his every thought, his every breath. He felt the same chain of sleepless nights fast approaching on the horizon, but he knew that just beyond that horizon, just past catching the killer, lay his salvation, one that took the shape of something he had lost long, long ago. It was his family, and it was right there for the taking. Deke Durgess had his eyes set on the prize.

Chapter Ten

Deke's cell phone rang precisely at 4:45 A.M. and made him jump from his loose sleep. The caller ID identified the caller as Captain Murray's cell phone. He sat up so his feet could hit the floor and turned the light on over the bed. He flipped the phone and began talking.

"Why you callin' me from your cell?"

"I'm still home, dammit. I just got the call. Our boy hit in Brooklyn yesterday."

Deke interrupted. "You sure it was yesterday? Maybe he hit on Christmas."

"Deke, relax. I talked to CSU. He hit yesterday, sometime between 4:00 and 6:00 P.M. I want you to head straight to the scene and see what you can pick up."

"Gimme the address."

"It's 922 Georgia Avenue."

"Georgia Av? Isn't that in Bed-Stuy?"

"Yup. He goes where he goes."

"All right, let me get Joseph over here. We'll be there in an hour or so."

Deke hung up on the captain and quickly called Joseph on his cell. The bleary-eyed Fed picked it up on the second ring.

"Rise and shine, cupcake. Get your ass over here."

"What? What time is it?"

"C'mon," Deke said urgently. "The killer hit again."

Joseph was suddenly thrust into consciousness. "Where?"

"Brooklyn, Bed-Stuy. That's all the info I got so far."

"All right. I'm on my way."

"The lights and siren button is right under the dash. Move it! I'll be downstairs waitin'."

The ride from Brooklyn to Manhattan for Joseph and then from Manhattan back to Brooklyn for both of them was relatively uninterrupted, as the only other vehicles on the road at that hour were a few Sanitation salt spreaders handling icy streets. Deke and Joseph rolled onto Georgia Avenue, which was comprised mostly of commercial stores with an occasional house sprinkled in every two hundred feet or so.

The area was a carnival, multicolored lights flashing everywhere and news reporters filling every empty space on the street. As usual, the attention turned to Deke in a big way once recognition set in among the reporters. They flocked to him and shot questions from every direction into his ears. He and Joseph pushed and shoved their way through the crowd and past the police barriers. Once inside the cordoned-off area, Joseph jokingly commented to Deke that he wanted to play himself in the movie version of this crisis if it ever went to film.

"This thing'll be a movie, guaranteed," Deke answered. "Let's see if we can make it a happy endin'."

When they got near the door, Deke encountered something he had never seen before—CSU guys crying.

"This ain't gonna be good," he said to Joseph.

Inside the house was the single most heinous thing either

man had ever seen. There were ten bodies in all, two adult women and eight small children ranging in age from six months to eight years. The women had been killed first, according to CSU, and the children had been picked off one by one as the killer marched through the halls of the house. Two of the kids, a girl seven years old and her little brother, age three, were found huddling under a table in the entrance hallway. The girl had her arms wrapped around the boy as if trying to protect him. Both were shot in the head. All the other kids were individual kills and were found in closets or under beds, some shot once, others multiple times. Only the baby's body was found where it should have been, in its crib under a blanket.

It was a hard scene for even Deke to process. There was way too much death here. Everywhere people looked, there was a body, and more often than not, it was a tiny one. Adults being killed doesn't bother cops too much. It's a scene most of them have seen at one time or another. Besides, at least the adults understand what the hell is going on and take a shot at defending themselves. The kids are always a different story. They rely on the adults in the house for protection, and when that first line of defense fails, they try to hide instead of getting out. Cops always equate the kids to their own home life and their own kids. It's never easy seeing the little ones take the hit.

Deke couldn't even walk the whole house for fear of stepping in all the blood and contaminating the scene. Instead, he grabbed one of the guys taking pictures and looked through the photos on the back of his digital camera. The carnage was nothing he'd ever seen before. The killer was either getting more brutal or making up for the day he had off. One thing was for certain, he wasn't in Central Booking when Deke was there. He wasn't in any hospital either. Whatever made him skip a day of killing was in his head and his alone. The Christmas thing might have to be thought about after all, and all its religious components. Why this family, though? Of all the places to go in the city, why pick a welfare home? These were people trying to do good. They weren't bothering anyone. The twisted method this guy was using to pick his victims had to be deciphered. The death toll had long become intolerable.

As usual, there were no witnesses to the carnage and no viable forensic evidence left behind. No one could even figure out the method the killer used to gain entry into the house. Considering the number of toys lying about the place, he could have come in as a delivery truck guy for all they knew. There was definitely no sign of forced entry.

The other usual signs were all about the place, though. There was the methodical way the killer went about his business. There was much body trauma, insinuating a high-caliber weapon, and as always, there was the note, BETTER LUCK NEXT TIME, and it was dropped right on top of one of the adult victims.

Deke took note of the number of bodies he was now faced with. The count stood at thirty-two. He thought that it could somehow be running along racial lines. Up until this murder scene there had been fifteen white victims, three black victims, three Hispanic, and one Chinese victim. This murder scene alone added ten black victims into the mix. If it was a racial thing, then Hispanics could be the next group targeted. Deke immediately called Captain Murray and had him beef up the police presence in the Hispanic areas.

He went back outside and found Joseph leaning against a tree, head down and tears in his eyes.

"You all right, bud?"

"We need to stop this," he said imperatively. "All of this has to stop right now."

"C'mon, Ku-Jo. I need ya to hang tough with me here. You gotta keep it together."

Joseph was angry. "Hey, listen, I'm not accustomed to see- ing little babies with bullets in their heads. You might be used to shit like this, but I'm not." He took a second to compose himself. "I'm not falling apart here. I just keep thinking that it could be my kid in there, that's all."

"You can't let it screw up your head, though. You gotta keep thinkin' clear."

"Well, that's kind of an impossibility now, isn't it! What I saw in there will screw with my head for the next forty years. When I'm seventy and sitting in a retirement home somewhere, the memories of those kids will be just as clear as they were ten seconds ago."

"You don't think it bothers me, too? There ain't a chance I'll ever forget this shit! It don't go away, but you gotta be able to put it in the back of your mind so you can keep thinkin' straight."

"Well, if it's all right with you I think I'll keep it in front. I'd like to use it as motivation," Joseph said as he pushed himself off the tree and began walking to the car. "Let's go get this fucker!"

The news reporters picked up right away on Joseph's change in attitude, thanks to their powerful camera lenses. They were zoomed right up to him and Deke as they had their conversation. As Joseph got close, all the microphones and questions were di- rected to him and him alone.

"Detective, what did you see in there? How many bodies are there? Was this the work of the Daily Killer?"

Joseph ignored every one of them and didn't even give his trademark "No comment" line. He even smacked away a few of the microphones that got too close to him.

Deke followed, happy not to be the center of attention. He also kept a close eye on Joseph in case he needed to grab him if he went after one of the reporters. They worked their way through the crowd, got in the car, and hurried away. Deke was back behind the wheel, and Joseph sat in the passenger seat, slightly reclined, eyes closed. Deke could tell Joseph was working it out in his brain.

He knew he needed to distract his own mind a bit, to get it away from the thoughts and pictures of the last murder scene. "So," he began, "who you think should play you in the movie?"

Joseph sniffed deeply through his nose and cracked his neck. "I don't know. Tom Cruise is too short. Maybe I'll just play myself. Nobody out there is good-looking enough."

"Yeah, OK. Who you think should play me, then?"

There was no hesitation. "Arnold Schwarzenegger."

Deke laughed. "Are you nuts? He don't look nothin' like me."

"I know."

"Then why him?"

Joseph had him set up perfectly. "Neither one of you can speak a word of English."

Deke nodded approvingly and looked out his window. He'd been had, and he knew it.

Joseph smiled victoriously and went back to playing things in his mind. There was just no way to shake it.

Deke drove the car down Flatlands Avenue and made a left onto East 108th Street toward the Belt Parkway. The morning rush-hour traffic coupled with the sun rising just over the horizon and blinding the drivers gave Deke all the incentive he needed to divert from his present course onto an alternate route. He made a right onto Rockaway Parkway and took the long way back into the city. He took notice of all the people just going about their normal routines. Most were going to work, some were taking kids to school, others were just strolling along. The killer could have been any one of them. Somehow, some way he was meshed in with the rest of society, passing himself off as one of them. People out there knew him for what he presented himself to be, a co-worker, a friend, a family member. No one was picking him up as the cold-blooded murderer he presented himself as to the police.

That in itself was a problem for Deke. Tips were coming in like wildfire from citizens trying to cash in on the reward money offered for the capture of the killer, but hardly any of them were credible. Sure, they would all have to be checked out, wasting countless man-hours for detectives who could actually be on the street chasing real leads. People were calling in tips on neighbors they didn't like, folks who owed them money, and sometimes even making things up just to feel important and like they were part of the action. It happened all the time, and the more important and publicized the case was, the larger the number of false leads that would usually come in. What troubled Deke was that none of the tips were leading him to the killer. Whoever he was, no one out there was seeing him for what he was. He had whatever circle of people existed around him convinced that he was just as much a victim as they were. That was the scariest kind of killer that could be out there, as far as Deke was concerned. That kind of guy could just flip a switch and go from a normal, law-abiding citizen one second to a ruthless, uncaring baby killer the next, and it chilled him. That kind of guy possessed the potential to just lose it anywhere. What was it that caused that switch to trigger itself?

The car was on its way over the Manhattan Bridge when Deke's cell phone alerted him that a call was coming in. It was Captain Murray again.

"Go, Cap."

"Where are you?"

"We're just gettin' into Manhattan. We'll be there in ten."

"Negative, do not come here! You gotta go straight to Third Avenue and East Fifty-sixth Street."

"What's goin' on there?"

"He hit again."

"What! Are you kiddin' me?"

Joseph's eyes opened, and his attention was focused on Deke's conversation.

Captain Murray was exasperated. "The bastard hit twice yesterday. This shit's gonna be all over the airwaves in twenty minutes. Get over there and let the news people see that we're on top of this. Call me back when you get something." The phone was abruptly hung up.

"What's going on?" Joseph asked, straightening his seat.

"We got a second scene."

"What? Where?"

"Up on Third Av. We're a few minutes away."

"When were the victims killed?"

"I don't know. The cap says it was yesterday, but I don't see how this guy did two locations in one day. One of these two's gotta be from Christmas."

Joseph threw his fists over his eyes. "Jesus Christ Almighty! What the hell is it with you New Yorkers!" He looked at Deke. "Does this state have a death penalty?"

"Not anymore," Deke replied. "The legal eagles put a stop to it 'cause stickin' needles in the arms of murderers was considered cruel and inhuman."

"Really? Well, guess what. I just reinstated it."

"What's that supposed to mean?"

"When we find this guy, there will be no arrest. If you're with me, you better look the other way, because I am going to kill him on the spot. I don't care what happens to me. No way he lives the rest of his life getting three square meals a day."

Deke threw a little chuckle at him. "That's a pretty long line you're gonna have to get on the back of."

"Good. As long as we understand each other, then."

Deke didn't like the look in Joseph's eye. He was absolutely serious. There was a definite change in him since he saw the bodies of the kids at the last scene. If he and the killer ever did cross paths, Joseph was going to waste him, no doubt about it. Deke wasn't sure how to process this information. He pushed it to the side. It was a bridge that would have to be crossed only if he got there.

The crime scene was another circus. Reporters were everywhere, some taping segments, others doing live feeds. Everything turned on Deke as the police barriers were pulled back and his car rolled through. He drove slowly in case one of the reporters jockeying for position slipped on the icy curb and into the path of his vehicle. Not that he would have cared. It would make great TV to have one of these scum-suckers getting run over on film. He just didn't need the sideshow of an accident investigation derailing him from the case he was on.

Deke was able to drive right up to the front door of the murder scene like a Hollywood star pulling up to a movie premiere. The big-time NYPD investigators in charge of the area were well aware of the media presence and wanted it made known that there was someone competent running the show. As always, in the public eye, everything was based on appearance.

Deke and Joseph exited the car and headed straight into the house. CSU was rapidly processing the scene and even had a forensics team from the FBI assisting them. Somewhere along the line Deke ran into the lead CSU guy, and they discussed the particulars of the scene.

The murders did indeed, according to the medical examiner, take place the day after Christmas. They also took place in a Hispanic area, giving weight to Deke's theory. There were only two victims this time, though, a man and a woman, both roughly thirty-five years of age. It still left the Hispanic victim total way behind the whites and blacks. Deke felt that the next hit could also be in a Hispanic area and ordered the police presence maintained.

Deke and Joseph crouched in front of both bodies and noted the similarities to all the previous cases. Almost everything with this guy was a head shot. He seemed to revel in blowing people's faces off. They knew it couldn't have anything to do with trying to conceal the victim's identity; there were too many other ways to ID the bodies. It appeared to be his gimmick, another kind of MO to show the police who they were dealing with, as if the sick note dropped on the woman's body here weren't quite enough.

Deke pointed out to Joseph that the man had to be the first one shot because the woman fell slightly on top of him. It wasn't much of a revelation considering that, at all the other scenes where a man was found, that man was always the first one shot. It could have been that the killer wanted to take away any chance of the victims defeating him. He might not be comfortable with the possibility of physical confrontation.

Deke thought right away of Jesper and his small size. He quickly dismissed the thought. He still felt that Jesper was not capable of pulling something like this off and didn't want his eager-to-solve-this-case brain talking him into it. What they really needed was the marine guy. Whether he was the killer or not, it would be good for the public perception just to see him coming in for questioning. He had a background that the news reporters could happily focus on. He was nowhere to be found, and however, at the moment that put him at the top of the list of suspects.

Deke and Joseph finished their business at the scene and went back to headquarters to brief Captain Murray. When they walked into his office, he looked physically and mentally drained. The case was wearing on him probably more than on anyone else due to the pressure put on him by the people both above him and below him on the chain of command. It was an unfair hassle, but it was one that came with the territory.

He sat in his chair licking the wounds from another chewing-out session with the commissioner. They were becoming more redundant and more hostile with every murder. The only thing keeping the commissioner from outright replacing Murray as the head of the Homicide Unit was that, deep down, he knew that it would be viewed as strictly a face-value move. Captain Murray wasn't doing anything less than anyone else in his position would have been doing. At the moment, the killer was just better than the police. It was simple arithmetic.

The three men walked over to Ronnie's desk, where all of the information was gathered. Ronnie had been sent over to Brooklyn to conduct interviews at the Bed-Stuy murder scene, although he wasn't enamored with the idea of seeing eight dead kids in one spot.

Deke couldn't make heads or tails of Ronnie's system for sorting the information. Rather than digging around and screwing up all that Ronnie had done to that point, he tried calling Ronnie on his cell phone. The call wouldn't connect.

"Yo, Cap," Deke said. "You got Ronnie's cell number? Mine ain't goin' through."

Captain Murray pulled his phone and gave it a shot. Wherever Ronnie was at the moment, he was either out of signal range or just in a bad signal area.

Joseph suggested they get the phone number of the house where the murders took place and call that. It was bound to still be working, and one of the CSU guys just might answer it. It was as good an idea as any, so Captain Murray went with it. He grabbed one of the rookie detectives, one of the guys just promoted and assigned to go-for duty. They weren't yet seasoned in the art of investigation, but they sure could do things no one else wanted to do, like file papers, run errands, and get coffee.

He returned a few minutes later and informed Captain Murray that someone did pick the phone up at the murder scene and said that Ronnie had shown up there but left soon after.

"Did he tell anyone where he was goin'?" Deke asked.

"Not that they told me, Deke. He might be on his way back."

Deke looked at Captain Murray. "He probably went to the other scene on Third Av. Ronnie wouldn't cut it short." He spoke again to the rookie detective. "Same thing as before. Get the number of the other scene and see if Ronnie's there. If you get him, transfer the call in here."

"OK, no problem."

Deke looked at the mess on Ronnie's desk. He knew there was some kind of method to the madness but resisted trying to figure it out. Any kind of disruption to Ronnie's system could set things back a few hours while it was being redone. Deke tried Ronnie's number again to no avail.

"Where the hell is this guy, China?"

"That's where I'd be if I were him." Joseph smiled.

"Hey, Cap, we gotta do somethin' with all these reporters sniffin' around every crime scene. They're like friggin' cockroaches all over the place. I'm startin' to get really pissed with this nonsense."

"Well, get used to them, Deke. There's nothing you can do about it. You want to stop them? Catch the guy they're following you about."

"Thanks, Cap. I never woulddda thought of that."

Deke grabbed one of Ronnie's suspect lists and noted how he really did seem ahead of the curve when it came to nailing down potential leads.

Joseph took out the new recording device he'd gotten from another agent and whispered into it. "Deke doesn't have a clue," he said and then soft-tossed it over the desk. Deke caught it and played it into his ear.

"Funny," he responded and then recorded his own insult to Joseph and threw the device back over the desk. It was childish, but it was a way to pass some time until Ronnie was contacted.

Deke had the device in his ear playing Joseph's latest insult when the rookie detective hurried back into the room. There was a look of urgency on his face, and his breathing rate was up.

"What's the matter?" Deke asked, rolling his chair backward and turning it to face the detective. "Somethin' happen with Ronnie?"

"I think you need to see this," he said, holding out a few papers.

Deke took the papers and scanned them quickly. Joseph watched as the rookie detective first pointed to a spot on one page for Deke to see, then to another on the next page that would gain his interest.

Deke's eyes went back and forth between the two, making sure he absorbed them correctly. His head snapped immediately in the direction of the rookie detective. "Is this right?" he asked. "You sure about this?"

"Yes, sir. I checked it a few times," the detective said. "There's no mistake."

Captain Murray started moving in their direction. "What is it, Deke?"

"It looks like our first big break." He turned to the kid again. "Go double-check this some more. I want a hundred percent on this!"

Captain Murray and Joseph came around the other side of the desk so they could see what Deke had. He pointed it out carefully to them.

"Look right here," he said, alluding to the phone number

from the Bed-Stuy scene. "Then look at this one," he said of the Third Avenue number. "They're the same. Different area codes but the same number. This guy might be goin' by phone numbers!"

"Phone fucking numbers?" Captain Murray said. "That's how he's picking them?"

"If that's the case," Joseph said, "then Jesper has to go back to the top of the list. He's got the easiest access to that kind of information."

"Motherfucker," Deke replied. "It's gotta be him! All this time and he was right in front of us. What the hell was I thinkin'?"

"Hang on," Captain Murray said. "Don't be so quick to drop your instincts, Deke. This could still be someone randomly picking people from a phone book."

Deke kept staring at the numbers. They were jumping out at him for some reason.

"What is it, Deke?" Joseph asked.

"I don't know. I've seen these phone numbers before. Can't place 'em, though."

"Do you remember where you were when you saw them?"

"It feels like I was right here."

Joseph took the papers from Deke. "Let's try something. I've seen this done before. Go sit down over there and close your eyes, and I'll read them off to you. If you hear them enough, it might trigger something."

Deke moved to a more comfortable chair, sat down, and tried to clear his mind. It didn't do much good.

"You ready?"

"Not really, but give it a shot anyhow."

Joseph read the numbers carefully. He didn't want to get any wrong. "555-0870." He repeated it over and over. "555-0870. Anything?"

"Not yet. Keep repeatin' 'em, though. It'll come eventually."

The rookie detective came back and told Deke that the numbers had been checked and rechecked and that there was no error. While Deke listened to him, Joseph stood off to the side, continually repeating the numbers in hopes that Deke's subconscious would somehow click. It didn't take long.

A look of bewilderment came over Deke's face. "Holy shit, Ku-Jo," he said calmly. "That actually fuckin' worked. I got it." He took hold of the rookie detective's arm and walked out of the room with him, filling his ears with instructions the whole way. On his way back in, he stopped and dug through all the wastebaskets in the office.

"What the hell are you looking for?" Captain Murray shouted over.

"This," Deke yelled back as he pulled out a copy of the newspaper and held it up.

"Deke," Captain Murray said, exasperated. "Tell me the goddam answer!"

"Lottery numbers! He's usin' the fuckin' lottery numbers! Look here," he said, pointing to a panel in the newspaper that showed the previous day's drawings. "Five five five was the number in yesterday's midday Pick Three—"

"Yeah," Joseph said. "That's right. I remember, we had five oh nine and five five five came out."

"Hold on," Deke said. "It gets better. Look at the Win Four. Zero eight seven zero."

"We need to go back over every murder scene file and get a list of the phone numbers and see if they match up to the daily numbers," Captain Murray said.

"I just sent the kid out to do that, Cap. He's gettin' all that info now."

"The friggin' daily numbers," Captain Murray repeated. "Unbelievable."

"So much for pickin' 'em randomly from the phone book, huh?"

"We need to go find Jesper," Joseph said.

"Let's see what the kid brings back first. I don't feel like hearing from Jesper's lawyers on top of all the other crap that's been in my ears," Captain Murray said.

The rookie detective came back with a list of all the phone numbers from the murder scenes in one hand and a list of the previous week's daily numbers in the other. In every case they matched perfectly. The number that came out in the midday drawing coincided exactly with the phone number at the victims' address on every occasion. The connection had finally been made. The system of how the killer chose his victims had been cracked. Everything kept coming back to Jesper. He was the only one on the list who had access to phone numbers, names, and addresses.

"Why would he skip Christmas, though?" Joseph wondered aloud.

The kid was already on that one. "There's no numbers drawn on Christmas Day in New York," he answered. "The guy in the booth downstairs told me."

Deke looked at his watch. "It's one thirty, shit! The number came out already. It's not on the list here. Go now! Find out that fuckin' number and get it back here!"

"There's a number on there you can call and get the daily number," the kid answered.

Deke found the number and dialed it quickly. He scribbled down the numbers and slammed down the phone. "Two five seven and one five two zero."

"What now?" Joseph asked.

Deke pulled some business cards from his wallet and fumbled through them. He found the one he was looking for and dialed the number on it. "Yeah, gimme Mr. Trebor, right away, police business. Yeah, tell him it's Detective Durgess."

The phone call was transferred.

"Line repair, Trebor speaking, how may I help you?"

"Mr. Trebor, it's Detective Durgess, me and my partner were in your office the other day."

"Yes, Detective, I remember. What can I do for you?"

"Listen, I need to know where Jesper is right now."

"He's out in the field on a repair job . . . in Bay Ridge, I think. Why?"

"We need to talk to him immediately. Some new information just came in that he might be able to help us with."

"OK, I'll page him and have him call you—"

"No! Do not have him call me. Just find out exactly where he is, and you call me back and tell me."

"What is going on with him, Detective?"

"Nothin'. We believe Jesper might somehow be involved in a situation we're dealin' with right now. Just call him, find out where he is, and let me know. Whatever you do, don't tip him off we're lookin' for him. If he gets an idea that we are, I'm comin' after *you*."

"OK, Detective. There's no need for threats. I'll call you back. I still have your card."

"Good. Listen, there's one more thing I want you to do for me."

"I'm listening."

"I'm gonna give you a phone number. I want you to gimme the names and addresses of the people at those numbers in all the area codes in the city. How long will it take you to get me that info?"

"I can do it immediately. Give me the number."

"555-1520. You get that? 555-1520."

"Hold on, I'm running it."

Deke could hear the sound of Trebor typing the numbers into his computer keyboard. He was actually humming Christmas songs while he did it.

"OK, here we go," Trebor said. "Only one address comes up in the five boroughs. 555-1520, right?"

"Right. Where is it?"

"That number is assigned to a Michael Marotta, address is 4343 Amboy Road, Staten Island, New York. You need the zip code?"

"No," Deke said as he wrote down the information. "Just find Jesper and don't forget what I told you."

Deke threw the phone on the desk, and Joseph took it and hung it up. Deke sat down and tapped his knuckles on the desk. "Ku-Jo, are any of your FBI buddies good at computer hacking?"

"I can find a few real easy, yeah. What do you need?"

"Get a couple over to Jesper's office and have them go through his computer and see if he traced any of the victims' addresses through his computer. It's time to start tyin' him into this thing."

"OK, right away."

"Listen!" Deke yelled as Joseph was leaving the room, stopping him. "Make sure they get Trebor's permission to do it so we don't gotta deal with no legal mumbo-jumbo from him. Have him put it in writin'."

"Anything else?"

Deke thought for a second. "No. I'll have one of my guys call a judge and get him to fast-track a search warrant in case we find somethin'. I don't wanna run into no illegal search and seizure crap."

"Gotcha," Joseph said, then left.

Captain Murray, who had stepped out a minute earlier, returned. "I just got off the phone with the Staten Island detective squad. They're sending a couple of detectives to the Marotta house right now. Let's come up with a plan to nail this bastard."

"Already got one, Cap."

"Let me hear it."

"When we get Jesper's whereabouts, we'll stick a tail right on him. Multiple tails, we don't want him gettin' suspicious that we're followin' him. One tail can pass him off to the next. We get ourselves set up in this guy Marotta's house, take the family out, and me and Joseph'll be in there for the arrest. We close down the whole street, hidin' cops in bushes if we have to. Soon as he knocks on the door, we swarm him and take him down. He won't know what hit him."

"OK, sounds good. Call the Aviation Unit at Floyd Bennett Field. I want a helicopter with infrared standing by just in case Jesper somehow slips through."

"He ain't slippin' anywhere this time, Cap. Today, it's *his* turn to become the victim."

"Listen, Deke, you're in charge of that scene. Take only the guys you know you can trust. I don't want anything slipping out that can screw this collar up. Remember, you're in a residential area. No shooting unless absolutely necessary. I want this guy brought in alive. The public is going to want to see him dragged through a trial."

Deke's first thought was of Joseph and his promise. "I just gotta keep Ku-Jo from pullin' his gun," he said with a smile to the captain.

"I'll be right back," Murray said. "Let me go bring this to the commissioner and get everybody off our backs."

"Listen," Deke yelled to him as he was on his way out. "When you hear from Ronnie, tell him to call me. I want him there on this one."

"Yeah, will do!" Murray shouted back.

Joseph returned and informed Deke that an FBI team of computer wizards was on the way to Jesper's office to search his computer. Deke sat Joseph down and convinced him not to take any aggressive action against Jesper other than arresting him. If Jesper just happened to get a broken jaw or leg or something during the arrest due to a slip of Joseph's powerful arm, well, that was his own tough luck, but he *would* be taken alive. Joseph agreed, so long as he knew he could get a couple of free fists in on Jesper's face. Again, he was informed he'd be at the back of a very long line.

Deke assembled a crew of fifteen cops and detectives that he was familiar with and felt he could trust. They were a gritty, hard-nosed bunch that could be counted on not to lose control and blow the takedown of a suspect by moving in too early.

They all loaded into an NYPD passenger van for the ride to Staten Island, and Deke briefed them on the situation and how they would handle it. At some point on the Gowanus Expressway, Deke got the call from Trebor telling him exactly where Jesper was and what stops he had left. Joseph took that information and called it in to Captain Murray, who set off a string of tailing teams that would never let Jesper out of their sight no matter where he went. One team would follow him for a while and then pass him off to another that was just ahead of them. There were over fifty detectives and a helicopter assigned to the tail at varying points along the way. Jesper, on his very best day, would have no chance of shaking those following him, even if he knew they were there.

The van arrived at the location, and Deke could see right away that it was the perfect setup for him and his men. There were trees and bushes all over the street that were ideal for concealing men ready to pounce. The streetlights were the dim kind and set far away from each other. The house where the potential victim lived had a small front porch that was enclosed on two sides, leaving the front door and the steps leading down to the sidewalk as the only means of escape. Once Jesper got in there, he could immediately be taken down before he even knew what was going on.

Deke rang the front doorbell and was greeted by the two Staten Island detectives sent in earlier. Once the ID thing was done and everybody knew who everyone was, Deke got down to work assigning people to different spots on the block so as to trap Jesper in a web of cops no matter where he was on the street.

News from the tail came in. Jesper was still in Brooklyn, under surveillance and having a cup of coffee at a restaurant on Eighty-ninth Street and Fourth Avenue. Some of the guys wanted to take him down right then and there, but Deke knew better. No one knew if he had the weapon on him at the time; as crafty as he was, he could have planted it somewhere along the way to be picked up just before he arrived at the scene. It wasn't by accident that there was never any evidence left behind at these scenes. Deke now believed that it was due to very careful preparation, hurriedly done, but careful nonetheless. This Jesper was a real cutie-pie, Deke thought, in the way he charmed himself through the interview at headquarters. He really passed himself off as a schlep, one who couldn't even balance a checkbook, let alone plan to kill thirty-four people and then do it. Deke would never make the mistake of underestimating him again.

Deke walked into the house and met Mr. Marotta and his very shaken wife, Eileen, sitting on the couch. He pulled up a chair and sat in front of them. "Mr. and Mrs. Marotta, I'm Detective Durgess of Manhattan Homicide. Did these other detectives fill you in on what's happenin'?"

"A little bit," the husband said. "Mostly they've been guarding doors and windows and moving all over the place."

"OK, good. That's what they're supposed to be doin'." Deke took notice of Mrs. Marotta. "Are you OK, ma'am?"

"She tends to get rather nervous, Detective," Mr. Marotta answered. "She'll be all right."

"I'm OK," she said.

"OK, listen, everything is fine now, I want you to know that. You're not in any danger whatsoever. You guys have heard of the Daily Killer, right?"

They both nodded.

"OK, we have reason to believe that your address was to be the next one hit."

"Oh my God," the wife said in a shaky voice.

"Relax, honey," Mr. Marotta said. "What do you mean, our address, Detective?"

"The guy that's killin' people seems to be usin' phone numbers and addresses to choose his victims. Yours, we think, is next, probably tonight."

"What are you planning to do?"

"Well, first thing we're gonna do is get you and your wife outta here. You got any kids gonna be comin' home?"

"We have one, a daughter. She has autism, Detective, and she's asthmatic. She's upstairs. We can't be taking her out of the house. All her medication is here, and the nebulizer she needs to administer it is, too."

"We'll see to her care, sir. We really would be more comfortable if you guys weren't in the house."

"Are you expecting this guy to make it inside my house?"

"Not at all. We'll be takin' him down outside."

"Then my family and I should be safe inside. My daughter won't handle the disruption well, Detective, if we move her. We'll stay inside while you do your job outside."

"Unit 63 to Car 509, K."

Deke excused himself, got up, and pulled his walkie-talkie out of his back pocket. "Car 509 go, K."

"Detective, this is Unit 63. Be advised that the suspect is on the move, K."

"10-4. Gimme his current location, K."

"He just hopped an express bus at Fourth Avenue and Ninety-second. It's headed for the Verrazano Bridge, K."

"Are you in pursuit, K?"

"10-4. We have him until the other side of the bridge. Unit 49 will pick him up at the tollbooths, K."

"Unit 49 on a break to Car 509, K."

"509 go."

"Deke, it's Jimmy. We're at the tolls. We'll get him when he comes over."

"OK, Jimmy, very good. Listen, get the route number off that bus. I want the MTA called, and I want a car at every one of its stops. I wanna know exactly where he gets off, K."

"10-4, Deke. We won't lose him. Let's try to keep this channel clear so I can get right through to you if anything happens, K."

"10-4, will do."

"Unit 63 on a break to Unit 49, K."

"49 go."

"We're approaching tollbooth twenty-three. It's an E-ZPass booth, K."

"Yeah, 10-4, we see you. OK, you can let the bus go now. We'll take him from here, K."

"10-4. Unit 63 breaking off."

Deke continued to monitor the conversation until the bus hit the Staten Island Expressway. The sun was beginning to go down, and he realized that the time was fast approaching when the killer would make his appearance at the Marotta household.

Deke grabbed Joseph and had him try to talk some sense

into the Marottas while he was outside making sure everyone was in position and, at the same time, going over any last-minute details.

Everybody knew his role in the thing, and they were all champing at the bit to get to the killer. They all knew this was history in the making, and each man was completely committed to getting it right. No one would take even one second off until this guy was facedown on the street with cuffs slapped on his wrists.

Deke returned to the house and was greeted by a downtrodden Joseph.

"No luck, huh?"

"They refuse to leave, Deke. I don't know what to do with them."

Deke looked at his watch and then at the setting sun. "Shit. We ain't got no time to force these people outta this place. We're gonna have to work around 'em."

"Yeah, OK. We'll stick them up on the second floor. They'll be safe up there."

Both men went and talked to the homeowners and told them exactly what was expected of them: to stay out of their way and harm's way. The daughter was nervous and upset by the presence of the two strangers in her house, but her parents did their best to quell her fears, eventually getting her to sleep.

It was a waiting game. They were all in position and on their toes, but the anxiety of the wait was getting to them. The guys in the street had earphones connected to their walkie-talkies so no sound would be emitted from the speakers. They practiced holding their breath so that the killer wouldn't notice any misty clouds coming from behind bushes and trees and such that would tip him off. Everything was set and ready to go.

Deke stood by the front door and peeked out the window. The block was empty as far as he could see. He knew where all his guys were hiding, and he couldn't see any sign of them. It was a perfect setup.

The walkie-talkie in his pocket was called by one of the outside units.

"Unit 49 to Car 509, K."

Deke pulled it from his pocket and held it to his mouth. "509 go."

"Deke, your guy just got off the bus at Richmond Avenue and Amboy. He's walking your way. Unit 52 has got him now. They're on foot a half block behind. They can't contact you, though. He might hear, K."

"Did he make any stops, K?"

"Negative. Straight trip so far. He is wheeling what appears to be a tool case of some sort behind him, K."

"OK, 10-4. Listen, stand by at that location in case he does a turnaround, K."

"Will do, Deke. Good luck and be safe, 49 clear."

It was game time, and Deke was at the ready. He put the talkie to his mouth again. "509 to all units, 509 to all units. Be advised suspect is approximately two blocks away. Everybody get ready, and don't move until my order."

All the other units quickly and quietly responded that the order was received and understood. Deke pulled his gun and took the safety off. Joseph stood at the ready next to him, his gun also drawn.

Deke checked the doorknob to make sure he could pull it in a flash and get outside before the suspect knew what was happening. A whisper came over his walkie-talkie.

"All units, be advised suspect has entered the block. He is walking down the center of the street."

Deke pulled the curtain a bit more and saw Jesper come into view. He moved up the street like he didn't have a care in the world. Perhaps it was his way of not drawing any suspicion to himself.

The hearts were pounding in Deke's and Joseph's chests. The endgame was upon them. Deke's hand gripped the doorknob tightly as he watched Jesper ambling up the dimly lit street.

His head bobbed from side to side as he scanned the addresses on the houses, looking for his target. As he neared the Marotta house, Deke whispered into his walkie-talkie for all units to stay ready.

Suddenly, Jesper's head turned to the other side of the street, and he moved his head forward as if struggling to see something in the distance. He stood there for a second or two looking around from side to side and front to back. The breaths from his mouth formed sticky clouds in the cold winter air that would hover for a second or two and then dissipate into nothingness.

"What the hell's he doin'?" Deke muttered to Joseph. "Come this way, asswipe. We're over here."

Jesper unbuttoned his coat and started for the house across the street. Deke's stomach nearly exploded as he saw the suspect moving toward an address that was occupied by innocent, unsuspecting, *unprotected* civilians.

"Fuck!" he whispered to Joseph. He grabbed his walkie-talkie again. "Five oh nine to all units, move on him, move on him! Take him down now!"

In the blink of an eye there were people all over the street. Jesper saw cops everywhere, running toward him, holding up badges and guns and telling him to get down on the ground. He immediately reached into his pocket and was blindside-tackled from behind by a burly 6'4" cop who used to be a linebacker in college. It was the old shock-and-awe technique that cops all over the country loved to employ, to completely overwhelm a suspect before he has the chance to react. The cop kept his 243 pounds on top of a stunned and now incoherent Jesper while others came over and cuffed him.

Deke and Joseph had burst out of the house shortly before Jesper went down and were now standing over him, guns drawn. The NYPD helicopter was hovering high above, shining its bright spotlight on the madness below.

People had heard the commotion going on outside and were sticking their heads from doors and windows. The cops were on loudspeakers urging them to go back inside.

Jesper was beginning to come around, and Deke knelt down next to him and had the officer pinning his face to the ground relent so he could see his eyes clearly.

"Hey, Jesper. I bet you're pretty fuckin' surprised to see me, huh?"

Jesper was still somewhat in shock, his voice not yet available after getting the wind knocked out of him. He tried to speak. It just wasn't there.

"Search him," Deke said forcefully, "and search that tool thing there. Find me that gun."

A couple of the detectives did as ordered and went though Jesper's pockets and tool case. No gun was found. No note either. The only things he had on him were his wallet, phone, and tools. In his front right-hand pocket was a piece of paper with the address of the house he was headed to. Deke ordered a search of the entire street for the gun in case Jesper had planted it there at some earlier time. It was time to interrogate.

"Get him up and sit him on the sidewalk over there," Deke ordered. "Somebody get this guy some water. Let's bring him around a bit."

One of the cops squirted a bottle of spring water onto Jesper's head, and Deke softly slapped his face a few times. Deke saw coherence come back into his eyes.

"Where'd ya put the gun, Jesper?" Deke asked, right in his face.

"What gun?" was the groggy answer. "What is all of this?"

Deke took a fistful of Jesper's collar. "Listen, don't fuck with me. The game's over. Where is the goddam gun!"

"I don't have a freaking gun!" He started crying. "Why are you doing this to me?"

Deke slapped his face again, this time a little harder, to bring him back. "Cut the shit. I ain't fallin' for it."

"I don't have a gun!" Jesper yelled.

Another slap. "Then what are you doing on this street?"

A complete look of confusion came across Jesper's face. His voice got very soft. "What do you mean, 'what are you doing on this street?' You sent me here. Don't you remember?"

"What the fuck are you talkin' about? Why would I send you here?"

"I don't know. You called me about three o'clock, didn't you? You told me to be here by six."

Deke grabbed him tighter and lifted him to his feet. Jesper was on the tips of his toes as Deke held him to his eye level. "I never called you. Stop the shit. Tell me where the gun is."

Jesper was panic-stricken, and Deke could see it was real. His eyes held Jesper's, and he listened intently to Jesper's shrilly and shaky voice as he repeated his claims that a phone call was made to him that sent him off to that address, a phone call that came from Deke himself.

Deke's brain went into overdrive. What if there was some truth to this? Jesper's body language didn't indicate subterfuge— but why the hell would Jesper receive a call sending him to this address when he was already expected at the one across the street? There would be no reason. Suddenly, a cold shiver ran down Deke's spine, and his eyes widened as big as anyone had ever seen.

"Jesus Christ! No!" he hollered and pushed Jesper down onto his backside. He pointed to two of the cops standing there. "You two guys watch him!" He took off running to the other side of the street. His head spun back quickly. "Everyone else come with me! Now!" he screamed.

Deke bounded over the four short steps leading up to the door of the Marotta household as he jumped to the porch. He noticed that the front door was ajar, although he couldn't remember if he left it that way when he and Joseph tore out of it a few minutes earlier. He threw up his left hand, stopping Joseph and all the other cops in their tracks. Slowly, he pushed the door open the rest of the way and peeked inside. An oblong puddle of red liquid was slowly oozing its way across the floor from an area Deke couldn't quite see unless he stuck his head in farther. He didn't need to see the origin of the puddle, though. The puddle was one he was all too familiar with, one he had seen too many times in the last week. He turned his head to all the cops standing at the foot of the stairs. They all could see the urgency in his face. "Half of you that way," he shouted as he pointed to one side of the house. "The other half go that way," he yelled while pointing to the other. "Seal the sides and back of this house off! No one comes out! Ku-Jo, you're with me."

Both men had their guns pulled, and Deke gave Joseph a little nod that alerted him they were going in. Deke ran in first and threw himself up against a wall for protection in case anyone was still in there. Joseph moved quickly into the doorway and covered the room so Deke would be free to move around.

The first thing Deke noticed was the cause of the oozing puddle. He followed the trail right back to the head of Mr. Marotta. He was lying on the floor by the front windows, his still fresh brains sliding down the wall above him. Strapped into his hand was the video camera he had been using to secretly tape the arrest of Jesper, a video he figured was going to be priceless to the news organizations. The camera had been smashed and stepped on, the tape in it destroyed.

The body was still twitching slightly, and on top of it was a haphazardly placed note, one that looked like it was dropped in a hurry rather than gently set down. BETTER LUCK NEXT TIME, it read.

Deke's thoughts immediately turned to the wife and daughter. He and Joseph moved slowly from room to room in search of anything that stirred, their guns out ahead of them in direct line of sight with their eyes. They could hear the other cops outside the locked windows, talking and planning with each other what to do if the killer found a way out. That wasn't going to happen, as far as Deke and Joseph were concerned. If the guy was still in the house, he'd be going out on a stretcher or, better yet, in a body bag.

With the front of the house behind them and cleared, the kitchen in the back was next up. Deke started to make his way in and then threw up a quick fist to Joseph, stopping him cold. He turned and mouthed the word "body" and then continued forward, very slowly. On the floor near the refrigerator was the body of Mrs. Marotta. She had been shot once in the chest at fairly close range. Her body had fallen in a heap, and her leg was grotesquely twisted behind her, but it was her face that captured Deke's attention most. "Look," he whispered to Joseph. "Look at the face. He cracked her with the gun. See the bruisin'? Fuck knocked her cold before he killed her. Probably did that so he could cap the husband so he wouldn't hear the shot when he took her out. Knocked her out, went and blew him away, then came back here and finished the job."

"Where is he?" Joseph whispered back urgently. "He didn't have a lot of time to do this. Gotta still be here."

Deke looked out the back window and could see more of his men as they took up positions in the yard. "Upstairs!"

The stairs were going to be a difficult task to accomplish. If the killer jumped out from above while Deke and Joseph were still coming up, they would be trapped like fish in a barrel. They walked up slowly, back to back. Deke had everything in front of them while Joseph covered everything behind. As they neared the top of the stairs, the faint hum of medical equipment made its way into their ears.

No words were exchanged between Deke and Joseph. A tap on the shoulder and a nod in the direction of the sound was all that was needed. Deke slowly pushed open the door to the daughter's room. It was dimly lit by a small lamp with a fifteen-watt bulb in the corner to provide just enough light to keep her calm at night.

Both men entered the room, moving silently. Joseph turned and focused on the door in case someone snuck up from behind. Deke slid over to the daughter and had a look at her. He could see her chest rising and falling in the dim light, and there appeared to be no signs of trauma on her whatsoever. He quietly checked the rest of the room for the killer and then got on his walkie-talkie. Whispering into it, he called for a team of four cops to come in and do a sweep of the entire house. The others were to remain outside and make sure nothing slipped past. He also told someone to contact the medical examiner and get him there on the double.

Deke and Joseph moved outside the daughter's room and carefully pulled the door shut. They continued through the second floor, which was also the top floor, looking for any sign of the killer. It was clear. Joseph looked at Deke and shrugged.

"He didn't have no time to go killin' the kid," Deke said. "He was probably in and out."

Deke took one of the cops and stationed him outside the kid's door. If by chance she woke up, there was no need for her to go downstairs and see Mom and Dad like that. It also didn't hurt to have a cop there just in case they missed something during their search.

Joseph and Deke went back outside, and Deke immediately got on his cell phone to Captain Murray.

"What's going on there, Deke!" Murray asked angrily. "I'm hearing there's problems there."

"I'll tell ya what's goin' on, Cap," Deke answered, just as angry. "We got a fuckin' leak somewhere! That's the problem!"

"What are you talking about?"

"I'm talkin' about a dirty fuckin' cop doin' this shit."

The comment was met with silence. Captain Murray was steaming on the other end. "I thought you settled on Jesper!" he finally yelled. "How the hell are we back to square one again?"

"Relax, Cap. We ain't back at square one."

"Well, if you're gonna accuse a cop, Deke, you better have something solid."

"Listen, someone with inside information called Jesper and changed the plan. We got taken out of the house on the distraction, and someone went in and killed the homeowners. They probably got .38 caliber slugs in their heads, and most of the guys here are carryin' .38s. This is the first place to look."

"You're gonna make a lot of enemies with this shit, Dckc. Cops don't like being accused."

"I don't care. Look, it might be one of us at the scene here, it might not, I don't know yet—but someone with intimate fuckin' knowledge of the situation pulled this off." He paused a moment while he gathered his thoughts. "Listen, as much as I hate to say this, Cap, I think we're gonna have to take a look at Ronnie

234

maybe. I mean, we ain't heard from him since this mornin'. Where the hell is he?"

"Don't know. He's still MIA."

"OK, if he shows up, make sure he calls me. I'll find out what's goin' on with him. He's probably just doin' his own thing."

"OK, will do. Listen, did you do a sweep of that house there?"

"It's bein' done now. Nothin' in there so far, and I'm willin' to bet nothin' will be found, neither."

"Are all your guys at the scene accounted for?"

"Yeah, I know where everyone is. If it is one of us, I don't think he'll be stupid enough to make himself conspicuously absent."

"OK, I'm sending a team of forensics cops there now. No one leaves the scene! We'll grab all their guns for ballistics tests and check their hands for gunpowder residue. If it's someone there, we'll nail him."

"Good, good—but listen Cap, it might not just be a cop here. How many people up there knew, not countin' Ronnie?"

The question was met with resentment. "Just me and the commissioner, Deke. I'm pretty sure I know I didn't do it. You think I should go up there and arrest *him*?" Murray answered snottily.

"No, Cap, c'mon, stop bein' ridiculous. It's just that we got a leak somewhere with this thing. If it ain't Ronnie, then it could be someone else up there. I'm just tryin' to nail it down, that's all. Maybe if someone up there overheard you guys talkin' about it. That could be it."

"Yeah, whatever. I'll check it out. You make sure no one leaves that scene."

"Understood." Deke stuffed the phone back in his pocket and called Joseph over.

"What the hell's going on here, Deke?"

"C'mere," Deke said, pulling him off to the side. "Listen, we got a leak somewhere here. I don't know who it is yet, but everyone's under suspicion. They could be workin' alone or workin' with someone, I don't know."

"Well, Jesper's off the list now, that's for sure."

"Unless he's workin' with the killer. Could be an accomplice. Anyhow, someone here is definitely in on it."

"What are you gonna do?"

"I got a bunch of forensics guys on the way. They're gonna test everyone's gun and hands."

"Here you go," Joseph said, handing over his gun.

"Keep it," Deke told him. "I know it ain't you."

"You sure? I'm the one no one here really knows."

"It ain't you. Stop the shit. You been with me constantly. I can't have you out of the loop. You're the only one here I trust right now."

"Thank you," Joseph said genuinely.

"Listen, get back in the house. Stand outside the kid's room with the cop that's there. If it is one of us, I don't want him sneakin' in and finishin' the job."

"Got it," Joseph answered and ran off in the direction of the house.

Deke walked back over to Jesper, who was still sitting on the curb with cops standing over him. "Get him up," he said to the cops.

Jesper was lifted to his feet. Deke took hold of his arm. "C'mon, Jesper, we're goin' for a walk. You guys stay here," he said to the cops.

Deke and Jesper walked off into the darkness, and when Deke was sure they were out of sight and sound, he pushed Jesper up against a telephone pole. "I'm tellin' you right now, come clean with me or I'll shoot ya right here. Who the fuck called you and sent you there? Who you workin' with?"

Jesper looked at the gun in Deke's hand and had no doubt he was for real. "No one! I swear to God. I thought it was you that called me."

"Bullshit!" The gun was raised and shoved under Jesper's chin.

"No! Don't! I'm not lying. Some guy called me up, said it was you, said he needed my help to catch the killer. I thought I was doing the right thing."

"Where'd he call you?"

"On my cell phone. It came up UNAVAILABLE on my screen."

"Gimme the phone."

"I don't have it anymore. One of the cops back there took it when they went though my pockets."

The gun was shoved harder into his jaw.

"Please! Stop! I'm telling you the truth!"

Deke's head dropped. He knew that if the dirty cop had the phone, it was certainly gone forever. Before they went back to the scene, he lowered the gun and grabbed Jesper by the throat. "I'm tellin' ya right now, you're gonna take a polygraph. We'll find out if you're tellin' the truth. I kid you not, I see one squiggly line on there and I'm blowing your head off. We clear on that?"

The forensics team arrived at the scene and confiscated the guns of all cops and detectives on location. Many of them were not very pleased at the implication that they were dirty. Deke didn't much like being the one accusing them, either. There was no choice in the matter. One of them was dirty, probably a killer also if he didn't have an accomplice carrying out the deed for him. The lines had to be drawn. The innocent cops would under-stand later.

Deke called Captain Murray before deciding to head back

to the hotel. The whole night was a half inch short of the straw that broke the camel's back. He was drained, mentally and physically, and needed a night in quiet surroundings to recharge. He considered going over to Frannie's house, but he knew she'd pick up from his face that the job was in his mind more than ever.

Captain Murray answered the phone; he sounded weird.

"Yo, Cap, it's Deke. You OK?"

"I've been pulled out of the Homicide Unit, Deke. I'm being reassigned."

"Why?"

"The commissioner didn't like being made to look like a fool. We told him we had it nailed down, and now two more people are dead and it might be a cop doing it. Someone's head had to roll, and it wound up being mine."

"That's bullshit, Cap, and you know it! I'll talk to the commissioner. My head should roll, no one else's."

"Deke, you'll do nothing of the kind. We need this guy found, and you're the best shot to do that. Don't waste time fucking around with the stand-up guy routine. Go do your job."

"But it shouldn't be you."

"Well, that's the way it goes. You wanna redeem this fucking situation? Go catch this bastard!"

Deke paused a second. "Will do." The phone was hung up, and he reflected on the situation. Kicking Murray out was a knee-jerk reaction by the commissioner, but it was one that was fairly common when public eyes were watching a situation very closely. Someone always had to fall on the sword to appease the blood-thirsty masses. In this case, Captain Murray filled the bill.

Deke called Joseph on his cell phone. "Ku-Jo, what's goin' on up there?"

"It's quiet. The little girl's still sleeping."

"Geez, the poor kid," Deke said sadly. "What's her life gonna be like now?"

"Probably not too good. What do you need?"

"They just kicked Captain Murray out of homicide. They made him the sacrificial lamb."

"Really?" Joseph answered, surprised. Then reality set in. "Yeah, I guess you could see that one coming. Not very fair, though."

"Not at all. Listen, I gotta get away from all this shit for a while. I need to go somewhere quiet where I can clear my mind and think about what's been goin' on here. I'm gonna head back to the hotel for a bit and sit in that Jacuzzi thing and relax. It's gonna take a couple hours for the forensic results to come back anyhow on these guns and powder burn tests. I really need to clear my head."

He didn't sound good, and Joseph knew he needed a break. "OK, Deke. Go do it. If anything comes up, I'll call your cell."

"All right, listen . . ."

"What?"

"Ronnie's still missin'. No one's heard from him."

Joseph knew where he was going with it. "It's not him, Deke. You've always trusted him, always could vouch for him. I mean, I thought about maybe checking him out, but then you set me straight. Now that I've gotten to know him a little, I just can't see him being involved in this. I doubt he went bad."

"Yeah, me, too, but if he don't show up or check in within the next hour, I want you to get a picture of him over to the girl in the hospital and see if it triggers anything. Do it real quietlike."

"Understood. Will do."

"Thanks, Ku-Jo. I'll catch ya later. You goin' to my place again or back to the hotel?"

"Your place. What am I gonna do? All the stuff I need is there now."

"Yeah, OK. Keep in touch!"

"Done."

"Hey, don't lose my key! It's the only one I got."

The ride back to the hotel was filled with nothing but flashbacks for Deke. He tried remembering the faces of all the cops that were on top of Jesper during the takedown to see if anyone was missing. It all happened so fast and was such a blur that he couldn't truly be sure about anyone. He parked the car in front of the hotel and marveled at the good fortune of finding a parking spot right outside. Usually there was a twenty-minute ritual of going around Manhattan blocks four or five times until something became available. After that it was the old hydrant maneuver. *At least something went right for me tonight*, he thought. He went upstairs, stripped down, and hopped in the tub. He sat there and felt truly frustrated at being upstaged by the killer at every turn. No one had ever given him a run like this. It was almost like he was chasing a carbon copy of himself.

Joseph, meanwhile, locked down the rest of the crime scene and then headed back to Deke's apartment. He unlocked the front door and turned on the lights. The apartment Deke had set up was filled with a ragtag assortment of furniture and other odds and ends. It was plain and unpainted, nothing fancy like the hotel room, but that was what was so special about it. It was more than a place to sleep, it was a home, and that was what Joseph found most appealing. It wasn't just a mass-produced, hurriedly thrown-together room designed purely for commercial use. This was individualized by someone in an effort to put the mind at ease after a long and trying day. Well, sort of. Joseph knew Deke hadn't put that much effort into it, but at least it was personalized.

He took his gun out and placed it on the table near the door.

He put his cell phone there, too. He reached into his pocket and pulled out the small leather wallet containing his badge. He stared at it for a second and then flung it across the room in frustration. It really pissed him off when the bad guys were one up on the cops. It pissed him off even more when the bad guy turned out to be a cop. He took a few steps into the living room and plopped down into the most comfortable-looking chair, an old brown La-Z-Boy recliner. He set it all the way back and kicked his feet up on the little pedestal thing that popped up. He closed his eyes and tried again to place faces at the scene even though he didn't know the names to go with them. His mind drifted to his daughter; she would soon be going to sleep, and he would need to call her to deliver her good-night story. He lamented that he'd left the phone on the table near the door and would actually have to get up to retrieve it. The La-Z-Boy really felt that good.

As he lay there with his head back and eyes shut, the faint scent of cigarette smoke entered his nostrils. He wasn't sure if it existed in reality or if it was his brain playing tricks on him. His eyes opened slowly, and he noticed a cloud of smoke pass him on the left, coming from behind him. Another one then came from the same location. A chill ran though his body, and his stomach felt sick. He wasn't alone in the room! Worse, whoever was there with him wasn't trying to hide. There was an intensive effort to be noticed.

Joseph's hand went right away for his waistband. *Shit!* he thought as he looked at the table near the front door and saw his gun lying there. He reached for the lever on the chair to lower himself so he could quickly spring up and get it.

"I don't think I'd do that, Detective," came a cold, gravelly voice behind him, one he'd clearly heard before but couldn't quite recognize. He then heard the sound of a gun being cocked.

His head turned slowly around to allow him a glimpse of his tormentor. The face hit his memory bank in the blink of an eye. Every fiber of Joseph's being seemed to collapse in on him as soon as he saw those pockmarked cheeks. They sucked in hard on a cigarette, and another plume of smoke flew arrogantly past Joseph's nose. It all made sense now. Jesper was just a patsy, an unwitting decoy in the whole thing. The real mastermind was standing behind Joseph with a gun pointed at his head, all the while smiling deviously and puffing on a filterless cancer stick.

"Why, you're not Detective Durgess," the man said with that nasty smile. "I got the FBI guy instead. Can you tell me where the good detective would be, please?"

"Trebor," Joseph said, disgusted with both the killer and himself. "How the hell did we not pick up on you?"

The gun was aimed angrily. "I said, where is the detective?"

"He's on his way; parking the car. He'll be here any second."

"Well, I guess I should make quick work of you, then," the man snarled as his grip on the gun tightened, "and get ready for our Rhodes Scholar."

"No, no, hold it." Joseph relented. "He's at the hotel with my FBI team."

"Will he be coming any time soon?"

"He's there for the night. Dammit," Joseph said angrily. "You slipped right through the fucking cracks!"

"I guess you only looked where you wanted to look, Mr. Agent," Trebor said in that trademark raspy voice. "You didn't look where you *should* have looked. Bad for you, good for me."

"You ever watch the show *Let's Make a Deal?*" Joseph asked, clearly behind the eight ball and looking for any way out.

The smile was gone from Trebor's face. "I've seen it once or twice. Two problems, though. One, you have nothing to trade, my friend. Second, only one door's gonna open here, and that's the one *I'm* gonna walk out of. You, I'm afraid, are gonna come up a loser."

Joseph slipped his hand into his pocket while he spoke, in hopes of finding anything in there that could be used as a weapon. The only thing he pulled out was a set of keys with a little electronic device on it. He admonished himself for not even bringing his ankle gun with him. After all Deke had told him, there just was no excuse for this lack of readiness, and he knew that it was going to cost him dearly.

Joseph started getting lightheaded as the reality of the situation began to set in. This was his Alamo. The time for action was fast approaching. If he was going to go down, he made up his mind that he was going to do it swinging. There was no other way he knew. If he could somehow get within arm's reach of Trebor, his hand speed would negate Trebor's gun; he'd be disarmed before he could pull the trigger. Then it would be fun time, when all that FBI anger-management stuff would go right out the window. Joseph could take a nation's worth of frustration and animosity out on the man's face. He was in no position to do that at the moment, though. He needed to get Trebor distracted somehow, needed to get him closer. The thought of throwing his keys at the man in hopes of disorienting him briefly spun through his mind. The idea was quickly dismissed.

Trebor's icy voice was back in his ears. "You were close, Mr. Agent. I gotta give you that. I thought you two had it figured out."

"I can't believe it," Joseph responded. "Izzot Trebor is the killer!"

"Fucking right, Dick Tracy! All this while. And guess what? I'm not done yet." He walked around the chair to face Joseph head-on. The gun was trained directly on Joseph's nose.

"How the hell did you find out where Deke lived?" Joseph

asked loudly, hoping someone somehow would hear him. It was useless, though. Deke rented in this building because the walls were extra-insulated and resistant to sounds coming through them. Neither man knew that, though.

"Hey, keep it down. You shout like that again, and I won't play with you anymore." The voice was so sinister and so unfeeling that Joseph wondered how Trebor fooled so many people. "If you must know, I found the place by the phone number the good detective was stupid enough to put on a card for me. Couldn't have been easier. I wanted to keep this game going on a bit longer, but you guys were starting to get a little too close."

Joseph felt a little let down by Deke. It was a stupid mistake putting his home number on his business card.

"Did you like the way I sent Jesper over to the house across the street? I figured that would get both of you out of there. Boy, did I laugh when I saw you guys jumping on that schmuck. Didn't you see me there?"

"You think if I did you'd be here today?"

"I guess not. Funny, though, I could have sworn you looked directly at me just before I went inside and blew those fucking people's heads off."

"Why'd you leave the kid?"

"Time constraints, Mr. Agent. I wasn't at my leisure there."

"Go finish her now."

"I don't think so. I'm sure all your friends are taking care of her just fine without me."

Joseph was really irritated with himself. Seeing Trebor standing there with the gun now made so much sense to him he couldn't believe it got by.

It never should have gotten past Deke either. Nor would it have at any other point in his career. The fact that it happened in a case like this was just as surprising as finding out exactly who the killer was. Not that it mattered, though. The chips were down, way down. The only thing Joseph could try to do was keep Trebor talking.

"So, you were the one who called Jesper pretending to be Deke, huh? I didn't even know you did fucking impressions," he said nastily.

"He's not real hard to imitate, Mr. Agent. I just hadda sound like a retard when I talked. Jesper fell right for it."

Joseph's heart was pounding. He knew that if he got the gun away from Trebor the situation was a gimme. He would beat the daylights out of him. The gun was the great equalizer, though. It sat out there as big as Mount Everest.

Joseph tried to think of any kind of move that could be made. The thought of his life ending here and never getting the chance to be with his wife and little daughter again terrified him more than the bullet itself. He knew his only chance at the moment was to stall until an opportunity presented itself. It all depended on how long Trebor would stay engaged.

"Why are you doing all of this? What did any of these people ever do to you?"

"Yeah," Trebor responded. "I guess I owe you that much, my friend. I'm sick of all of these fucking people out there! They all live the perfect life, doing their little shopping and family dinners and crap. I almost had that once until they took it from me!"

Thoughts, pictures, and memories all blew into Trebor's mind at the same moment. Thoughts of his joyless childhood, the way he was sent off to school every day with sneakers so worn out that his toes would bleed from being scraped on the concrete, thoughts of the humiliation he suffered when the other kids would make fun of the bread-and-ketchup sandwiches he brought each and every day for lunch, thoughts of the way girls would look down on him because he wore clothing stolen from a church's poor box.

Pictures rolled by his mind's eye of his father smacking his mother all over the room for not having enough money to put decent food on the table at night, the way she would cry and tell him it was her fault so he would stop hitting her, the pitiful way she would whimper while lying on the floor helplessly, her beautiful eyes begging for help through the tears.

The memories set off a firestorm in his head. There was the way his father blew out of the house one night after beating Mom yet again, the image of him having a heart attack and dying right there on the front lawn, the complete indifference shown by a young Izzot and his mom at the funeral.

Things should have gotten better after that, especially once the insurance money rolled in. They didn't. They wound up getting worse. Men started showing up at the door, evil men who would take Mom into another room and demand money from her, slapping her harder than Dad ever did if she didn't pay. Izzot sometimes overheard them talking as he hid in his closet. He heard things he didn't understand, like "laying points" and "exactas" and "trifectas." He heard her begging for more time, asking if she could go "double or nothing." There would be talk of breaking legs and fingers if money didn't come across.

Sometimes they would go into her bedroom, and the door would be closed for a while. Things would get real quiet then, except for a few moans and groans and maybe a heavy breath or two. After that, the angry men would come out not looking so angry anymore. There would be a half-smile on their faces and a look of gratification that Izzot couldn't quite grasp.

As Izzot grew, the knocks at the door came less frequently and eventually stopped altogether. He didn't care what the reasons were that those men stopped coming by. He didn't know why they were there to begin with. All he knew was that Mom was safe and would give him all her attention. The euphoria didn't last long.

A new set of evildoers soon replaced the old ones. They would come in early in the morning and stick Mom with all kinds of needles. They told Izzot it was necessary, that things were growing inside her and the needles would take her pain away. Then they'd roll her wheelchair to the window, where she'd sit all day staring out at the street. When Izzot would go to work, she'd be at that window from the time he left until the time he came back, just staring out and waiting for him.

When he finally walked through the door, it was always the same ritual. Mom would be sitting there in her own urine and feces, drool flowing down her chin and saturating her shirt. Izzot would remove her to the bathroom, where he would sponge-bathe her and dress her in fresh clothing. The wheelchair would be cleaned and Mom would be placed back in it, where Izzot would then spoon-feed her baby food. No words would be spoken during these times. They sat in silence, Mom wondering what she did to get here, and Izzot wondering what *others* did to get her here.

The cigarette smoke Izzot blew in her face from time to time did little to rouse her from her doldrums. He wasn't even aware he was doing it, but then again, chain-smokers have little compassion for those around them.

Mom always sat there, her face blank and expressionless, and gummed her mush slowly, some of it going down her throat, some going back onto the spoon below her mouth. It was the same thing, night after night.

The only time life would spring back into her eyes was when Izzot would wave a daily dose of lottery tickets in front of her face. Then it was like all the drugs had been removed from her system. She would perk up and regain the capability to interact, even smiling as she went through them. The tickets were mostly comprised of daily numbers, but Izzot often would sprinkle in some of the instant scratch-off variety that she adored so much. The ones that really tickled her fancy went for twenty dollars a pop, and it usually didn't take long for Izzot to blow through her Social Security check in order to keep her daily fix going. Once her money was gone, his funds became the source, and, like always, the result was less food on the table. It was just like the good old days.

It would be just a matter of time, she told him, until they hit it big. Then they could get out of that place and pay for real doctors to take care of her instead of the ones at the free clinic who were trying to kill her. The money would come rolling in as soon as Lady Luck smiled in their direction. She was convinced their phone number would come out in the daily numbers, usually demanding that Izzot play at least ten dollars per drawing on the front three and back four digits of it. Once it hit, they'd be on easy street, she said. It was her daily mantra.

After the numbers were drawn and the tickets scratched, with less than stellar results, all those losing tickets Izzot purchased would be thrown into the garbage. Mom would retreat back into her shell until the following evening, when he'd once again return from work with a new arsenal of tickets in his hand. Day after day. Night after night. Their lives had become nothing more than an endless loop of nonexistence.

Joseph sat there and observed as Trebor drifted in and out of the moment. Every time it appeared Trebor had his attention somewhere else, Joseph would try to squirm out of his chair in hopes of getting to his gun. The movement would always bring Trebor back, and the gun would be steadied on Joseph's face.

"Sit right there and don't move, Mr. Agent," Trebor said angrily. "Don't think for a second I won't end this game right here, right now."

Joseph raised his hands submissively and let Trebor know through body language that all was cool. It wasn't working. With each passing word, Trebor's calm, condescending demeanor deteriorated. He started complaining about a "she" and "what they did to her," ranting and raving at all the injustices that affected his world.

Joseph could see that Trebor was beginning to lose it, could see in his eyes that he was becoming detached. The grip was tightening on the gun, the finger fidgeting precariously on the trigger. Joseph knew he had to pull him back carefully.

"Who are you talking about, man? Your wife? I have a wife myself."

Trebor's eyes locked into Joseph's. "Wife? No wife. What the fuck would I need one of those for! My mother wouldn't have it!" A look of interest came over his face. "Did you say you have one, Mr. Agent?"

"Not anymore." Joseph changed his tune, fearing the obvious. "She left me."

"Would she still be alive?"

A cold chill ran down Joseph's spine. He wasn't quite sure how to answer the question. "I don't know," he said sheepishly. "I haven't seen or spoken to her in a year."

A wry smile came across Trebor's lips. "Don't worry, my friend, I wouldn't kill her unless she was here, and, believe me, I already looked around the place; she's not. No, only you are the chosen one."

"Chosen for what?" Joseph asked rhetorically. "What did I do to you? What has *anyone* done to you to start this shit?"

"You ever wipe your own mother's ass, Mr. Agent? You ever have to clean dried piss out of her snatch? You ever take your mother's clothes off and wash her body in the bathtub? Well, I did! I had to do it every day because you fucks came in and shot her full of drugs. You shot her full of drugs and left her to die by the window." He clenched his teeth. "Well, you know what? Now it's my turn to do some shooting."

"You're killing innocent people! You fucking asshole!"

"There are no innocent people! If they were so innocent they wouldn't have been chosen." His voice had a demonic undertone. "My mother wanted to be one of those do-good people. All she ever wanted was to have what they had, to do what they did. The doctors said she couldn't, though. They made her stay on that medication and let her stare out the window all day. They made her nuts!"

"Listen, man, these people didn't do anything to you. Your mom might have really been sick. People shouldn't have to die—"

The gun was shaking in Joseph's face. "Shut up!" Trebor yelled. "My mother wasn't nuts."

Joseph sat quietly, but he was seething inside. More than anything he wanted his hands around Trebor's neck. The FBI anger-management course was in a direct tug-of-war with the hothead days for control over Joseph's mind. His patience was rapidly wearing thin while listening to the crap Trebor was sputtering out, while at the same time his mind replayed the pictures of the murder scenes he'd been at, little children blown away at the hand of this asshole. His eyes locked on Trebor in a maniacal stare. Somehow, some way, he had to get to him.

Trebor himself was teetering on the edge. In his mind, he was in the right in this whole thing. What they did to his mother was inhuman, he thought, and no one had any right to disparage her. It took a few seconds for him to calm himself down. "Every day, she played our phone number in the lottery," he continued. "She always told me she was gonna hit someday and we'd move away and start over, get away from these fucks. When they had her too doped up, I played the numbers for her. Well, one day, they came out, both in the same drawing on the same day. It was a fucking miracle, a million-to-one shot. It was her dream come true. I ran home from work to show her." He stopped talking, and Joseph could see he was picturing things in his mind. "She was dead," he said softly. "I came in, and there she was by the front window, dead. These fucks came in and killed her because they knew she was gonna get out!"

Joseph was treading carefully, waiting for an opening. "Look, Trebor, I'm sorry about your mom. Put down the gun, and I promise I'll help you find out what happened to her."

"Shut up!" he yelled again. "They'll tell you the same thing they told me. She was old and she was sick. I don't believe it. Her numbers finally came out, more than a hundred grand. She never got to cash the tickets. They're in the coffin with her."

Trebor's eyes were gone. Joseph could see the situation crumbling before him. Any move to be made had to come right there and then, and the choices weren't abundant. He quickly rolled them through his mind; either head directly for Trebor and try to take him down, or try to make it to the gun on the table. Unfortunately for Joseph, neither of the two was particularly close to him. Even though the table was a couple of steps closer, and the gun on it wasn't moving around the room the way Trebor was, the more hazardous decision was made. Joseph was going right at the killer. Anger and adrenaline might just carry him through and allow his viselike hands to get a grip on Trebor's throat. Right or wrong, it was the way it had to be. Straight on like a bull.

All the while Joseph was pondering his move, Trebor had been rambling from his soapbox, waving the gun all about the place. Joseph slowly lowered the chair so it was back into its normal upright position. His feet were now on the floor, and his fists were on the arms of the chair. It was as good a time as any to take his chance.

Trebor, as he rambled and paced, had wound up standing next to the table by the front door where Joseph had left his gun. The two were just inches apart, and Joseph was ready.

As soon as Trebor's gaze once again seemed deflected, Joseph sprang from the chair and headed straight for him. A loud shot rang out, and Joseph felt an intense, white-hot pain in his chest as a bullet tore through. It immediately knocked him to the floor, just below the table holding his gun. With all his remaining strength, he tried reaching up for it.

Trebor reached over and grabbed the gun for him. "Is this what you need, Mr. Agent?" His voice was much calmer now, much more evil, much more in control. "Ooh, I like this one. It has a good feel. Maybe I'll take it with me and use it next time."

"Go fuck yourself," Joseph said, blood mixing with saliva in his mouth and oozing out onto the floor. "Deke will get you." He tried reaching for the killer's feet. "You won't get away with this."

The barrel of the gun was pressed against the front of his head.

"Don't be so sure. You're a hotshot FBI guy, and you were too stupid to stop me. What makes you think that retard detective can? It doesn't really matter, though. Let him come after me. Then I'll kill him. After that, I think I'm gonna take a little break from all this. Maybe I'll go on vacation for a while. I'll move to another city and start all over again. I think this is fun." The gun was cocked. "Have a pleasant day, Mr. Agent."

"I have a baby," Joseph said, fading. "She needs me."

Trebor paused a second for cruel effect. "Hey, it's not like she's not gonna see you again." A thought breezed through his mind. "Probably be in a casket, though. Oh well. I'll see you on the other side."

Joseph felt his eyes burst from their sockets as everything got very bright and then went completely dark. The bullet that ended his life passed straight through his head and into the floor below.

Trebor took Joseph's gun and wiped all the prints off it. He placed it on the floor next to him and smiled. "I don't need your gun, pal. I don't carry souvenirs. Thanks for the fun time, though."

He stood up and gave a hard kick to Joseph's ribs. "Don't ever fucking talk about my mother again!" he said harshly. He took a note from his pocket with his gloved left hand and placed it on the body. When he got to the front door, he snuck a look out the peephole and, seeing all was good, pulled the door open. He thrust his middle finger into the air in Joseph's direction as a final good-bye and then walked defiantly out the door into freedom.

Joseph's body was found the next morning when the apartment was checked after no one could reach him on either his cell or Deke's home phone. CSU was already processing the scene when Deke and Captain Murray arrived. They entered the apartment pensively and stopped in their tracks at the sight of Joseph's lifeless body on the floor. To Deke, this scene was different from the rest. The blood seemed redder; the smell, more intense.

"Son of a bitch!" he hollered. "The kid didn't deserve this, Captain. He shouldn't even have been here."

"None of them deserved it, Deke," Murray said softly. "Not him, not any."

"Never shoulda been here!" Deke shouted again at Joseph's body and then kicked the recliner a few steps away. "He switched with me 'cause he hated the freakin' hotels. That should be me on the floor there, not Ku-Jo."

"You don't know that, Deke. He could have just followed the kid and got in somehow."

"No way. The kid was a good cop, had good instincts. He wouldn't just let that asshole in." Deke's gaze drifted off into space for a moment. "How the hell did he find me?" he whispered audibly enough to be picked up by Captain Murray.

"It's pointing more and more to someone on the job," he said. "Real easy for a cop to run you through the database."

Deke's head dropped. "What kinda cop kills another cop, even if he's FBI?"

"I don't know," the captain said, frustrated. "I don't know anything anymore."

Deke kept staring at Joseph's body, seemingly drawing strength from it. "I'll go through 'em one by one if I have to. I'll check out every fuckin' cop on the force until I find this guy."

"Well, you could start by wiping off everyone at the last scene, Deke. All the tests came back negative on those guys. Even Ronnie's been cleared, poor bastard. This whole investigation needs to be started over."

"Yeah, Ronnie," Deke said somberly. "How's he doin'?"

"He's still in intensive care, but he's coming around a bit."

"What about the guy that hit him?"

"I haven't heard anything in a couple of hours, but last I knew, he was gonna be arraigned on a DWI rap. The DA was thinking about upping the charges to attempted manslaughter since he still had an open bottle of Scotch on the seat." Captain Murray checked the face of his cell phone for any messages. "It really pisses me off. The guy T-bones Ronnie in the driver's side and walks away without a scratch while Ronnie ends up in ICU."

"Always seems to happen like that."

"Yeah, well, they better nail this guy to the freakin' wall. I don't want to lose two good cops in one day."

"You gonna tell him about the kid?" Deke asked grimly.

"Yeah, might be a cop we're looking for. I don't think he'll handle that real well, but eventually I'm gonna have to tell him it could be one of our own," Murray responded as he stared down at Joseph's body. "Can't do it now, though. I still can't get it straight in my own mind."

"How you gonna give these CSU guys orders? They gotta know by now you're outta the unit."

"I'm still a captain, Deke, and they're just cops."

"Yeah, but the commissioner—"

"Fuck the commissioner! I'm on my own time here. This thing just got real personal for me."

Deke wasn't happy about having to go back to the starting line on the case. Just the thought of it was irritating to him. The bubbling acid in his stomach was only compounded once he caught sight of a piece of paper placed carefully on Joseph's body. "Look at this shit," he said, sickened. "Look at the note he left this time."

The note was short, nasty, and to the point. It was cold and it was calculated, and it differed from the rest. YOUR LUCK HAS RUN OUT, it read. No one knew if the note was meant for Joseph or for the cops. It was just as mysterious as the others.

"I don't know how we're gonna find this guy," Captain Murray said, dejected.

"I'll find him," Deke answered. "Don't you worry about that."

Captain Murray rubbed the back of Deke's head and nodded approval. "I hear you." He then walked to the other side of the room to talk to the guys who were dusting the windows for prints.

Deke, meanwhile, knelt alongside Joseph and touched his hand to say a little prayer. As he bowed his head, something in Joseph's other hand caught his attention. It was his keys, and attached to the end was a tiny black electronic device, one that Deke had recognized immediately. Joseph's fist was wrapped around it tightly.

Deke called the lead CSU guy over and asked if he could

move the hand to get the keys out. The CSU guy had some pictures taken of the hand from different angles. Once he was sure the hand, its contents, and its position on the floor had been properly documented, he gave Deke permission to move it and get the keys out. The hand was cold and stiff and didn't want to release its grasp. Deke pried the fingers open, and the keys fell to the floor. He picked them up, closed his eyes, and said another prayer before pushing the small button that said PLAY. Joseph's voice was heard right away, distressed but clear.

The recording was only three seconds long, but Joseph had timed it perfectly, and it contained everything Deke needed. There were two separate voices, one right after the other. Deke recognized both of them. "Izzot Trebor is the killer!" "Fucking right, Dick Tracy!" And then it stopped. Joseph had found a way to leave the most valuable clue of all.

All the puzzle pieces fell right into place for Deke. The whole thing made sense in an instant, not necessarily the *whys* but the *hows*. Trebor had the same access to the same information that Jesper had, a computer with the phone numbers and addresses of every person in the city. It was crystal clear. When Deke cracked the code of the selection process and called Trebor to find out where Jesper was, he accidentally tipped off the killer that he was onto him. From there, it was set in concrete. The detective had to go.

The switch in sleeping arrangements was a twist that Trebor never saw coming. Not that it mattered to him, though. A body was a body, especially when it fell within the four walls of his funhouse. It actually sweetened the pot for him, knowing that Joseph was there strictly by coincidence. It was a horrible irony that had dealt Joseph's last hand.

Deke's brain immediately played back the promise Joseph had made to him if he himself ever found the killer. As Deke looked at the crumpled body on the floor, the words kept playing over and over in his head, along with the pictures Joseph had shown him that day in the car of his little girl, Samantha. Something in his brain clicked. Anger had finally intertwined with intolerance.

He carefully and quietly removed the recording device from Joseph's keychain while Captain Murray was off talking to the CSU guys and quickly shoved it in his pocket. He took his own recording device, cleared it, and attached it to the keychain where the other one had been. He then stuck the keys back into Joseph's lifeless hand and gave him a little pat on the back.

Captain Murray turned just in time to catch sight of Deke's back as he walked out of the apartment. Not paying any mind to it, he continued his investigation of the scene.

Another two days would pass before the next murder scene was discovered. This time it was at the house of one Izzot Trebor. CSU was once again called in to process the scene. It was by far the most gruesome and bloody of all. Trebor's body was found badly beaten and tortured. His eyes were swollen shut, and all his front teeth were knocked out. Some were found in the back of his throat, while others were embedded in his cheeks. They appeared to have been kicked there. Chairs, lamps, and tables were found broken all about the place, and it would later be determined that the killer had used each one of them to pummel his victim. There were broken ribs, a severely fractured skull, and a jaw that would have been wired shut eight ways to Sunday if the victim had survived. There was never a chance of that happening, though. A .38 caliber blast to the forehead was the finishing touch on this masterpiece. Ballistics would show the bullet to be from the same gun as the rest of the murders. On the body there was found a note. It read, YOU AND YOUR LUCK ARE DONE.

The murder was chalked up as one more by the Daily Killer.

No one ever figured out why they suddenly stopped after the Trebor killing or why Trebor was targeted when his phone number wasn't even close to matching the daily number. Only Deke was privy to those answers.

Jesper once again found himself thrown to the top of the suspect list after it was discovered that his boss was the latest victim. Despite numerous, symbolic attempts by Deke to tie him to the murders in any way possible, he always came out unscathed. There was just no evidence whatsoever linking him to any of the scenes. Not that Deke looked very hard anyway. He didn't believe in patsies. You were either guilty or innocent in his world. There were no fall guys.

Jesper's computer never showed any record of having researched any of the addresses in question. No one ever did check Trebor's computer. Ultimately, it would end up going missing, never to be seen again.

The murders would forever be etched into New York lore as the Daily Killings, America's version of the Jack the Ripper spree in London more than a hundred years earlier. As in those killings, suspects in this case would always have their names linked to the murders, but none could ever be solidly connected to them.

Joseph's death added a tremendous weight to Deke's mind, and he knew it would be a huge, burdensome link added to the chain he'd be forced to carry through life. It was impossible for him to shake the feeling of responsibility for it. Knowing the case was over from his standpoint, he immediately put in for disability retirement, citing emotional distress from the case and the loss of his partner. Deal or no deal with Frannie, this case would have been the end of the line for him, regardless.

Both the commissioner and Deke's new commanding officer in the Homicide Unit fought feverishly to keep Deke from retiring until the case was officially closed. The thought of having the mayor breathing down their necks again if they were forced to assign a new lead detective to the case was not at all appealing. Deke let it all run right by. There was no way whatsoever he could have told the higher-ups that the killer was already dead, or he would be facing a murder charge himself.

Ironically, it was Frannie who would ultimately convince Deke not to retire until the killer was caught. She was as oblivious as the rest of the world to the status of the man who had killed so many, and she knew there could be no closure for Deke while he was still out there. Deke didn't like lying to her about the whole thing, especially when she was being so up-front with him, but what else could he do? It's not exactly a smart move to tell the woman you're trying to win back that you've just brutally murdered a man who could have more easily been arrested.

The pain in his face merely at the thought of Joseph was authentic, though, and Frannie wanted all loose ends tied up for Deke if they were going to restart their life together. She amended the agreement they had made on her front porch on Christmas Day, and Deke reluctantly agreed. He would be allowed to come home yet still keep the job, and she would support him in his efforts so long as he agreed not to take on any new cases the police tried to throw his way. Finish this one case, she said, get involved in no others, then retire and move forward as planned. She loved him that much. Besides, she'd already told the kids that Daddy would be coming home soon and knew she couldn't disappoint them.

Deke was caught between a rock and a hard place. The guilt in his eyes that Frannie assumed was for Joseph was really for her. There was no way out for him.

Joseph was given a full NYPD inspector's funeral, which was broadcast live throughout the city and simulcast in his native California. As his closed casket made its way from the funeral home to the church and then to the airport, all the reporters that had hounded him and Deke constantly while the case was in full swing stood silently by and let the pictures tell the story. That story didn't last very long. The strobes would flash a while longer, and the cameras would continue to roll here and there, but inevitably Joseph's name would fade from the headlines. In New York, interest always begins to wane once the story is over and a new, more important one pops up just around the corner. Reporters never deviate from their golden rules. Always get there first, and never, absolutely never, get too involved in a story, lest you miss the next big byline on the horizon.

Joseph's wife and daughter received many donations of different kinds from all over the country as word of his story spread. Most were monetary, but every once in a while a teddy bear or a bicycle would roll its way in. One day an anonymous package showed up. In the box were fifty tiny recording devices just like the ones she used to get from her daddy. It was a secret gift from his last partner, and it wouldn't be the last. Little Samantha was set up with a scholarship and a trust fund designed to grow right along with her as she went through life without her father.

A few days after the funeral, Deke moved back into the house with Frannie and the kids. Shortly after that a civil service would mend their broken marriage.

Deke would continue to go to work every day and marvel at the fact that he was chasing an imaginary fugitive. He was ordered by the NYPD commissioner to dedicate himself solely to the capture of the Daily Killer and not to let up until he was in custody. He considered it gainfully employed retirement and chased down all leads and suspects, knowing ahead of time that they'd all wind up being dead ends.

Every night he would return home, on time and stress free, and truly enjoy his family. No police-business phone calls were allowed in to him when he was off duty. None would be accepted, anyway. In Frannie's eyes, he was upholding his end of the bargain by working a straight eight-hour shift and not letting it interfere with his private life. The more Deke could see that Frannie was truly happy being back with him and having normalcy returned to her life, the less guilty he began to feel about his lie. Especially when he considered the biggest fringe benefit it brought. Every night at 8:30 P.M. he would tuck little Lauren into her bed and read her favorite bedtime story to her. At the end of every story, he would kiss her nose and run his fingers through her hair. "Remember, baby, Daddy loves you like the whole universe, and you? You are its prettiest star." It was a tribute to a man he had not known long enough but wished he had. In Deke's mind it kept the memory of him alive.

For the Daily Killer's thirty-seven victims, justice had ultimately been meted out by the one who was sworn to uphold it. No one ever said the game was fair. No one even sought to play it that way. Murder is murder. Those who witness it are just as much victims as those who experience it. No one wins.

The end result of the Daily Killings had come and gone with no recognition by anyone other than Deke. It was a case that would stay open for all time and would be debated for eternity.

Suspects would always be questioned but none ever named or officially charged.

The gun would never be found. The movie . . . never made.